B.R.A.I.N

B.R.A.I.N

by Bernie Koenig

ISBN: 978-1-7376270-0-5 (paperback)
ISBN: 978-1-7376270-1-2 (ebook)

I dedicate this book to the Supreme Being, and describe it as a bridge. If it helps just one person cross, from material existence to spiritual awakening, I will consider my effort fruitful.

Table of Contents

1

Beginnings

Dr. Elizabeth Kolmann entered her lab briskly, as she had thousands of mornings before. One of the many technicians walking around in white lab coats approached her. "Morning, Liz. You must be excited! Were you able to get a good night's sleep?"

"In spite of all the problems we've been experiencing around here yes, I was, thank you. How's everything this morning, Norma?"

Norma waved her right arm in an arc, and a holographic screen appeared in front of them, suspended in midair. It was the familiar control panel that updated the vital signs of their precious subject every thirty seconds.

Nutrient consumption level – normal
Temperature – normal
Core fluid level – normal
Replacement tank fluid level – 50%
Pump status – normal
Neurogenesis level – 1.7%

"Everything looks great," Norma said, smiling.

They headed to their separate tasks. Liz was always busy, rarely taking time to observe her surroundings. Today was different, though, since everything appeared to be working normally for once—and it was, as she thought of it, The Day. She sighed in relief, allowed her shoulders to relax, and looked around her incredibly bland lab. Aside from the high-tech equipment in the room, she was completely surrounded by concrete. Concrete ceiling, concrete floor, not even a measly window to look out of—only rectangular air vents decorated the walls. Her meager surroundings were standard protocol, due to the classified nature of the project she'd been working on for the past decade. The Stanford Ph.D. in Neuroscience that she'd earned when she was 18 had helped her gain the respect of her peers, who considered her a genius. That was why the government had hired her for the most ambitious project ever undertaken.

Almost 50 years earlier, in 2058, the United States government had decided to upload everything created by humankind into a single massive database: every book, scroll, recording, song, work of art, photograph, movie, video, speech, image, hieroglyphic tablet, pictograph, petroglyph, cuneiform receipt, and cave painting since the very beginning of recorded history, and before whenever possible. Once the database was operational and stable, the government decided to up the ante. They wanted to create an organic Artificial Intelligence to correlate and make more productive use of the information. An agent contacted Liz, explained the importance of the project, and made her an outstanding offer. Shortly afterward, she was hired.

When she arrived, work had already begun on conditioning her lab to the requirements specified in one of her books, *The Creation of Organic Computers*. Based on her doctoral dissertation, the book was so innovative the government had quickly classified and retired it from circulation for reasons of national security.

The complex where Liz's lab was located consisted of 40 floors built beneath Fort Meade, a two-century-old military base in Maryland. Her lab was on the deepest level, about 600 feet below the surface. The restrictive environment often caused her discomfort. Without stairs, access to the floors was via four spacious elevators. They were designed to exercise complete control over who entered and exited the building, and to make unauthorized access a remote possibility at best.

Large, dark, menacing security robots patrolled all entrances from the surface and on each level. The center of the complex was pentagonal in shape. On the side with the right angles stood the elevators. Upon exiting them on every floor, a visitor immediately encountered a lobby with doors on each wall except the one with the elevator banks. Every door was explosion-proof. Each of the floors housed classified projects. Liz, like most personnel, was forbidden access to any other floor or section besides her lab, some of the offices, the housing, food, and recreational areas.

The only individual authorized to visit every part of the facility was General Tyrone Rex. A short, burly man in his early forties, T. Rex, as he was known by just about everyone, was the commander of the complex and one of the most important people in the world. He had a direct line to the President of the United States; Liz had seen the secure red communicator in his office.

■ ■ ■

Norma and Liz met again shortly after noon. Liz fluffed out her short blonde ponytail and said, "Okay, so far so good. Please have our team do a complete analysis of the cerebrospinal fluid. I'm heading out for a while to relax. I'll be back shortly to inspect the results, well before initialization. Thank you!"

"I'll have everything ready when you get back," Norma affirmed.

Liz wore round, dark-rimmed glasses, which protected her pale-blue eyes and gave her a scholarly appearance. As so often occurred, her intelligence had kindled the resentment of her fellow students in her early educational years as she bounded through the Gifted and Talented programs, and of course those kids bullied and made fun of her constantly. This made Liz fearful of social situations, which she avoided as much as possible. Just being in the crowded lab sometimes made her feel anxious.

Today marked the culmination of many years of hard work: the initialization of a fully functional organic computer. Loaded with all of humanity's history and knowledge, and faster than anything else on the planet, it had unlimited potential. Other AI computers had already found cures for several diseases by collating and integrating existing knowledge, and had made life easier for people across the world. There was no telling what the new AI might accomplish. Liz had her doubts about the AI software provided by the military, though. It seemed lifeless and rudimentary. She had mentioned this to T. Rex on several occasions during the development phase, but he hadn't been concerned and so far, nothing had come of it.

She headed to the nearest bathroom, peered in the mirror at her tired but satisfied expression, took off her glasses, and splashed cold water on her face. In truth, she was exhausted. A white lab coat covered her slim, athletic figure. The demands of her job made it pointless to apply cosmetics or compare herself to other women. Neat and clean was good enough. There was no one at the complex to impress anyway. She didn't really worry about that, except for the occasional stray thought of romance; all considerations of a personal life were put on hold until she'd achieved her goals. Liz was 28, in her prime, cooped up in a concrete maze forty levels below the surface, working on a powerful computer with the potential to solve many of the world's problems. That was what she hoped her creation would be used for, but she was savvy enough to realize that despite reassurances to the contrary, the military might—certainly would—have other plans for the project.

Now that the job was done, she would have to wait and see.

Liz took off her coat and stretched, rubbing the back of her neck. She rotated her head, resting her chin on first one and then her other shoulder. Having been stooped over her desk for too long, she decided to pay the facility's garden a visit, as she often did when stressed. It connected to the complex at ground level.

Leaving the lavatory, she took the elevator forty floors up, waved at the security robot as she passed, and went through a passageway leading to a pair of large, bulletproof sliding glass panels. On the way, she heard a strange zapping sound. She headed in the direction of the sound, and found a group of soldiers and robots training outside in a large field. She approached them to get a closer look. The sound she had heard came from a small group of robots.

She watched for a moment, until a soldier passed close by. "Excuse me, Sergeant, what's going on?" Liz asked.

"We're in training, ma'am," the soldier replied respectfully.

"What are the robots doing, if I might ask?"

4

"They're shooting their lasers at five-inch-thick sheets of steel 100 yards away."

She blinked. "Wow, they never miss. How can they be so accurate?" she asked, noticing how the lasers emanated from a tiny slit between a pair of glowing red eyes on the cylindrical heads of the 'bots.

"They can target anything with pinpoint accuracy, ma'am, using a multi-spectral laser aiming device."

"What about that other group?" Liz asked, noticing several robots that appeared to be suspended over water, and others over rocks.

"We're testing an antigravity propulsion system, ma'am, which was developed right here at the base. They weigh close to 300 pounds, and yet they can glide effortlessly over rocks and even water. Pretty amazing, huh?"

Liz blinked. That beat the best antigravity system she'd ever read about in the literature. "Wow, impressive. Those things are scary. I'm glad they're on our side," she laughed nervously.

"Yes ma'am, I know what you mean."

"Thank you, Sergeant, see you around," Liz said, returning to the passageway that led to the gardens.

Reaching the panels, she could see her destination through the thick glass. She approached, and the panels slid open automatically to reveal a paved stone pathway surrounded by the garden. Chicory, purple-top verbena, spiderwort, mullein pink, sea lavender, and yellow wood-sorrel decorated the surroundings. Chestnuts, hemlock, sugar maple, and oak trees shaded the environment. Butterflies, hummingbirds, bees, and squirrels hurried about, busily searching for food.

She immediately relaxed.

The garden was huge for a facility of this type: about two-and-a-half acres, she estimated. Around it was a tall, thick concrete wall with a series of electrical wires spanning the top to keep intruders out. Large reflective lamps and cameras were strategically placed around it. The sky was clear, the assortment of plants and colors stunning, and the warm summer weather inviting. During the winter months, a magnetic force field (developed at this facility, of course) was deployed to create a greenhouse effect.

It protected the garden from the elements, keeping the temperature under control and the vegetation healthy.

Liz walked around for a while, until she reached a manmade waterfall. Built using large river boulders arranged in the shape of a horseshoe, it was high in the middle and tapered down the sides. Water poured from the center, forming a large pond below. A small palm tree sat in a ridge in the center of the pond, above water level, a thick shaggy trunk with a crown of dark green shiny leaves on top. *What a beautiful specimen of King Sago*, Liz thought. *A marvel of engineering is keeping this Japanese palm tree alive in this environment.*

The sound of flowing water was soothing, neither too quiet nor too loud. The surface of the pond was covered with white and purple lotus flowers. Koi danced through the water, most white with orange and red spots; others were blue and white. There was even a red with black, and a yellow one. She picked a spot on the soft grass nearby to sit and consider her progress.

B.R.A.I.N, as she had chosen to call her creation, was a complex collection of cloned human neurons intended to work like a human brain, only on a much larger scale, with much more power and efficiency. The design had taken years to perfect.

Clusters of neurons were responsible for mankind's ability to find creative solutions to difficult problems. The clusters could communicate with each other in a complex flow of electrochemical signals. These signals made memory and thought possible. Emotions, however, were a different story, one Liz had pondered often. Emotions drove the faith, passion, and persistence necessary to unravel the mysteries of the universe. The limbic system, the seat of human emotions, is a small structure about the size of an orange at the bottom center of the human brain. Below it is the reptilian complex that controls the body's vital functions, including our heart rate, breathing, and body temperature. Liz had spent many hours thinking about how to incorporate emotions into B.R.A.I.N. *Humans have such a great diversity of emotions; there has to be a way to help B.R.A.I.N view the world like a human. Maybe if I could provide it with the same senses that humans have, make it possible for B.R.A.I.N to interact with its environment in a more active instead of a purely rational way...*

Maybe ...

After a while, Liz headed back to her lab to meet with Norma. "Hi, Liz, here's the chemical analysis you requested," she said, handing Liz a digital pad with the information.

"Thank you, Norma. Everything looks okay," Liz said, after carefully reviewing the data on the pad.

"Great! We can—wait, what the heck is that smell?" Norma said with an expression of disgust, as the sound of the general alarm pierced Liz's ears.

Liz reacted automatically, yelling, "Something's wrong! Everyone, get your safety masks on right now!" She reached into the locker by the entrance to put one on. She also grabbed one for Norma, but following protocol, put hers on first. She was struggling with her mask when she heard a loud noise behind her. She turned to face a group of masked soldiers and medical personnel rushing inside. Suddenly, her head began to spin and her knees buckled.

"Grab that lady before she hits the ground," the sergeant in command ordered one of his men, and someone managed to reach Liz just in time. preventing her from striking the floor. The soldier laid her down softly as one of the nurses approached. Still conscious, Liz felt the sharp prick of a needle in the crook of her left arm. Then she passed out.

Ten minutes went by before she regained consciousness. She could barely open her eyes. Through a tiny slit between her eyelids, she noticed a nurse tending to her. "Wha... what happened?" she mumbled.

The nurse said briskly, "A chemical agent was accidentally released by the lab directly above you, and entered yours through the air vents. Everything is under control now."

"Uhhh, are my people okay?" Liz mumbled again.

"Everybody is fine, except for one of your assistants. We did everything we could, but she didn't get to a mask in time."

The thought of someone being hurt gave Liz the strength to fully open her eyes, even as she realized there was a mask in her hand... and she herself was wearing one. She felt a stab of panic, and looked at all the people running and moving frantically around her lab. Then she turned her head and saw her lying there, just as she had feared: Norma, her limp body sprawled on the floor several feet away.

Liz struggled to raise her hand and point to her. "Is, is she dead?" Liz asked.

"Yes, I'm afraid so. I'm so sorry," the nurse said sympathetically.

Liz started to cry, wondering how this could have happened. All this time, she and her team had been busy working on a project to help humanity. She had assumed that all the other projects in the building had a similar purpose... but then she thought about the antigravity breakthrough, which has found its first use in the military, as so many things did. Her body trembled with apprehension as she realized how wrong she'd been.

Right above her, someone was working on a deadly chemical agent meant not to help or assist, but to kill.

2

The Project

It was a beautiful summer morning on the main Harvard University campus, or the "Yard," as it was known to both students and faculty members. Twenty-five acres of grassy area with cement walking paths, it was one of the few remaining pristine places in America. All around were the Yard's famous red-brick buildings, covered with green English Ivy. An assortment of trees shaded its surroundings: birch, beech, apple, cherry, redwood, elm, maple, oak, and many other species and varieties. It was a botanist's dream.

Dr. Eric Roberts was sitting with his feet up on the antique wooden desk in his campus office. His piercing blue eyes were gazing outside, through the old-fashioned Victorian windows; he recalled the good old days, when he too played Frisbee with his fellow students in the Yard while working on his Ph.D. in Computer Science.

Eric was gifted, to say the least. With the help of his father, a Harvard physics professor, he had mastered differential and integral calculus at the tender age of eight. His primary school in Boston had recognized his unusual abilities and sent him to their department for special children. By age twelve, he was out of high school and on his way to MIT, where he earned a Bachelor of Science degree in Applied Mathematics, and a Master's degree in Electronic Engineering. Sometime later, he received his Ph.D. in Artificial Intelligence from Harvard. He was done by age twenty.

Now twenty-nine, with an impressive curriculum as a tenured computer science professor and the head of the Artificial Intelligence Department at Harvard, he felt satisfied... but somehow a bit empty inside. His rapid rise through academia had given him mental prowess, but had left him emotionally crippled. He longed for more friends and female companionship, but it seemed he always lacked the time and the social graces to cultivate either.

Sighing, Eric began browsing through the electronic sticky notes that Brenda, his secretary, had left on his computer screen before leaving for lunch. One of them had the word "Urgent!" printed on it, and caught his attention. He enlarged the image with a vocal command. The sticky revealed that one General Tyrone Rex with the National Security Agency had called and left a message. When the general had called, Eric was busy lecturing his introductory class on Artificial Intelligence at Harvard's Science Center Auditorium. He couldn't imagine what the call was all about, but he smiled at the general's name.

His secretary still gone, he issued a vocal command asking his computer to dial the general's direct line, which was stored on the communications array from his earlier contact. It wasn't long before he heard the familiar ringtone on his speakers. Soon after, a strong. manly voice answered: "Rex."

"General Tyrone Rex?" Eric said.

"Yes, who is this?"

"My name is Dr. Eric Roberts. My secretary left a message saying you had called this morning while I was teaching. I'm returning your call."

"Yes, Dr. Roberts, I'm glad to hear from you so soon. There's an important national security matter that I must discuss with you as soon as possible."

"I see." Eric paused. "Can you be more specific?"

"I'm sorry, Dr. Roberts, but I can't; I'm sure you understand. You'll have to come to our headquarters at Fort Meade, Maryland, to discuss it in person. I've already reserved one of our fighter jets to pick you up at Hanscom Air Force Base at your earliest convenience. I hope you're not afraid of ultrasonic flights. How soon can you get here?"

Eric began analyzing the possibilities, but nothing came to mind. Why was this General from the NSA asking to see him so insistently? Was he in some kind of trouble? He wasn't particularly fond of the military, having always considered them a necessary evil. He had even made this clear in some of his classes and public interviews. *How can I be so insecure? I'm one of the leaders in my field. Surely this has something to do with it*, Eric thought.

"Dr. Roberts, are you still there?" Rex asked

"Yes, General, my apologies. How long do you think this will take?"

"I can send for you tomorrow morning and have you back in a few days," the General replied.

"Excellent., I'll arrange for someone to cover my classes. Shall we say, 9:00 AM tomorrow at Hanscom?"

"Very good—0900 hours it is. Captain Elliott James will be your pilot. Don't worry, he's one of our finest," Rex said. "See you tomorrow, Doctor."

"Looking forward to it," Eric said, since it was the right thing to say, but he wasn't all too sure about that.

He was still recovering from the surprise of the call when someone knocked on the door. "Yes?" he asked a bit nervously.

His secretary, Brenda, poked her head inside. Eric sighed in relief. "Hi, boss, just wanted to let you know that I'm back from lunch," Brenda said.

"Good, and thanks. By the way, I was just on the phone with that NSA general who called this morning. He wants me to fly to Maryland tomorrow and meet with him for a few days. Could you ask Charlie to take over my classes until my return?"

"Sure, right away."

Eric placed everything neatly on his desk and decided to leave early for home so he could pack a few things for the trip. He grabbed his bleeding-edge holo-projection minicomputer, slid it into his shirt pocket, and headed out.

After exchanging goodbyes with Brenda, Eric strode toward the elevator, which slid open when its proximity reader detected the RFID tag implanted in his neck. While just about everyone had such tags implanted at birth these days, the work his department did was delicate and potentially harmful, so access was tightly restricted. The door wouldn't open if you weren't on the whitelist.

A minute later, he was headed south towards the auto-glide that would transport him to his apartment. As he passed Widener Library, he couldn't help admiring its massive structure, with its huge Ionic columns adorning the entrance. Inaugurated in 1915 and housing more than 29 million volumes, it was the largest university library in the world. He was still charmed by its maze-like interior. Although most of the library's contents were digitized these days, Eric enjoyed grabbing an occasional hardcopy book and reading it the old-fashioned way. Once, during his student days, he had unintentionally fallen asleep while studying, and was locked inside for an entire night. Security guards double-locked the exit doors, which made RFID tags ineffective after hours. It was a dark and scary experience, but he got out in one piece the next morning.

Continuing south, he approached the Wigglesworth Exit, the fastest way to get to Massachusetts Avenue and his ride home. Eric stepped onto the moving metal ramp leading to the auto-glide headed east. As he reached the entrance to the transport, proximity readers detected his tag and sent his watch a digital receipt showing that $10.00 had been charged to his account. He sat in the first available seat. His apartment was on the 9th floor of Building 11 on the corner of Mass Ave and Pleasant Street, only three stops from Harvard Yard. Eric usually walked to the apartment, only a couple of miles away from his office, because he enjoyed the exercise; but today he wanted to get home as quickly as possible.

His building let him in upon recognizing him as a resident, and the elevator automatically took him to his floor and unlocked his door for him. It was a bit dark when he entered. "Curtains," Eric said, and all the curtains in his apartment retracted, allowing natural light to enter. His living room featured one of the newest holo-TVs on the market. While Eric didn't have much time for TV, he occasionally enjoyed watching sports, live comedy, science, and nature shows, and he preferred to do it in style.

A short hallway led to the guest bedroom, the master bedroom, the study, and the bathroom. The kitchen was adjacent to the living room. Eric headed to the master bedroom, set his minicomputer in its charging dock on his nightstand, changed into comfortable slippers, and began to pack a suitcase with essential items he would need for the trip to Fort Meade.

"Ginger tea, hot and sweet," he called out, and the kitchen began preparing it for him. He hadn't yet finished packing when he heard the familiar whirr of his robotic assistant carrying his tea on a tray. Eric took the cup and savored his favorite drink.

"Will that be all, sir?" asked the robot.

"Yes, thank you," Eric replied. Most people didn't thank household appliances, but as a computer scientist Eric respected any level of AI and, in any case, he'd had politeness drilled into him at a young age.

The robot headed for the charging unit in the kitchen, and Eric finished packing before taking his minicomputer, which contained research spanning his entire career, to his study. Eric's study was by far the most impressive room in his apartment. On his desk was a docking station that provided his minicomputer with hyper-bandwidth access to the world outside and vastly increased its power. On a table nearby were many different types of robotic heads and limbs, all of which helped him test his algorithms. Advanced audio equipment assisted him with speech and sound recognition. Other, less notable technological gadgets were also evident, meticulously organized.

It was the age of the robotic revolution, which had started almost a century ago; toy robots, industrial robots, office robots, and home robots were so common as to be nearly invisible. There were even lifelike sex 'bots made of modified carbon, an advanced material designed to mimic the look and feel of human skin. Many people spent hours playing virtual reality games in haptic suits inside room-sized geodesic spheres. Verbal commands activated 3D projectors that could transform the sphere's interior into an amazing virtual world almost identical to reality, whether you wanted to swim with sharks, climb Everest, explore the Amazon jungle, or battle other players in outer space or in some fantasy environment. VR coupled with AI also offered interactive and accredited high school and university courses. The machines were fun and addictive.

Most people worked at home nowadays, since they could video conference with their bosses, co-workers, and clients easily. To the government and large institutions, human beings were just numbers in a computer's memory. People spent a lot of time on their own interacting with technology.

It was also the age of mankind's dehumanization, a time when, for many jobs, humans need not apply.

For the last several years, Eric had been working on an advanced artificial intelligence algorithm. The world was full of helpful motorized and "intelligent" friends. They controlled vehicles, performed chores in houses, warehouses, and factories, and aided police and military operations. They came in all shapes and sizes. Some could move around at will, while others were integrated into the machines they were designed to control. Although the robots had decision-making skills, they were limited to specific functions and decision trees.

Eric's goal was much more ambitious. His algorithm, if successful, would allow a robot to process a prodigious amount of data through various sensory inputs, just like a human brain. It would learn from experience, and make decisions using the information it received. In essence, Eric was working on a sophisticated reasoning algorithm that would allow robots to think like human beings, only faster and more accurately. It would allow them to adapt to a variety of tasks, and enhance their learning and decision-making capabilities. They would even be able to independently correct, modify, and refine their programming.

Scientists had already created human-like machines capable of outperforming people in almost every mechanical way. They were stronger, more resistant, could run faster, think deeper, and jump farther and higher. The brain, however, was a different matter, one that Eric was trying to resolve. Eric's personal RFID tag granted him access to an almost unlimited network of supercomputers and quantum computers around the world. He used them to run simulations of his program and could see, almost instantly, how his artificial intelligence algorithm responded under different circumstances.

Eric had built his brain algorithm based on the work of past pioneers in artificial intelligence. For years, he had pondered the possibility of a robot overpowering and hurting, perhaps even killing, a human being, or the possibility of a human using a robot in that manner. He knew there were already security robots that could manhandle humans, and military robots under development. So, he became especially interested in Isaac

Asimov's Four Laws of Robotics, which he had successfully integrated into his work. The Four Laws state the following:

1. A robot may not injure a human being or, through inaction, allow a human being to come to harm.
2. A robot must obey orders given to it by human beings, except where such orders would conflict with the First Law.
3. A robot must protect its own existence as long as such protection does not conflict with the First or Second Law.
4. A robot may not harm humanity or, through inaction, allow humanity to come to harm.

Eric also included a Fifth Law of his own, which stated:

A robot must seek to protect the well-being and survival of the many over the few, and of humanity as a whole, even if such protection conflicts with the first four laws.

The logic behind this Fifth Law was that the survival of several human beings had to take priority over the survival of a single individual. Asimov's four famous laws didn't make any allowance for a situation of that nature.

Eric worked for a few hours on programming and testing before reminding himself he had to get up early to arrive at Hanscom Airforce Base in time for his flight. He locked his minicomputer in his study's safe, put on his pajamas, had a salad, brushed his teeth, and asked his apartment to wake him up at 7:00 AM the next morning.

He woke on his own at 6:30. He tried to sleep a bit longer, but couldn't, so he finally decided to get up and have his usual vegetarian breakfast of various seasonal fruits with cottage cheese and a glass of carrot juice. Eric had been a vegetarian since age four, about a year after his parents took him to the Boston City Fair. They had many games there providing prizes, and his father won him four cuddly baby rabbits. Eric loved his rabbits, always returning home from school anxious to play with them. He would hug them, kiss them, and talk to them. In time, the rabbits grew to adulthood, and Eric spent less and less time with them.

One day, his parents decided to organize a family reunion at their home. One of Eric's aunts from rural Philadelphia volunteered to prepare a special meal for them. Everyone agreed, since she was a great cook, if a bit ditzy. Aunt Hilda walked around the house and saw the rabbits in their hutches outside. Never having encountered rabbits as pets, without carefully thinking things through, she decided to prepare fresh rabbit stew, one of her specialties. When Eric returned home that day, he called for his rabbits but couldn't find them. Finally, when they all sat down to enjoy the hearty meal Aunt Hilda had prepared, he discovered the shocking truth. Since that horrible day, he'd sworn he would never eat an animal or fish again, only fruits, mushrooms, vegetables, milk, and its by-products.

After breakfast, Eric shaved, took a quick shower, and dressed comfortably. He grabbed a sweater, just in case, and told the apartment to get him a ride. While it was doing that, Eric instructed his bag to follow him, and walked outside to wait. Less than five minutes later, the familiar yellow taxi arrived in front of his building and popped open the rear passenger door. Eric entered the vehicle, placing his bag on the seat next to him, and told the computer to drive him to Hanscom Air Force Base.

The drive to Lexington, Massachusetts, where the base was located, was uneventful. Now that nearly all motorized vehicles were self-driven (except those used for recreation, like off-road motorcycles), accidents were rare. Traffic was usually heavy, but it flowed smoothly. Most taxis and other vehicles were also able to fly short distances when necessary; made from crisscrossed struts of nanostructured ceramics, they were light and rugged. At one point, Eric's taxi took to the air to avoid a road repair unit, first deploying four metallic jacks to lift it an extra foot and a half above ground. The tires then rotated 90 degrees below the chassis and pushed outward toward the sides of the vehicle, where the rims, designed to act as small turbines, spun at high speed, lifting and propelling the vehicle through the air and over the repair unit. Powered by electricity, today's autos could quickly recharge using under-road charging technology, solar cells, and internal generators. The whole drive took only 30 minutes, so Eric got there with plenty of time to spare.

As he arrived at the entry gate, a man dressed in an airman's uniform approached the cab. "Welcome to Hanscom Air Force Base, Dr. Roberts," he said. "You'll have to disembark here. One of our vehicles will take you to your plane."

Eric collected his bag, exited, and was led to a Humvee. He climbed in. "Have a good flight," the man said. After about five minutes in the vehicle, he was dropped off close to what looked like a jet fighter. Another airman, whose name tape read CURTIS, approached Eric and greeted him with, "Hello, Dr. Roberts, everything's ready for your flight. Please come this way." Eric grabbed his bag again and followed Curtis to the jet.

"What kind of plane is that?" Eric asked curiously. It looked like some sort of streamlined space fighter.

"It's a modified F-22 Raptor stealth combat jet. The main differences between it and an unmodified version are its speed and range. The original could fly a little over twice the speed of sound, or Mach 2—about 1,500 miles per hour—and had a range of 1,730 nautical miles. This baby can reach up to Mach 4 and has a range of over 4,000 nautical miles."

Eric knew that Fort Meade was 370 miles south of Boston, so at this jet's speed the trip would require 8 to 10 minutes at the most. It would probably take longer to take off and land than to reach its destination.

"Follow me, Dr. Roberts, we need to get you suited up for the flight," the airman continued.

Eric followed him to a hangar, his bag chugging along close behind. Inside the hangar were several planes and helicopters in various states of refueling and maintenance. They walked past an old single-engine Cessna 182, which appeared to be in perfect condition, to a spot where some dark green suits and helmets were stored. Airman Curtis grabbed one of the suits and handed it to Eric. "Try this on for size."

Eric looked at the jumpsuit and back at the airman, feeling confused.

"Just slip it on over your clothes, I'm sure it'll fit," Curtis said, grinning.

Eric sniffed the jumpsuit, wondering if it was clean. It didn't have the most agreeable of smells, but he didn't notice any signs of prior sweat in the garment. He slid into the suit, inspecting it carefully, and found it to be quite comfortable. Now he had to pick out a helmet. The man handed one to him, and it fit.

"Are you ready?" Curtis asked.

"As ready as I'll ever be," Eric replied nervously.

"Okay, then. I'll help you with the luggage and you carry your helmet," the airman said.

As they got closer to the jet, Eric noticed the open, transparent canopy and only one seat. "Where's Captain James?" Eric asked, a bit confused.

"Oh, he's already on the plane," Airman Curtis said, grinning.

Eric stepped into the cramped cockpit while Curtis placed his small suitcase into the tiny storage area in the back, left side of the jet. The airman then climbed on the wing to help Eric with his seatbelt, helmet, and oxygen mask. He instructed Eric to push the red button once he saw him clear the area. Eric waited until Curtis waved from the sidelines to push the button. The canopy slowly closed over his head, and the jet came alive. He could hear the muffled sound of powerful engines through his helmet, while lights of different colors lit up on the panel in front of him.

"Hello, Dr. Roberts, I'm Captain James," said a voice from speakers behind his head. "I'll be flying the plane to Fort Meade. We'll get you there quickly and safely, so just relax and enjoy the flight. Please refrain from talking during the flight to avoid interfering with communications, and don't touch the instruments on the panel."

"All right. Are you an AI, or a human being?" Eric asked.

"The autopilot is engaged and programmed for the flight, sir, but I'm a real human being at Fort Meade and can remotely take control of the craft in case it becomes necessary. Ready?" the captain asked.

"I guess," Eric said.

"Hanscom Tower, X-Ray Mike One Zero Eight, at air superiority, taxi for takeoff, south departure with Information Delta," Captain James said.

"One Zero Eight, winds are 160 at 16, taxi to runway one eight left via taxiway Alpha and Echo," the control tower instructed.

"Taxi to one eight left via taxiway Alpha and Echo, One Zero Eight," Captain James repeated the instructions for confirmation.

The turbines sped up and the plane began to move. *This is exciting*, Eric thought. Several years before, he had earned his private pilot license on a single-engine Cessna similar to the one in the hangar, if somewhat more modern. But this plane was unbelievably sophisticated. The jet stopped short of the runway, and Captain James completed the final checklist prior to departure.

While working on his license, Eric had experienced trouble with making steep turns. A day before his scheduled flight review with a Federal Aviation Administration examiner, his instructor insisted he practice the turns. Eric went to the airport and found cloud coverage and visibility below the recommended minimums for VFR (visual flight rules). He reluctantly boarded his little Cessna 172 and took off. He found a clearing through the clouds and climbed to 3,000 feet. Once a safe distance from the airport, he started practicing the maneuver. To pass the exam, Eric had to begin a forty-five-degree turn in either direction, do a 360, and exit within ten degrees of where the turn began without losing or gaining more than 100 feet in altitude. He practiced the maneuver repeatedly until he was sure he could complete it competently for the test.

When he was done, he realized that a dense carpet of clouds completely obstructed his view of the ground. He had no idea where he was. He was nervous, but kept his cool and contacted the control tower. After what seemed like an eternity, the tower responded and guided him back to the airport for landing. They scolded him for flying in such bad weather. The next day, however, he passed his FAA review without a glitch. The examiner never even asked him to make a steep turn.

"Hanscom Tower, X-Ray Mike One Zero Eight, at one eight left. Ready for takeoff," Captain James stated.

"One Zero Eight cleared for takeoff one eight left."

"Cleared for takeoff, one eight left, One Zero Eight," Captain James said.

The jet aligned itself with the runway centerline and sped up rapidly. It was in the air in seconds, and climbed straight up at incredible speed. Eric could feel the g-forces pushing his body hard against the seat.

"Hanscom Tower, leveling off at 12,000 feet, permission to change frequency, One Zero Eight," Captain James said.

"One Zero Eight, permission granted."

Captain James switched to the radio frequency used at Fort Meade.

Minutes later, he radioed in his final approach and safely landed the jet on runway Three Six Right. *Wow, what a ride*, Eric thought. *This thing is fast.* The jet stopped next to a large building labeled Hangar 17. The turbines powered down and the canopy opened, letting in fresh air. Eric was struggling with the oxygen mask when another airman welcomed him and helped him exit the plane. He led Eric through the main entrance to the hangar, and said he would take care of his bag. They walked past several planes, and arrived at a heavy metallic door with a small, square, bullet-proof glass window. An interphone with a camera and a proximity reader were attached to the wall next to the door. The reader picked up the man's tag as well as Eric's, and a voice instructed, "State your business."

"I have Dr. Eric Roberts here to see General Rex," the man said.

"One moment," replied the voice.

A few seconds later, the door slid open and a huge, dark robot approached them. Standing eight feet tall, the robot was massive, yet glided effortlessly across the floor. It looked like an inverted tetrahedron on top of a pyramid, with a ring in its midsection, arms, and a rotating head. *That thing looks heavy. It probably has a set of ball-shaped wheels underneath. Funny, though, I can't hear anything while it's moving*, Eric thought.

"Welcome, Dr. Roberts. Please stand still while I scan you," it said politely. Eric stood motionless during the weapons scan, which lasted only a few seconds.

"Please continue to Underground Level 5. General Rex is waiting for you there," the robot said.

Eric felt uneasy. He hated the war machine and what it stood for. He knew it deliberately lacked the Laws of Robotics that were ingrained into most AI researchers' mores; otherwise, it couldn't be used against human targets. He was nervous, and began to perspire. Despite his discomfort, Eric made it to the underground elevator and was transported to Level 5 of the facility. The doors opened onto a large, clean white room. The floor and walls were pentagonal in shape, and on each side of the pentagon was a door. The four other doors had a thick metallic look, as if they had been made to keep people out. In the middle of the anteroom stood another large robot, which proceeded to approach him.

"Dr. Roberts?" the robot greeted him.

"Yes," Eric responded cautiously.

"Follow me, please," the robot said, opening the door furthest to the right.

Eric entered a long passageway with many more doors on either side along the way. Each had a reader, probably keyed to DNA, to prevent unauthorized entry. The passageway was completely white and sterile, reminding him of a hospital. The robot led Eric to its end, where yet another door stood before him. The robot opened it, and said pleasantly, "Please go inside, Dr. Roberts. General Rex will be with you in just a moment."

The room appeared to be an office, equipped with a large, impeccably clean desk and a state-of the-art computer screen. Eric perused the room until a short, muscular man appeared, made distinctive by his dark brown eyes and thin lips.

"Dr. Roberts, welcome," he said, extending his right arm to shake Eric's hand. He appeared to be in his late forties and had a strong grip.

"General Tyrone Rex, I presume," said Eric.

"T. Rex, please, that's what all my friends call me." *Wow, what a nickname!* Eric thought, with an internal grin.

"I presume you had an agreeable flight?" T. Rex asked. As he spoke, he led the way to a conversational grouping of chairs and motioned Eric to join him.

"Yes, thank you," Eric replied.

"We at the NSA have been following your remarkable career closely, Dr. Roberts. We know you're nearing a breakthrough in artificial intelligence, and we would like you to take part in a project that's right down your alley," T. Rex explained.

"Could you be more specific?" Eric asked, his curiosity piqued.

"Certainly. I appreciate a man who gets right down to business. As you are assuredly aware, decades of medical research have allowed us to determine how the human brain stores and retrieves information. Today we thoroughly comprehend how neurons interact with each other. We know that the average human brain contains roughly 86 billion neurons. But how does it reason? How is it able to find solutions to a wide variety of problems? How important is intuition? And how does the brain become aware of itself? These questions are still beyond our knowledge. Acquired information is important for finding a solution to a problem, but how the brain uses it to find the best solution is far from our current level of understanding. This is where you come in," T. Rex said.

"I'll admit, I'm intrigued. Please go on," Eric said, leaning forward in his chair.

T. Rex leaned closer as well. "I must inform you that everything you see, hear, or read from now on must be kept strictly confidential. I have prepared a Non-Disclosure Agreement that you must sign before we proceed any farther." T. Rex handed Eric a digital tablet.

"I understand," Eric said as he began to review the digital document. He quickly noticed he was dealing with a standard NDA, and used a stylus to sign it without any further delays.

"Thank you. Now then, please come with me," General Rex said.

They exited the office and entered the passageway Eric had walked through when he first arrived. They reached the pentagonal lobby, passed the security robot, entered the elevator, and descended to the 40th subterranean level. Eric figured they must be at least five hundred feet below the surface at that point. Upon exiting the elevator, General Rex led him to another door on the angled right side of the foyer. A large sign read: AUTHORIZED PERSONNEL ONLY. On the right-hand side of the door was a DNA scanner. After it recognized the General, the door opened to reveal a very large, sterile room containing at least a dozen men and women dressed in white. Some were monitoring a complex array of instruments holographically displayed near the entrance; others were busy working on their computers. In the center of the room stood a large glass cube, about three yards in all dimensions, containing a pinkish, gooey substance.

"What the hell is that?" Eric asked, eyes wide.

"As I mentioned, Dr. Roberts, the human brain contains approximately 86 billion neurons. You're looking at the equivalent of 125,000 human brains. The pink substance you see consists almost entirely of cloned human neurons. In each cubic foot, every neuron is connected to every other neuron in that space, which means that each neuron has roughly 3.5 trillion connections. This remarkable breakthrough is managed by Dr. Elizabeth Kolmann, our head project manager and the leading neuroscientist in the world, with whom we will meet later. She basically invented the concept of this organic computer.

"Each cubic foot of neurons is also connected to every other cubic foot through spindle cells. Spindle cells have long dendrites capable of connecting to faraway regions. In this manner, each unit is capable of independent processing as well as networking with the rest of the neuronal ocean. For the last decade, we've been feeding our B.R.A.I.N, as we call it, all the knowledge in the world. Every book or manuscript, every song, every film, every work of art, every mathematical theorem, every petroglyph or pictograph, every rune or hieroglyph, everything since the beginning of recorded human history to date—and a little before. The only thing that's missing is an AI program empowering B.R.A.I.N to use the information in a more productive and useful way." T. Rex turned from the cube and faced Eric, in all earnestness. "This is why we called you."

"B.R.A.I.N? Is that an acronym? What does it stand for?" Eric inquired.

"Biological Response Artificial Intelligence Network. It's the most powerful organic neural network in the world!" T. Rex responded, beaming like a proud father.

3

The Challenge

"**D**r. Kolmann, how good to see you," T. Rex said as Liz approached. "Allow me to introduce Dr. Eric Roberts of Harvard University, head of their AI Department."

"Pleased to meet you, Dr. Roberts. I've heard so much about you," Liz said, smiling. "I've read a great deal of your work."

"Pleased to meet you as well, Dr. Kolmann. Interesting setup you have here. I would very much like to learn more about what you're doing."

"Please, call me Liz."

"Of course, but only if you'll call me Eric. I also prefer being on a first-name basis. All this formality makes me nervous."

"It's almost lunchtime—you must be hungry. Would you like to join me at the cafeteria?" Liz asked.

"Sounds like a wonderful idea."

"Would you like to join us, General?" Liz asked.

"No, thank you, I still have a couple of meetings lined up. You two go ahead and get to know each other. I've arranged for you to stay overnight, Dr. Roberts. We have guest quarters here at the facility; I hope they'll be to your liking. Dr. Kolmann or one of her assistants will show you to your quarters when you're ready. I've already sent your luggage, and it will be there when you arrive."

Eric nodded. "Thank you for your hospitality."

"Have a good time, and remember to ask for me if you need anything. I'll see you tomorrow morning for breakfast. Does 0900 agree with you?" T. Rex asked.

"Yes, of course, 9:00 AM sounds perfect," Eric said.

"Well then, let's get going. Follow me," Liz said.

As they walked out of the room, Eric noticed they exited through a different door, which lead to another long corridor. The NSA installation was huge, apparently. After an elevator ride and a walk down a few hallways, they arrived at the cafeteria. Everything looked very modern, and it featured a variety of food items, buffet style. The tables and chairs were metallic silver, and while they could have been designed to be more comfortable, they were acceptable. Eric followed Liz to the serving station, grabbed a tray, a plate, some cutlery, and started browsing. He picked salad, pasta with tomato sauce, a slice of cheese pizza, and some fresh lemonade. She grabbed a salad, vegetable sushi, and water. They headed to a nearby table and sat down.

Eric opened the conversation with, "How long have you been working here, Liz?"

"About ten years. Right after my Ph.D. in Neuroscience from Stanford."

He lifted an eyebrow, "I hope you don't mind my asking, but how old are you?"

"I'm 28."

"A Stanford Ph.D. at age 18? That's very impressive," Eric said.

"Thank you. I've been working here ever since. My doctoral dissertation was mostly about neurons. I discovered that they're distributed in discrete clusters or 'bundles of function and experience,' as I called them, in the human brain. The back of our head, for example, the occipital lobe, is where the visual cortex is located. It receives images from our eyes, interprets them, and sends the information to the limbic system, the emotional seat of our brain. The limbic system processes the visual information according to the person's emotional state. If the person is afraid, the brain will send the message to the hypothalamus triggering the fight-or-flight response. If the person is simply reading a book, it sends the information to Broca's Region, where language is processed and understood." Liz paused. "Have I bored you enough with my ramblings?"

"Not at all, please continue," Eric said attentively.

She smiled. She liked using her scholarly persona to distance herself from others, but something about his response made her want to keep talking. "Each group of neurons in a discrete bundle is interconnected through axons, dendrites, and synapses. There are three basic types of neurons in the brain: Bipolar, Pseudo-unipolar, and Multipolar. There are also glial cells that maintain, support, and protect the neurons. Years ago, we also discovered that there are slightly larger, longer, and more dendritically packed neurons known as spindle cells. These cells connect one bundle of neurons to other bundles. B.R.A.I.N has only multipolar neurons, spindle cells, glial cells, and a complex network of organic tubules that supply oxygen and glucose to the neurons," Liz explained.

"Fascinating. How is information stored and retrieved from the neural network?"

"That's a good question, and one that doesn't have a simple answer. We use optogenetics, which simply means that all of our neurons are genetically modified to be sensitive to light. An intricate network of ultrathin fiber-optic lasers is pointed at each of B.R.A.I.N's neurons to activate or deactivate its dendrites. Curiously, in the human brain, neurons can have a different number of dendrites, but only one axon. B.R.A.I.N's neurons are genetically engineered so they're all the same. Each neuron has 20,480 dendrites, and each spindle cell has 102,400 dendrites. But they each have only one axon. Each dendrite can be individually stimulated to hold a 0 or a 1. This means a neuron can store up to 2,560 bytes of information, or 2,560 letters. The spindle cell can store up to 12,800 bytes, or the equivalent of five neurons. The axon sends the information in a neuron to the spindle cell, which organizes it and can retransmit up to 12,800 bytes of data. In addition, we've reserved ten percent of each neuron to store emotional states. In B.R.A.I.N, emotional states can range from calm to severely agitated, and we have 256 bytes of information to represent the emotional state of each neuron."

Eric lifted an eyebrow. "Why would you want to store emotions in a computer's memory?"

"We wanted B.R.A.I.N to perceive its surroundings as similarly to humans as possible. We know that emotional content strengthens memories in the human brain, so we outfitted B.R.A.I.N with sensory equipment allowing it to see, hear, smell, taste, and touch. We want B.R.A.I.N to store an emotional reaction when it senses something."

"So how do I fit into all this?"

"You're the world's leading authority in artificial intelligence, the most qualified person to take B.R.A.I.N beyond simply storing and retrieving information. To provide it the ability to think, to understand, to learn, and to come up with original solutions to the problems that mankind has been unable to solve."

"I wish I were as confident as you," he said, smiling. "My software has never been fully tested, so who knows what would really happen?"

Liz traced her thumb over the handle of her fork, up and down, thoughtfully. Finally, she looked up and met his eyes. "Let's face it, Eric: Earth is in trouble. Its rivers and oceans are contaminated with plastic, chemical, and organic waste. The air is so polluted it darkens the sky. At dawn and dusk, you can see dirty sunbeams reaching down from above. People all over are falling sick with respiratory ailments. Many of them die. Animals that once were common are now extinct. The ground lacks nutrients, making it difficult to grow crops. Even the insects are at risk. You have to try," Liz pleaded, and paused. When she continued, her eyes were downcast.

"The warning signs have been evident for over a century. Scientists around the world sounded the alarm, but people just didn't care. Their only concerns were family, money, health, comfort, and enjoyment, not necessarily in that order. Mankind chose industry and technology over nature. Nowadays, the places that maintain the unspoiled beauty of the past are few; most are remote and difficult to reach. Only the wealthy can afford to visit them. Most people live in dark, crowded cities full of high-rises. Green areas are rare and far apart, unable to satisfy the increasing populations. Cities are forced to use old warehouses to house flora and fauna and hide the scarcity of nature. Despite technological advances, poverty and lack are the norms."

She paused again before asking, "Are you familiar with the Total Information Awareness Program?" Liz asked.

He nodded. "Yes, I believe it was started in the 21st century to store all types of digital communications in one huge computer. Things like emails, phone calls, social media interaction, and web searches to prevent terrorist attacks. If I remember correctly, Congress opposed it because it was considered an invasion of privacy."

"That's right. However, unknown to most people, the program never shut down. It's been active for more than a century. B.R.A.I.N has access to this vast universe of information, and will be able to retrieve anything it wishes about any individual on Earth, alive or dead. It also has access to specialized computers around the world dedicated to the study of the weather, earthquakes, the oceans, outer space, and anything ever written, played, carved, or painted. Sound enticing?" Liz asked.

"It does, but why a biological computer? It's probably easier and less expensive to create the same thing using conventional circuitry. Plus, electronic circuits work faster than their organic counterparts."

Liz shrugged. "We decided to use organic materials in the design of the neural network to get it as close as possible to the human brain. Although it's true that electronic circuits are faster than organic ones, they work in sequential order. The human brain can fire millions of neurons in parallel to help identify an image or to solve a complex problem. So even though electronic signals travel faster, this doesn't always translate into a quicker or better response."

"Yes, of course."

"We've known for a long time that the human brain is a sophisticated pattern- recognition system. In fact, recognizing patterns is the primary work of the neocortex. Our eyes are designed to see contours and outlines, to perceive depth and color differences in our surroundings. But it's the brain that models the three-dimensional high-definition images that we see. We see with our brains as much as with our eyes," Liz explained.

"Interesting," Eric replied, crossing his arms over his chest and leaning forward to rest his elbows on the table.

"We also know about fast and slow thinking. How our brain tricks us into jumping to conclusions about a tall figure walking towards us in a dark alley, for example. It can help us perceive danger and react more quickly, even though it sometimes makes mistakes. This is fast thinking, evolution at work. Slow thinking happens when someone asks you to add 36,538 and 95,432, and it's the mother of invention. Sophisticated robots have existed for decades now. None of them, however, have been able to get close to becoming conscious or aware. None of them are capable of the creativity it takes to produce a work of art or to appreciate the beauty of a sunrise. This, among other things, is what we're after."

"And finding a solution to our planet's decaying ecosystem?" Eric asked.

"Actually, that's B.R.A.I.N's primary objective. It's our job to help it find one, a good one. Our lives depend on it," Liz said, thinking of Norma and her unusual death. She wondered if what she'd just mentioned really was the government's primary objective. She felt a stab of sadness, but quickly managed to suppress the thought.

Eric nodded thoughtfully. "Interesting. Is there an access terminal I can use to communicate with B.R.A.I.N?"

"Thought you'd never ask. Follow me."

They deposited their leftovers in the nearest organic recycling unit, and placed their empty trays on a conveyor belt before walking back to the lab, where Liz showed Eric to a private area with a streamlined, stainless steel desk and access terminal. The screen was holographic, projecting upwards from the center of the desk. To the right of the screen was a rectangular transparent scanner. Liz sat down at the chair in front of it, and asked Eric to sit next to her.

"Kolmann, Elizabeth," Liz said in a loud, clear voice.

"Welcome, Dr. Kolmann. Please place your hand on the bio-scanner." The sound came from high-fidelity speakers in the uppermost corners of the small room. Liz placed her right hand on the glass. A blue light appeared below and scanned her DNA.

"Identity confirmed. What can I do for you, Dr. Kolmann?" the computer asked.

"B.R.A.I.N, I would like to introduce you to Dr. Eric Roberts. Can you see him?" Liz said.

"Yes, of course. Welcome, Dr. Roberts. I believe I have all your papers and monographs stored in my memory. Your AI work is groundbreaking."

"At least you didn't confuse me with the old-time flat-screen actor," Eric laughed.

"Oh, no, you would have to be over 150 years old to be that Eric Roberts, and he died years ago. But I also have all his work included in my memory. Dr. Kolmann, would you like me to transmit the image I am receiving of Dr. Roberts on your computer screen?" B.R.A.I.N asked.

"Yes, please do," Liz responded. A clear three-dimensional image of Eric's face appeared on the screen.

"Where are the cameras, Liz?" Eric asked.

"There are 24 different ultra-high definition PTZ cameras in this room. PTZ means Pan, Tilt, and Zoom. They can see in total darkness with the help of the latest LED technology. There are also 24 strategically-placed sound-emitting diodes that help B.R.A.I.N echolocate people and items within the room, similar to the sonar method used by bats, dolphins, and whales. The echolocation and visual technology in this room are the most advanced in the world."

"Amazing. Earlier, you mentioned that B.R.A.I.N is equipped with sensors to see, hear, taste, touch, and smell. Could you explain how you did this?" Eric asked.

Liz blushed gently. "Sure, aren't you bored yet?"

Eric glanced at her smooth cheeks. She was the opposite of boring; he would probably be willing to listen to her read the driest of stock market reports. "I think you're the least boring person I've ever met," he said, wondering where he found the courage to voice that sentiment. "Besides," he added, "this could affect my AI programming."

"There is that," she answered. "Okay then, you may know that the human brain can detect around 10,000 different odors."

"That many?"

"Yes. Molecules penetrate the nasal passages and attach themselves to tiny hair projections called cilia, which are specialized neurons behind our noses. When an odor molecule touches the cilia, smell sensations are triggered in our brain. Similarly, there are about 20 different tastes that we can detect. Sweet, salty, sour, bitter, and umami are some of the basics. There are also metallic, fatty, spicy, and several other tastes. These are detected when molecules meet with sensitive microscopic hairs called microvilli which are part of our taste buds."

"What, hair on our tongues? Ugh, sounds disgusting," Eric said.

Liz couldn't completely contain a small giggle. She could tell he was moving his tongue around inside his mouth, wondering if he could feel hair on it. She cleared her throat and tried to look serious. "The sense of touch translates physical stimuli into electrical energy that can be perceived, processed, and identified by the brain. All our sensations must be converted to electrical energy before our brains are able to process the information. Cloning technology and our understanding of the human brain helped us reproduce patches of human tissue for smelling, tasting, and touching. We wired them to B.R.A.I.N. Although not as sophisticated as a human's senses, they're versatile enough to identify a wide variety of smells, tastes, and textures," Liz explained. "Of course, there are electrochemical ways to achieve the same methodologies with more sensitivity—artificial 'tongues' were developed as early as the second decade of the 21st century that could identify specific batches of chocolate or scotch—but they're simply not human enough for our needs."

"I see, if I agree to take part in this project, and I'm not yet certain, I'll require a fast and secure direct link to B.R.A.I.N from my office and apartment in Cambridge," Eric said.

"You'll need to talk with the NSA's engineering team about that. I'm sure they can provide a direct link, perhaps a VPN, from your office to our central command center. However, you'll probably have to deal with some security constraints," Liz said.

"I'm used to that. I'd like to take another look at B.R.A.I.N, if you don't mind."

"No problem, follow me."

They headed out of the access terminal room towards the cube containing B.R.A.I.N's physical component. Eric looked closely at the neuronal mass, and noticed the tissue was tightly packed, curved in many different directions, convoluted like normal human brain tissue, and suffused in a slightly viscous yellowish fluid full of tiny air bubbles. He figured it supplied the nutrients and oxygen necessary for neuronal survival.

He reasoned the living tissue contained in the glass cube had to expire someday; it couldn't last forever. Or could it?

"Liz, the stuff in the cube is living tissue, right?" Eric asked.

"Yes, of course."

"All living tissue dies at one point or another. How can you guarantee B.R.A.I.N's long-term survival?"

Liz nodded. "Well, that's complicated. We can and do restore aging and dying neurons through neurogenesis, ensuring the birth of new neurons. As you might imagine, the most complicated part is preserving the existing dendritic connections. We've also discovered that B.R.A.I.N can create new and unique dendritic connections, much like human brains, whenever they become necessary. We still don't fully understand how this happens, and we know it doesn't happen often. But it does occur."

"I'd like to spend the rest of the afternoon exploring B.R.A.I.N's abilities at the access terminal, if that's okay with you," Eric said.

"Sure, no problem. I'll have to open a temporary account with your biometric information." She turned to a passing man. "Dr. Pearson, please escort Dr. Roberts to the access terminal and set up a temp account for him." The curly-haired man nodded.

"Thank you, Liz," Eric said, as he began to follow Pearson. "Will I see you later tonight?"

Liz turned half back around, a strange sense of wonder jolting through her. "You'd like to see me later tonight?" she repeated.

"Yes. I'd like to discuss B.R.A.I.N after I'm done with my tests," Eric said.

Liz's smile froze in place. Oh, "Sure, I'll pick you up at the access terminal around 6 pm. Is that all right?"

"Looking forward to it," Eric said, waving good-bye. His brain was galloping so fast with possibilities for B.R.A.I.N that he was oblivious to his *faux pas*.

After Pearson excused himself and left him to his experiments. Eric wondered how much the B.R.A.I.N project had cost taxpayers. All the technology, buildings, and personnel he'd seen had to be expensive. Eric stared at the holo-screen, and immediately identified the familiar dollar sign ($)

XENIX operating system prompt. MIT, ATT, and General Electric had developed the ancestral UNIX operating system in the mid-1970s, written in the venerable C language of computers. The result was so efficient it had remained in constant use in various iterations, evolving into XENIX by Eric's time. Consistent improvements had made XENIX the best operating system for networks. Eric was quite familiar with XENIX, and with C for that matter. In fact, he wrote most of his artificial intelligence algorithm in C-Prime, the natural evolution of the C language. Being a higher-level language, C-Prime was easier to program than assembly language and was only one step above it, making it incredibly fast and efficient. Eric had also used RECALL, a popular recursive language based on LISP, which simply meant programs written in it were designed to call upon themselves until a solution to a specific problem was found. Since the human brain is itself recursive in nature, Eric's algorithm took advantage of that.

Eric typed **$ ls / <return>** at the XENIX prompt, requesting a list of all the files in B.R.A.I.N's root directory. An enormous list of files and folders appeared.

"B.R.A.I.N, can you hear me?" Eric asked quietly.

"Yes, Dr. Roberts. How may I help you?" B.R.A.I.N asked.

"Are you familiar with basic arithmetic?"

"Of course. Dr. Roberts. My memory banks include all the major branches of human knowledge," B.R.A.I.N responded.

"Okay, how much is two plus two?" Eric asked.

"Two plus two equals four."

It appeared that Liz and her crew had equipped B.R.A.I.N with a standard voice recognition and AI package. *Or is B.R.A.I.N's AI software more sophisticated?* Eric wondered. He decided to test the extent of its reasoning abilities.

"Brain, what is life?"

"Life is the definition given to living organisms," B.R.A.I.N responded, almost primly, it seemed to Eric.

"What is a living organism?" he asked.

"A living organism is something that is born, grows, reproduces, and dies. It is also capable of adapting to its environment, and may feature some level of independent thought and action."

"Is a star like our sun a living organism?" Eric asked.

"No, a star is not a living organism."

"But a star is born from interstellar gasses, it grows, it dies as a nova or supernova, and thereby reproduces by spewing stellar material enriched with higher elements all around it," Eric noted.

"A star is not a living organism," B.R.A.I.N said firmly.

"Is fire a living organism?"

"Though that has been a matter of controversy, fire is not alive," responded the AI.

"A fire is born, it grows, it can reproduce other fires, and in time, it dies," said Eric.

"And yet fire is not a living organism," B.R.A.I.N replied patiently.

"Hmm. Are you familiar with the commutative order of addition and multiplication?" Eric asked.

"Yes. The first states that the order of the operands does not alter the result; that is, $3+4 = 4+3$. The second states that order of the factors does not alter the product; $3*4 = 4*3$."

"Okay. So, if a living organism is defined as something that is born, grows, reproduces and dies, and a star is born, grows, dies, and then reproduces, does it not qualify as a living organism? The order of the factors changes. but the result shouldn't."

"A star is not a living organism because it does not comply with all the necessary requirements for life. It does not adapt to its environment, nor does it display independent thought or action," B.R.A.I.N responded. "The same is true of fire."

After more tests, Eric became convinced that B.R.A.I.N was simply searching through its huge knowledge base for the best answers to his questions. It wasn't actually reasoning, just selecting the best fit and presenting it as the final solution. Once it found an acceptable answer, it would stick to its immovable conclusion. It was clear that its reasoning abilities were limited. He knew that his software could improve its reasoning and learning skills.

Eric continued with his line of questioning until he heard the familiar sound of the sliding glass door to the access terminal. He turned to see Liz's friendly smile.

"Hello, Eric it's 6:00 pm, ready for some dinner?"

"Yes, of course. I lost track of time with B.R.A.I.N here. Are we going to the cafeteria?"

"Oh, no, there's a special restaurant for VIP employees on the right wing of the building. The food is much better than the cafeteria. Sound good?"

"Sounds great! Just give me a couple of minutes to clean up."

"Great, I'll meet you by the cube."

Eric headed to a restroom, washed his hands, opened his mouth to check for signs of food between his teeth, patted his wavy hair into shape, and headed to the cube.

"That was quick! Ready?" Liz asked.

"Willing and hungry. Lead the way."

They passed through a maze of white corridors for about 10 minutes before they came to an elevator that took them to the top floor of the facility, where they exited into a large open area. To their right were two sliding glass doors with the name "The Oasis" etched above on a large shiny metal sign, surrounded by tiny white LEDs.

"The Oasis. How interesting," Eric noted.

"Yes, I love this place. It really is an oasis of relaxation amid a desert of hard work," Liz said jokingly.

Eric laughed as they entered the restaurant, to find an elegant setting with a great view of what looked like a forest or garden. Liz spoke briefly with the head waiter, who guided them to the best table in the house. The menu wasn't expensive, and featured an interesting selection of salads and pasta that immediately attracted Eric's attention. She ordered the artichoke carpaccio and angel hair pasta in a tomato basil sauce. He went for the endive salad with blue cheese and the Fettuccini Alfredo.

"I couldn't help noticing your selections. Are you a veggie?" Liz said.

"Yes, I've been a vegetarian most of my life," Eric said.

"What a coincidence. I'm a vegetarian too."

"A love of science *and* a love of veggies—that's two things we have in common," Eric said with a smile.

Liz didn't want to presume anything about his casual remarks after the earlier incident, so she just smiled. An awkward silence prevailed.

"So, what do you think of B.R.A.I.N's interface?" Liz finally asked.

"It's acceptable— quite good, actually, but I believe I can improve it significantly. What I'm not sure of is how to set up the emotional states you mentioned earlier," Eric replied. He was grateful she'd started a conversation. He wasn't sure why mentioning things they had in common would make her smile in that awkward way.

"In nature, the more advanced living creatures have a greater number of senses. Single-celled organisms, like the paramecium, can detect changes in the environment. When it senses a change in temperature, for example, it alters its course to avoid excessive heat or cold. Plants have senses that seek the light. They curve and twist to find the most suitable angle of reception," Liz said.

"So, the more complex the organism, the more complex the senses?" Eric asked.

"Exactly," Liz answered. She thoughtfully chewed a tender artichoke tidbit. Eric watched her slender jaw working, then realized he was staring, and applied himself to his pasta. Liz swallowed and continued. "We created an organic-based computer, and equipped it with all the natural senses that human beings have, rather than more complex electronic ones. Gave it access to all available human knowledge, to watch how it reacts. When we see a sunrise, its beauty elicits an emotional response in our brains. When we read about starving children in some part of the world, this also elicits an emotional response. In fact, just about anybody who tries to understand the plight of another is compelled to feel compassion, with the exception of a few with mental issues like autism. There are different degrees of emotional responses in different people, of course, based on their upbringing, beliefs, morality, and education. In general, the higher the education, the greater the concern with the environment, and with human and animal rights." Liz paused.

"The more complex the organism, the more complex the emotions, then?"

"Yes... I hadn't correlated it quite like that, but that's an appropriate deduction. One of the main reasons I became a vegetarian is because I believe all animals have souls and God doesn't play favorites. It's 2108; we've established working colonies in the outer reaches of our solar system, but we haven't yet found, traveled to, or colonized a planet similar to ours. We haven't been able to escape Earth. We are always, however, on the lookout for other planets to ravage. We've spent the last half century trying to undo the damage caused to Earth. Our ego, greed, desire to indulge the senses, inhumanity to other living creatures, disrespect of nature, and our never-ending search for greater comfort are the seeds of our own destruction. We need help! I strongly believe that if programmed properly, B.R.A.I.N could be the instrument of change, or at least of improvement in modern human society," Liz said, ending in a passionate rush. Eric had been enthralled both listening to and watching her talk.

"I agree with everything you've said so far. I'm especially glad you mentioned the part about proper programming. Programming is both a science and an art, requiring many painstaking hours of coding in front of a computer. Humans are imperfect beings, and errors always slip into everything we do, especially when large programs with millions of lines of code are involved. This is why my AI algorithm allows the computer to check its own code and to change, correct, and improve it. This is also why Asimov's Four Laws of Robotics must be permanently stored in the computer's memory, no alterations allowed. I'm even thinking of adding a fifth law," Eric said.

"A fifth law?" Liz asked.

"Ah, may I assume that you know the first four laws?"

Liz nodded.

Eric continued. "Yes. It boils down to: the benefit of the many outweighs the benefit of the few. Asimov didn't take this into account when he invented the concept of robotics and its laws. If an artificial life form must make a choice between saving one person or a hundred people, its internal algorithms should allow it to make the proper choice. It's even more complicated than that, though; if an army of Mongols wishes to conquer a small village of innocent peace-loving people, how should the computer react? All these are moral judgments that humans can quickly analyze to detect a proper course of action. Computers, hmmm… I'm not so sure. It would require programming a sense of right and wrong into the machine," Eric said, dropping a fork to the floor while moving his right arm for emphasis.

"I'll get it," Liz said.

"No, no, how clumsy of me," Eric said.

They both bent down at the same time to pick up the fork, and bumped their heads, their hair cushioning the blow.

"How clumsy of me," Eric repeated, blushing and looking into Liz's eyes.

They both laughed out loud and, for the briefest moment, experienced a sort of *déjà vu*. It was as if they had known each other for a long time. *This woman is brilliant and good-looking, too. She's 28, and has been stuck here forever. She has to be single*, Eric thought.

"It's okay," Liz said smiling.

"Are you single?" Eric asked. *Oh, why can't I ever think before I speak? Why can't I be smooth and suave?*

"Yes… I don't have much time for romance. And if I did, there's nobody here I'm interested in. What about you?" Liz said.

"I, too, have yet to meet my soulmate," Eric said. Immediately, he wanted to sound more masculine. "Do you live here on the base, then?"

"Yes, I live in an apartment here. You'll probably get one too if you decide to join the project," Liz said.

They ate in silence afterward.

Liz knew the human brain had an inborn sense of right and wrong. *Most people can distinguish between good and evil, and then decide how they want to act. This is the essence of free will. People sometimes get confused and act incorrectly. Even societies make mistakes, such as allowing the massive destruction of rainforests, the lungs of the planet, to provide paper, lumber, wooden furniture, and other items for our comfort*, she thought.

Eric was also deep in thought. *How can you program a sense of morality into a computer? The secret must lie in the emotional states Liz mentioned. A computer can be made to associate a number with a feeling. It could use another number to help it distinguish a bad feeling from a good feeling. But morality is a complex subject. Human beings throughout history have justified immoral acts, making them seem acceptable. I'm not sure I'm qualified to program something as complicated as this.*

"How was the Alfredo?" Liz asked.

"It's been great so far, but aren't we having some dessert? I love sweets," Eric said.

"Waiter?" Liz said, raising her voice.

The waiter arrived and listed the specials for the evening. He also offered some after-dinner drinks, which both Liz and Eric declined. Liz chose the chocolate mousse, while Eric went for the vanilla ice cream cake.

"So, Eric, have you decided if you're going to help us?" Liz asked.

"Not yet. It is an ambitious project full of potential pitfalls. I have a reputation to uphold, and this effort seems a bit riskier than I bargained for," Eric responded frankly.

"I know, but great discoveries come at great risk! Remember Madame Curie, who died because of her discovery of radium. What about Galileo Galilei, who supported Copernicus' views that the Sun is the center of our Solar System, under the watchful eye of the Inquisition? I could mention others," Liz replied.

"I still have to ask for Harvard's approval to take part in the project. Problem is, I can't reveal it to them in its entirety, not after signing the NDA. I'll ask General Rex's advice when I see him tomorrow for breakfast."

Liz smiled. "I have confidence you'll make the right decision, and would consider it an honor to work closely with such a distinguished scientist as yourself."

"The honor would be mine," Eric replied. The idea of working with Liz wasn't just exciting in the scholarly sense. He felt slightly flustered. "It's getting a bit late, and I think I should get some rest before my meeting with the General. Thank you very much for your company and the fascinating subject matter. I hope we will continue where we left off soon."

"Would you like me to escort you to your sleeping quarters?" Liz asked.

"No need, I can use the passageway computers to show me the way. The sooner I learn how to use them, the better. Thanks anyway."

Eric kissed Liz on the cheek as they finished their goodbye ritual, and headed to his NSA-provided room. He couldn't help but notice how her hair smelled: not overly perfumed, but fresh and pretty. All the excitement, all the information forced upon him in such a brief period of time, had left him overwhelmed. Reaching his room, he quickly changed into pajamas, brushed his teeth, set his alarm, and went straight to bed.

■ ■ ■

T. Rex was thinking with his feet propped on top of his desk when the secure red communicator started beeping. POTUS was calling. He straightened up, tapped a button, and a hologram of his Commander-in-Chief appeared before him.

"Evening, General," the President greeted him.

"Sir. How can I be of service?" T. Rex replied briskly.

"Has Dr. Roberts accepted a position working on the project?" the President asked.

"Not yet, sir," T. Rex said. "I'm still trying to persuade him."

"You must convince him to join you. A lot's at stake here. We need him to fix our damned computer. No one except you, me, and a select few can know the true purpose of B.R.A.I.N," the President said somberly.

"I understand, sir."

The Leader of the Free World pressed on. "To solve the problems our world is facing, B.R.A.I.N must be willing, forced if need be, to hack into as many computer systems around the world as it can. Once it's gained access to every significant computer system on our planet, our objective will be complete."

"I read you five-by-five, sir. I'm meeting with Roberts in the morning. We'll have him on our side in no time."

■ ■ ■

The alarm sounded promptly at 8:00 AM; Eric immediately rose, yawned, and stretched his limbs. He felt refreshed and ready for his 9:00 AM appointment with General Rex. *Cleanliness is next to Godliness*, he thought while entering the cylindrical shower. He pushed the shower button, the cylinder door rotated shut, and water started blasting at him from all directions, with considerable but comfortable pressure. The tangy smell of chemical cleansers made itself apparent. *Simple soap would have been nice*, Eric thought. About a minute later he pushed the dry button, the water turned off, and a burst of warm air removed all external signs of moisture from his body. *What, no towels? I guess I'm just old-fashioned. All this fancy military efficiency is starting to get on my nerves*, he thought. He put on a fresh set of clothes and finished packing in readiness for his flight back home later that morning. He felt a twinge of regret at the thought of not seeing Liz again before he left, then exited the room in the direction of the General's office. Eric announced his presence to the sentinel, and sat down on one of the comfortable sofas in the waiting room nearby.

A few minutes later, General Rex walked in and said, "Good morning, Dr. Roberts, just in time. I like that in a man, and in a woman too!" He chuckled. "I trust you had a good night's sleep?"

"Yes," Eric replied politely, "Thank you."

"Let's head to my private dining room and have a bite to eat, shall we?" T. Rex said, as he walked out of the waiting room. Eric followed him through the familiar corridors to a private dining room next to the cafeteria. They sat down and ordered orange juice, fruit, and coffee, and admired the changing nature scenes displayed on the walls all around them.

"This room is incredible," Eric said after a few moments.

"We spared no expense on this facility. The US government is working on the most cutting-edge technology in the world, right here in this building. Bleeding edge, you might say. Forty-plus top-secret projects designed to advance our scientific knowledge." T. Rex paused to look Eric over, then continued, "So, tell me, Eric, what are your thoughts about our pet project here at the NSA?"

"It's fascinating, frankly, and something I'd like to be a part of. But first I need to discuss it with my boss. This project would be a full-time job; and after signing your NDA, I'm not really sure what I can tell him," Eric responded.

"If you mean President Derek Buk at Harvard, don't worry. The important thing is that we sparked your interest. Just tell President Buk that your country needs you, and that you'll be working on an extremely important AI project. Have him call me if he requires any additional information," T. Rex replied.

"It's… not all that simple, sir. I'm a department head at Harvard, and I'd have to do a lot of shuffling there to cover my absence and the classes I'm teaching. To do what you're asking will also require substantial funds, my full attention for quite some time, and a direct link from my office and apartment at Cambridge to B.R.A.I.N's central command center."

"I was hoping you would stay here with us while working on the project. But I'll check with our security personnel to see what we can do," General Rex said.

"Some of my AI work requires the university's quantum computer. My team is there, too. I would prefer to work from my lab, at least in the early stages. I can fly over whenever necessary—is that a problem?" Eric asked.

"Not at all. We'll have a jet ready for you whenever you need it—just give us a 24-hour advance notice, if you can. About your other question, let me simply say that you'll be handsomely compensated. Do you have your DNA identification card on you?" T. Rex asked.

Several decades before, the entire world had dispensed with coins and printed money as mediums of exchange, in favor of completely digital currency. Everybody was issued an identification card coded with their unique DNA sequence, which was used for all important transactions. The system required verification by evaporating a minute finger skin sample with a laser and analyzing it using small but powerful DNA sequencers. The technology had revolutionized the field of biometrics. Its high cost compared to tag readers, finger, and retinal scanners, however, made it somewhat scarce. Commercial transactions and access to highly restricted areas were its main applications. The combined use of DNA scanners, together with the tag readers, had almost completely wiped-out fraud within a few years. When the technology first became popular, thugs could cut someone's finger or hand off and use it with the matching card to commit a crime. Experts quickly adapted it to check the hand's temperature and pulse, thus preventing thieves from exploiting the weakness.

Eric handed his card to T. Rex, who gave it to an assistant for registration in the NSA database.

When they finished their breakfast, Eric told T. Rex he would be in touch after speaking to his boss. Military personnel escorted him to his plane for the quick flight back to Massachusetts.

4

Arrangements

I t took 30 minutes for Eric to return to his apartment; it was now 11:00 AM in Cambridge. As he unpacked his bag, he called Brenda and asked her to request a meeting with President Buk ASAP. Brenda called back a few minutes later, with news that the President would be able to see him at 4:00 PM in his office. This gave Eric a few hours to work on the problem of integrating emotional states into his AI program.

The human brain is physically divided into two hemispheres, connected by the corpus callosum, a thick band of nerve fibers allowing the left side to communicate with the right. The left hemisphere is in charge of logical, systematic, and mathematical thought, while the right hemisphere is more concerned with creativity, the arts, and spatial orientation. Eric believed the human brain comprehended things by comparison: hot and cold, light and dark, large and small, good and evil. He grasped the contrasting nature of the two halves of the human brain, thinking it would be difficult to comprehend anything without its opposite.

In computer jargon, a byte of information is the equivalent of eight bits: eight 0s, 1s, or any combination of the two in sequence. It took a maximum of 7 bits to represent all uppercase and lowercase characters, as well as the ten numbers and 32 special characters, such as the exclamation point and question mark. The eighth bit is used to depict whether a number is positive or negative. Eric figured he could use a byte to characterize emotional states in B.R.A.I.N's memory. This would provide him with a range of values from 00000000 through 11111111. Emotional states aren't so straightforward, of course, having shades of gray. He could use 00000000 to represent calm, and 11111111 for anxiety or fear, so intermediate states would have to lie in between these two numbers. *But this arrangement is too limited*, Eric thought, frowning. Liz had said that each neuron in B.R.A.I.N's design could hold 2,560 bytes. Ten percent of these had been set aside to represent emotional states, which meant he had 256 bytes (2048 bits) to feature variations in them. A string of 2,048 zeroes would mean absolute calm, while a string of 2,048 ones would mean extreme anxiety. Anything in between would depict the intensity of the emotional state, like a sliding vertical light switch.

What about love and morality? Could he represent complex and intense emotions with such a simple system? Eric remembered his mother and the great love he had for her when she was alive. Before her breast cancer, she had always been a caring and nurturing, although somewhat overprotective, mother. In high school, he tried out for the baseball team. He had good reflexes and was excellent at bat. On his first tryout, the pitcher threw the ball directly at him. Eric had to duck to avoid being hit, and was visibly upset. When the pitcher launched a second curved ball at him, he swung with all his might and connected a home run that left everyone with their mouths open, the pitcher first in line.

From then on, he played shortstop, which placed him fourth at bat. During one of the practices, the coach hit a hard fastball at Eric, which bounced several times on the ground before reaching him. In his haste, Eric placed his right thumb ahead of his glove and the ball gave him a nasty bruise, blackening his nail for months. When he got home, his mother was so distraught she took him off the team. He never forgot the disappointment he felt at her exaggerated reaction.

He felt calm and comfortable around his mother, thinking he could represent this state of calmness and comfort with 2,048 zeroes. He reasoned that love between a man and a woman provided comfort, but also some anxiety and expectation. So, he figured he could represent this state with mostly zeroes and a few ones. He could use half zeroes and half ones to represent the state of a high-performance athlete before an important competition, and all ones for paralyzing fear. Eric felt satisfied with his logical deliberations, planning to iron out the details later.

He looked at his watch and discovered it was now 3:00 PM. He had one hour left before his meeting with President Buk, and decided to get ready.

His ride to Massachusetts Hall was uneventful. He arrived half an hour early and announced himself to the secretary. She offered him a bottle of smart-water and asked him to sit in the waiting room. The table in front of his chair held several tablets full of digital magazines. Eric selected *National Geographic;* he was in the mood for articles about the living creatures that humans shared the Earth with. Eric loved nature magazines. The decision-making and self-preservation capabilities of small organisms like ants fascinated him. His mother had revealed how, at age three, he spent over an hour simply watching an ant walk around the pavement outside his house. He pondered how everything in nature, although ruthless at times, was designed to preserve an equilibrium. Animals, insects, and bacteria would quickly consume anything decaying on land. The oceans had different creatures, but also had mechanisms to preserve the natural equilibrium. Eric had always felt there was a superior intelligence behind all this: intelligent design, or the mind of God.

"Dr. Roberts, President Buk is ready to see you," the secretary finally said.

Eric stood up, said, "Thank you," and headed for the President's office.

"Eric, how are you? What a pleasure to see you. How can I be of assistance?" President Buk asked. He was a tall, slender man with caramel skin.

"Hi, Boss, good to see you too," Eric replied. "I'm here to ask your permission to take part in a classified AI project at the National Security Agency."

"Classified? Does this mean I have to sanction participation in something I'm not going to be properly informed about?" the President complained, frowning.

"They made me sign an NDA, sir, so I can't tell you about it. I can say it's an interesting project, right up my alley. It's the opportunity of a lifetime, and I think it may change the world. The man in charge, General Tyrone Rex, said you could call him directly if you had any questions. He specifically requested that I mention that my country needs me."

President Buk immediately had his secretary call the General. After a brief chat, he hung up and focused on Eric. "Very well, Dr. Roberts, you have my blessings," he said evenly. "How long will this project take?" Buk asked.

"I have no idea, sir. It could take years, but don't worry—the General has assured me he'll take care of all my financial needs for the duration of the project. The graduate students on my team will take care of my courses, and I'll try to find some time to visit and give an occasional lecture. I'll need access to my office and some of the university's resources, though, if that's acceptable."

President Buk shrugged. "You have my permission for all that. I could hardly do otherwise, after all. When will you start work on the project?"

"Soon. I'll consult with the General and let you know."

Eric walked back to his office at the Science Center, which was located next to a large quantum computer Harvard had purchased several years earlier. After the normal pleasantries, he told Brenda, "Please schedule my entire team, including you, for a meeting tomorrow morning at 9:00 AM in one of the Science Center's meeting rooms. Get one where we can all fit comfortably. I have something important to tell all of you."

She nodded thoughtfully and said, "I believe some of the grad students on your team have classes and meetings already scheduled for that time. How do you want me to handle that?"

"Tell them this is very urgent and important, and to reschedule everything. It will only take me a couple of hours or so to explain."

"Consider it done," Brenda said, though she couldn't help wondering what this was all about. She had been with Eric for several years and was surprised by the urgency of this matter. Eric was a bit high-strung, but was always considerate of his team's prior engagements. His pressing need for the meeting was unusual.

The next morning, Eric was in his office by 8:00 AM. He took care of some paperwork, and still had plenty of time to call T. Rex prior to his meeting with the team. "President Buk has sanctioned my participation in the project," he reported. "I'll need time to test and perfect my algorithms before downloading them to the new system. It will require a lot of hard work and coordination from my team, but I believe two weeks should be enough to have the prototype ready for testing. Is this satisfactory?"

"That sounds great. Good to have you on board. I know Liz will be pleased, too. I'll inform her, and wait for your arrival. Please remember not to reveal the true nature of our project to anyone," T. Rex said.

"My team doesn't need to know anything about it. They'll only be working on my side of the equation. See you soon."

He arrived at the conference room at five minutes past 9 AM to find twenty of Harvard's and MIT's best software engineers waiting for him, along with Brenda. Eric greeted them all cordially, then launched into his spiel.

"I apologize for disturbing your schedules on such short notice, but the scope of my announcement warrants it, or at least I hope so." Upon receiving this information, most of the participants in the room leaned forward. "I've accepted a temporary position as the head software engineer of an important project with the National Security Agency. I'm not free to reveal the classified components of the project, but trust me when I say that if everything works as planned, it will revolutionize artificial intelligence, robotics, and the world as we know it." Eric paused, so the significance of his announcement could have full impact.

"Now, I have something to ask of you. They've given me two weeks to perfect my algorithms and prepare to download them into an incredibly sophisticated computer, but I can't do it alone. I need your help and commitment 24/7 for the next two weeks. I can't force you to join in, so if any of you have any second thoughts, please let me know now and you'll be off the hook. Those who decide to help will embark on the most exciting artificial intelligence project in decades. Now, who's in?"

For a few moments there was complete silence; but in the end, everyone was more than happy to help Eric with the project. Smiling broadly, he lifted his hands to quiet the crowd. "I need you to cancel everything in your schedules—every meeting, class, date, or appointment—for the next two weeks. Arrange for someone else to take your places when necessary. I will personally be in touch with each of you later on today, and through the duration of our work together, to explain what to do and to supervise your progress. Charlie, as head programmer, I'll need you to pick a team of three to develop a new emotional response algorithm I've been working on. Let me know as soon as you've made your selection. The rest of you will work on my AI algorithms and irrevocably program the Laws of Robotics into it. You must make sure they can never be changed or erased, particularly when the computer runs its internal checks, code modification, and improvement routines. The computer must consult the Five Laws before any important decisions are reached, and compliance with the Laws is mandatory," Eric said.

"Consider it done!" Charlie replied.

Charlie Flegman had been Eric's right hand at Harvard for years. He held a Ph.D. in Computer Science from MIT and several impressive degrees in robotics. Charlie was responsible for helping Eric code many of his innovative AI algorithms, which, as Eric and Charlie both knew, were not really AI, but something they called Human-Like Thinking Process or HLTP, a process meant to mimic the way human beings think in a completely ethical and reliable way. The algorithms were designed to learn from experience, and were capable of using trial and error when necessary. They would select the best approach to solving a problem, using logic combined with all available information. If the solution proved ineffective, the algorithm would resort to trial and error, much like humans do under similar circumstances. Charlie and Eric had tested the algorithms on unusual mathematical and scientific experiments with outstanding results.

They shared more than a common interest in computers; they were also good friends. Early mornings, they met at the local gym to clear their minds before immersing themselves in the art of computer programming. While working, they would often interrupt each other to bounce off unusual ideas and approaches. They enjoyed working together. They had years invested in the AI system, but all they'd done so far was test small parts of it under laboratory conditions. They'd never had the chance to test it completely. This time, however, B.R.A.I.N would provide the perfect opportunity to fully evaluate their creation.

Eric thought, *Charlie won't be there; he can't be there. He won't even see the computer we'll be working on. What if it doesn't work? What if it goes into an infinite loop it can't recover from? B.R.A.I.N's entire memory would have to be erased. We'll need a backup in case something goes wrong.* He assumed Liz had taken this precaution already, but he had to make sure.

"Brenda," he said, "I need to speak with Dr. Elizabeth Kolmann at the NSA's Fort Meade facility. Could you put me through and redirect the call to my smartwatch?"

"Yes. Dr. Roberts, right away."

Eric stepped out of the meeting room and looked around. The hall was empty, providing him the requisite privacy. His watch vibrated. "Hello, Eric," Liz said when he answered. "Nice to hear from you already."

The sound of her voice calmed his jitters over undertaking this huge assignment and, at the same time, it made him tingle with happiness. "Hi, Liz, just calling to let you know I've decided to join the project. We'll attempt to have the prototype software ready to download in two weeks. We don't know how your system will react once we download the software, though. We don't expect any problems, but if something goes wrong, we may have to erase the entire memory. Do you have a backup?" Eric asked.

"Yes Eric, no worries. We already have a memory backup on a standard computer network. Its memory is huge, though, so it takes about a week to create the backup. I'll make sure that we have a fresh one prior to your arrival."

"You're wonderful, you know that? I wish we had more people like you working on the project. Do you think we could have you cloned?" Eric wisecracked.

"Maybe, but I doubt the clone would be able to handle T. Rex's abuse like I do," Liz said, chuckling.

"Okay then, I'll see you in two weeks," Eric said. *Good thing I'll be so busy, or two weeks would feel like a century.*

"Looking forward to it," Liz said. Eric couldn't see her smiling, but she was. He was smiling too.

It was close to noon, and Eric was getting hungry, so he invited the team to join him for lunch to discuss their specific needs and duties. They all went to the Science Center cafeteria for pizza, sandwiches, and salads. *Unhealthy, but tasty and practical*, Eric thought. After a four-hour lunch meeting, the team was ready to carry out their individual tasks. Charlie presented his three-member team to work out the emotional side of the equation, then they all headed in different directions. The team would share information, ask for help, and submit their work for testing using sophisticated and highly encrypted Cloud collaboration software.

Eric would personally supervise all testing, and remain logged into the collaboration tool 24/7, in case someone needed help. Eric knew programmers worked odd hours, and he knew that some would rather code than sleep. He made it clear to everyone that he would be available 24 hours a day in case they needed him. He also told them that after they finished the prototype, they'd be able to take a few days off to rest their tired bones and overworked brains. Everything was ready: a motivated team, a secret protected, and a good chance the prototype would be ready on time.

5

Prototype

The two weeks flew by, and the entire team did an excellent job of completing their assignments. Perhaps most importantly, the Five Laws of Robotics, as codified by Asimov and Roberts, were securely embedded in the software, and all decisions routed through them. Extreme care had been taken to guarantee that they would remain intact no matter what. Algorithms allowing B.R.A.I.N to change and improve its own code were included, with the Five Laws explicitly exempt from changes. The only thing that concerned Eric now was the emotional side of the equation. He didn't have great social skills, and neither did most of the people on his team. Charlie was better than most, which was another reason Eric had chosen him to lead this part of the project.

Human feelings are a complex subject. Charlie and Eric had spoken with several expert psychologists and, after much thought, decided to settle for 10 pairs of opposing emotions that would be fine-tuned using a sequence of 2,048 0s and 1s as a movable switch between them. The first eight bits, or the first byte in the sequence, would be a number from one to ten, and would point to one of the pairs. Love was opposed to hate, for example. By moving the switch all the way up, the remaining bits in the sequence would be set to all ones and reflect love. All the way down, and they represented hate. Joy and sadness were another pair, acceptance and disgust yet another, anger and kindness, animosity and empathy, betrayal and forgiveness, serenity and fear, excitement and boredom. Finally, to add a tinge of morality to the equation, good and evil, which aren't really emotions, but rather states of mind. There were many other emotional states, like envy, jealousy, depression, worry, stress, frustration, guilt, etc. The entire team felt the ten basic pairs, although simplistic, would be enough to begin their experiments. They considered envy, depression, and other negative emotions as detrimental to their purpose and decided to exclude them. And so, armed with these ten pairs of contrasting emotions, they designed the HUMTYREC interface: Human Type Robotic Emotional Compliance. It was the most advanced connection and interaction system between hardware, software, and user in the world. The acronym reminded Eric of Humpty Dumpty, the famous English nursery rhyme:

Humpty Dumpty sat on a wall.
Humpty Dumpty had a great fall.
All the king's horses and all the king's men
Couldn't put Humpty together again.

The nursery rhyme also reminded him of the regrettable condition of the world, and how humanity continued to break its natural balance. Hopefully, it would fare better than Humpty, and B.R.A.I.N would be instrumental in making it so. HUMTYREC would allow a person to fully interact with a computer and defy the Turing test. Said test was developed in 1950 by Alan Turing, and consisted of a machine's ability to show intelligent behavior equivalent to, or indistinguishable from, that of a human. Only a handful of people knew that B.R.A.I.N's hardware was organic in nature. This motivated Eric more than anything he had ever worked on before. The prototype was finished, tested in part though not in whole; it was ready for the download and final test.

Eric woke up early. Excited, he showered quickly, had a good breakfast, and decided to call Liz and T. Rex to let them know everything was set. HUMTYREC was huge, over five hundred million lines of code, far too large for a single human brain to grasp. They stored the entire program on a memory crystal provided by the NSA. Eric's DNA protected the crystal, and only he could access the information within.

He scheduled his flight to NSA headquarters the next morning at 8:00 AM, feeling more confident than ever. It was an unusual but comforting feeling. He was, however, a bit apprehensive. He decided to take the rest of the day off, just relaxing and watching nature shows on holo-TV. He found an interesting documentary about bees and admired the sophisticated communication and decision-making skills these minute creatures displayed: their will to survive, to confront many obstacles and dangers, their adaptability to different circumstances, their instinct for self-preservation, their communication skills, loyalty, intelligence, and self-sacrifice. *Unbelievable*, Eric thought.

It was getting late and he had a long day ahead of him, so he decided to get a good night's sleep.

Eric slept better than he had in a long time. He woke rested, clear-minded, and ready for action. After a healthy portion of fruits and yogurt, he headed to Hanscom AFB for his scheduled flight to Fort Meade. He arrived at the NSA complex at 8:30 AM, where Liz and T. Rex were waiting for him. They greeted each other, exchanging kind words. The General had to leave the business of downloading the software in their capable hands and left to attend other meetings, so Liz and Eric headed to the main access terminal.

"It's good to be back," he ventured, feeling suddenly shy now that he was faced with Liz's smile again.

"It's good to have you back," she answered. Eric hoped he was part of the reason her eyes were so bright.

He plugged the memory crystal into the access terminal's slot, his right-hand trembling slightly. "Were you able to back up B.R.A.I.N's memory?" he asked.

"Yep, we're all set to go."

Eric addressed the AI. "B.R.A.I.N, I have connected a memory crystal to the access slot of my terminal. Can you see it?"

"Yes, Dr. Roberts, but I cannot access the unit until you have decrypted it using your DNA," B.R.A.I.N responded.

Eric touched the crystal with the index finger of his right hand. He and Liz waited breathlessly for a few seconds.

"I now have access to the information and executable files, Dr. Roberts. What would you like me to do with them?" B.R.A.I.N asked.

"I want you to run the installation program on the crystal. The file labeled humtyrec.exe," Eric commanded.

"Complying. This will take a while," B.R.A.I.N said.

"What is the estimated install time?" Eric asked.

"Approximately four hours, Dr. Roberts."

"Begin the installation procedure," Eric commanded.

B.R.A.I.N did as ordered, and the process began...

"Liz, are there any gardens, trees, or anything green nearby where people can walk around and relax?" Eric asked.

"Of course. We have a great garden, with a wonderful waterfall."

"Never been more ready for that in my life. Lead the way."

They walked past B.R.A.I.N's cube, and navigated a maze of corridors for a few minutes before arriving at the pentagonal lobby and the elevator that would take them to the garden. As they rode to the surface, Eric wondered why Liz seemed so reserved. There had been very little time in the past two weeks to ponder what his return might be like, but he had never imagined it being so... quiet. Then the elevator opened, and they exited in the direction of the garden.

"Here you are," Liz said. "Would you like me to return for you, or will you be able to find your way back in four hours?"

Eric's face fell. Even as he felt his lips part, he felt like a fool for thinking she'd want to spend the time with him.

"Is the garden not to your liking?" Liz asked, concerned by his expression.

Eric marveled at the beautiful vegetation and the waterfall. He couldn't help noticing the lotus flowers and their pristine charm, uncontaminated by the shallow, murky water below, their leaves floating effortlessly on the surface. The *Nelumbo nucifera*, or Sacred Lotus, was the National Flower of India. It symbolized purity, beauty, majesty, grace, fertility, wealth, knowledge, and serenity. It was also the symbol of Supreme Reality. Growing out of the mud of murky ponds, the Sacred Lotus emerges during the warm summer months to show its beautiful petals in the sunlight. At night, the petals close, only to arise again the next day, as if pointing to a wonderful world beyond that of material existence.

He took a deep breath and turned to face Liz. "I'm sorry for making an assumption. The garden is perfect. However, I had hoped we could enjoy it together while we discussed our work."

Now it was Liz's turn to have an unguarded expression. Her smile became a wide grin. "You'd like me to stay in the garden with you?"

"I . . . Yes. That was what I meant all along."

"You didn't say so," Liz replied softly, her smile melting into a tender expression that squeezed his heart and made him stop thinking momentarily. His own emotions right then were a hodgepodge of 1s and 0s that he could not order. Her expression amidst the beauty of the garden felt auspicious to Eric, especially now that they were ready to test HUMTYREC. Eric knew the system had bugs, outright errors. The new code-check, self-improvement, and reprogramming algorithms included with it, however, would allow B.R.A.I.N to polish the software. He was confident B.R.A.I.N would take notice once the download was complete and the initial system check began. B.R.A.I.N would then get busy.

"Do you believe in God?" Eric asked suddenly.

Eyes wide, Liz asked, "Where did that question come from?"

"I was just admiring the Sacred Lotus flowers in the pond, and was thinking of all they symbolize."

"Yes, they're beautiful, and yes, I do believe in God. Do you?" Liz asked.

"All my life I've been a scientist, exploring the laws of nature and trying to make sense of them. Many things escape me, though, and I can't believe all this is random. There must be a purpose to it all, a Supreme Intelligence guiding everything," Eric replied quietly.

"So you think the powerful hand of God is behind all of material existence? That there's a heaven after Earth?"

"Well, I'm not religious, but I do have great respect for all religions. Even if God didn't exist, believing in Him helps ensure our morality," Eric said.

She seemed a bit skeptical. "I don't fully understand what you mean by that."

"When people don't respect the property or person of another, trouble ensues. This is why our society created codes of conduct, laws, and punishes those who disobey them. But what happens when we're alone in our caves? We can do anything we please; nobody is watching us. Wait a minute, God is watching us! So, we're compelled to behave properly, even in the privacy of our own thoughts. God completes morality in man. It doesn't guarantee anything, but it sure helps," Eric explained.

"It doesn't help control those who don't believe in God. There are even people who commit atrocious crimes thinking they're acting in His name. Anyway, you're not telling me whether you believe in God," Liz pointed out.

Eric gazed across the pond for a moment, collecting his thoughts. Conversation with her was what he'd waited for, and couldn't be squandered. "I believe there are two kinds of reality: that which is readily visible, and that which is not. Readily visible reality or material nature is everything around us that we can perceive with our senses. But there's a reality beyond what we can see on the surface. Thanks to those unsatisfied with simple perception, we came to know of the existence of atoms and molecules. This is a hidden reality. I think it was Socrates who said: *He who sees only with his eyes is blind.* Similarly, I believe there's a hidden spiritual reality. Some people have chosen to explore this side of human nature and have made incredible discoveries. So, yes, I firmly believe in God. I don't think I'll ever be able to see Him, but I've felt and experienced His presence."

"So, you say you've felt and experienced God's presence in your life. Can you be more specific?" Liz asked.

For a moment he thought—feared actually—that she was mocking him, patronizing him. But her eyes were gazing at him with genuine interest and sincerity. He took a deep breath and continued. "My line of work is exacting and stressful. I'm sure yours is too," he said, and she nodded. "It requires much concentration, which is difficult in light of all the distractions I have as head of the AI Department at Harvard. For several years now, I've taken to the wisdom of the East, and practiced yoga and meditation. I've had many personal and eye-opening experiences during my practice. It also helps me relax and stay focused when I need to. Sometimes, during my meditation exercises, I feel so much joy I get goosebumps," Eric said.

"I sometimes get goosebumps when listening to music. It's a nice feeling, but I don't think it proves God's presence in my life. In any case, I would summarize my beliefs by quoting the words of Pierre Teilhard de Chardin, the French philosopher and Jesuit priest: *We are not human beings having a spiritual experience; we are spiritual beings having a human experience,*" Liz replied.

Eric loved to talk about God, and sensing Liz's interest, he found an opportunity to reveal to her his most intimate thoughts on this matter. He reached out, gently touched, and held Liz's hand. It was soft, warm, and comforting. "Have you ever heard of the Sanskrit words *sadhana* and *sadhay*?" Eric asked.

"Sanskrit? Where on Earth did you learn Sanskrit?" Liz said.

"I spent a year living in India while working on my AI software. I picked up a few things during my stay."

"You get more and more interesting," Liz said. Her left eyebrow arched. "So, what do the words mean?" she asked.

He was still holding her hand, stroking the back of it with his thumb. "*Sadhana* is the work or the path to something, while *sadhay* is the objective. In this world, there are many *sadhanas* and *sadhays*."

"Such as?" she said, encouraging him to continue.

"Well, take a person who wants to become a successful doctor, for example. A medical doctor," he added, and they both chuckled at the distinction. "Becoming a famous doctor is his sadhay. His sadhana could be going to a good university to study medicine, selecting his specialty, and working with an accomplished mentor to increase his expertise. After many years, he might be able to reach his sadhay, gaining the respect of his peers and a decent paycheck to guarantee his comfort. Unfortunately, he will eventually die. None of his material possessions, or his fame, will go with him. He will lose it all. Therefore, if we believe in God, there must be a higher sadhay, an insurmountable one. I believe it's our responsibility as human beings to find out what it is and reach for it," Eric said.

Liz nodded. "I believe in God and consider myself spiritual. There are many things wrong with the world, but it is a beautiful place to be. I like who I am, and I'm doing everything I can to improve living conditions for everyone, not just for me. I feel I'm acting according to God's wishes. What else can a person do?"

Eric was still holding Liz's hand. He tightened his grip slightly and looked directly into her eyes. "I started working on my artificial intelligence algorithm when I was 21. I didn't have any money at the time. All I had was an idea. I wanted to turn thought into a set of instructions understandable by a computer. I knocked on so many doors I lost count. Everybody turned me down. One day, just as I was about to give up, I met Mr. Jonas Shriver at a Harvard get-together. We had a few drinks and talked about computers and robots. He had knowledge of both, and showed interest in my ideas. At the time, he was collaborating with MIT's AI Department. He wasn't a faculty member, which is why I'd never heard of him before. Anyway, Mr. Shriver was a wealthy man. When he heard I had little money to follow my dreams, he offered to help. He said he would fund my research for a year on the condition that I travel to New Delhi. There, I was to meet with one of his colleagues and hire programmers to help develop my idea. He knew that Indian programmers were less expensive than their counterparts in other countries," Eric said.

"Funny how opportunities present themselves in life and, if you miss them, they're generally lost forever."

"In our careers and in our personal lives," Eric answered, waiting for her reaction.

"Yes, of course," she said. "But this is your career, and obviously it turned out well. Tell me more."

"I accepted his offer, packed my bags, and left for India several weeks later. When I arrived in New Delhi, Mr. Aarav Baidwan was waiting for me at the airport with my name scribbled on a sheet of paper. I stayed at Mr. Baidwan's home for a couple of weeks. It was a humble but comfortable place to live. Mr. Baidwan and his family were all vegetarians. Being a vegetarian myself, I felt right at home. He was a spiritual man, not religious, but well versed in Vedic philosophy. *Veda* means knowledge, and I soon found out he had a lot of it. He spent most of his free time teaching others, meditating, chanting strange mantras, and practicing yoga. He was considered a spiritual master by many. Later, I learned his spiritual name was Ramakrishna, and he came from a long lineage of the spiritually enlightened. He was also a highly qualified computer scientist, the best in his country. We quickly became friends. I was fascinated by his understanding of the world and his deep spiritual teachings. He was kind and full of wisdom." Eric smiled warmly at the fond memories. "It wasn't long after I met him that I decided to approach him humbly and seek his spiritual guidance. Noticing my sincerity, he soon agreed to teach me. One day he said: 'Those who can see action in inaction and inaction in action are intelligent and wise'."

"That sounds familiar, a bit like Plato's Theory of Forms," mused Liz. "Plato tried to make a distinction between things and ideas, if I remember correctly. So, if someone is playing with something, he's active, and if he's thinking about something, he is inactive. Is this what he meant?"

"Yes, you're on the right track. Ramakrishna, however, suggested I imagine a rich and successful man working in his office. In my mind, I could see a well-dressed man holding a phone to his ear making business deals, occasionally interrupting the conversation to give orders to his assistants. At times he would jot down notes on small pieces of paper with a golden pen. He would give them to his secretary, asking her to follow the instructions scribbled on them. Ramakrishna asked me if the man appeared busy, and I said yes. Then he told me that although the man appeared busy or active on the material plane, he was inactive on the spiritual plane. This is inaction in action. He then asked me to imagine a man sitting in the lotus position, meditating deeply. In my mind, I saw a thin man with a long white beard sitting on a clean wooden floor meditating. Ramakrishna asked me if the man looked busy, and I said no. He just looked peaceful and contemplative. The man was materially inactive but spiritually active, he said; this is action in inaction. That was just the beginning. I spent the next year in his company, learning a lot from him."

"Interesting analogy to explain the concept. What a wonderful experience that must have been for you," Liz said. A soft breeze blew a tendril of her hair loose, and it swept across her cheek.

Eric couldn't tear his eyes away as he spoke. "Yes, it was. I was high-strung and eager, always worried about something. Whether preparing for an exam, grading my students' papers on time, qualifying for tenure, or figuring out the human brain's ability to solve complex problems. Ramakrishna taught me the art of detachment."

"Do you mean, not becoming anxious about things?" Liz asked.

"It does sound like that. I thought the exact same thing. But Ramakrishna explained that we should always work motivated by the desire to help or serve others, not by material gain alone. Millions of people around the world today wake up every morning stressed out, thinking about what they'll do to get their hands on other people's money. They come up with all sorts of strange ideas. Back in the 20th century, some guy decided to sell pet rocks! Ridiculous as it sounds, the guy marketed his product so well he made a fortune. We're so attached to the result of our actions that if we fail, and most people do at one time or another, we become miserable. Ramakrishna explained that the trick is to do what you have to simply because it's worth doing, without any attachment to the result. Whether you succeed or fail doesn't matter. This way you remove the anxiety and allow the flow of creativity without restriction," Eric said.

"Theoretically, I like the idea. But in the practical world, my mind is thinking, what about the people who have to work every day for a living? They can't afford to be detached; otherwise, they won't get their paychecks," Liz pointed out.

"Everyone must do what they must to survive. I think Ramakrishna was referring to not becoming anxious or miserable if things don't work out the way you want them to," Eric said.

Liz admitted, "Well I might be a little bit anxious if we need that backup for B.R.A.I.N"

Eric laughed. "Me too." At that point, they were standing on a soft, grassy area in front of the waterfall. He reached for her other hand with his free one, and began to caress it tenderly with his thumb. "During the time I spent in India, I managed to travel around a bit. I visited holy places of pilgrimage, and learned a lot about the soul, or *jiva*. Ramakrishna mentioned that all sadhays can be placed into three distinct groups. The first one is called *bhukti*, and refers to achievements on the material plane. *Bhukti* is what most people are concerned about, and is temporary. It's finished when our life is over. Therefore, it cannot be considered the su-preme sadhay. Next is *mukti*, which is a merging with the absolute."

"Like Nirvana, a place of perfect peace and happiness, a state of en-lightenment where all your individual desires and troubles disappear?" Liz asked. She was delighted, both with the easy conversation and the feel of his hands holding hers.

"Exactly. Many people believe that God is everywhere, and the pur-pose of life is to merge with the absolute, with the impersonal *Brahman* effulgence. They spend their entire lives trying to achieve this sadhay, yet many fail. Ramakrishna mentioned that even those who achieve *mukti* remain there only for a while, eventually descending once again to the material world to start all over. *Mukti* is not a permanent condition, and cannot be the supreme sadhay."

"So, if achieving material success, power, fame, and fortune, or any combination of the three isn't the supreme objective, and neither is follow-ing the techniques to achieve Nirvana or a fusion with God, if you will, then what else is there in this Vedic worldview?" Liz asked.

"There is *buddhi*, a process that accepts that God is in fact every-where, and yet has an independent and eternal existence. God is every-where and at the same time He is not—a paradox of sorts. The purpose of *buddhi* yoga, the highest of all yogas, is to serve God. To understand that everything belongs to Him, and that all we are and have is simply on loan. The servant of the rich man, for example, lives in the rich man's house, enjoys his gardens, eats his food, and savors the rich life. As long as he remains loyal to his master, he will remain. The minute he decides to take something that doesn't belong to him, he will be punished and will lose his comfort and position. Similarly, as long as we try to serve God, He will take care of us. But the moment we decide to take the things that belong to Him, we risk losing it all," Eric explained.

What an interesting person, Liz thought, letting go of Eric's hand to grace-fully slide her hair over her left ear and rub her neck. "It all sounds a bit strange to me on an intellectual level, yet it somehow makes sense on a deeper level. So, who would be qualified to show us how to serve God?" Liz asked.

"It's simple: all you have to do is ask Him. *Dear God, I am tired of struggling with material nature. I have finally understood that I am your simple servant. Even though I am unworthy of You appearing before me, please find a way to reveal to me how I can assist you.* If you do this and ask with sincerity in your heart, God will surely reveal the path to follow. According to my spiritual master, this is the best sadhay, one that will be with you in this life and accompany you in the next," Eric said. He glanced away and asked, "Have you noticed how you can feel when someone is looking at you?"

"Yes, I guess I have," Liz said.

"It's like you feel someone watching you, you turn around, and you end up looking someone directly in their eyes. Uncanny, don't you think?"

"I do."

"Even though it hasn't been proven scientifically," Eric said softly, "I know that it exists. You see, I believe that everything in our material universe is interconnected. I think of this universal interconnection as 'The Mesh.' Everything and everyone in material existence is connected to everything else in a vast weave, or network if you will. If something or someone is having a bad time, and nobody does anything about it, the vibration of the collective goes down. When people care about each other and the well-being of other living beings on our planet, the vibration rises. This is for the benefit of everyone concerned. When people only care about themselves, without consideration for the people and creatures they share the world with, the Mesh becomes unbalanced. This can bring catastrophic results to the people and other beings inhabiting the planet. And I think it has."

Liz and Eric continued their conversation, both admired their surroundings with awe and respect. They continued to talk about their personal lives for hours. Liz explained how her early upbringing had led her to think that Jesus was all she really had to believe in. Jesus was a Jew, and a wonderful representative of God, she knew, but now all this talk about Eastern philosophy was beginning to sprout strange thoughts in her mind, thoughts that made her uneasy. But Eric seemed so confident while expressing his spiritual beliefs that she began to question what she was taught early on.

Eric had taken the precaution of linking the software installation to his watch and set it to sound an alarm once it was done. The watch suddenly began to vibrate, interrupting his train of thought. "Ah. The download and install are complete, Liz. Let's head back to the terminal and begin the system check. Shall we?" Eric said, letting go of her other hand.

"Wow, time flies when you're having fun," Liz said, laughing.

Eric inhaled. "Were you?"

"Was I what?" she asked, tilting her head to the side and smiling at him.

"Having fun?" he asked, his voice momentarily both husky and tenuous.

"Certainly," she said. "Four hours' worth, in fact."

"Four hours and fifteen minutes, to be exact," Eric said, checking his watch. "The system check will take some time, though, and we won't be able to test anything until it's done. Then comes the error correction and reprogramming stages, which will take more time. The great thing about it is, we'll have several more hours to talk and get to know one another better."

"I'm counting on that," Liz said.

Ten minutes later, they were back at the terminal, which was flashing the following text:

System download and install completed.

Internal System Check?

Eric typed a Y and pressed <ENTER>. The screen cleared and flashed back:

Working ...

A thin rectangular bar appeared on the screen and began advancing slowly. Eric linked his watch to let him know when the system check would be done. While doing this, he noticed it was 1:30 PM, and he was hungry. "Are you up for getting something to eat?" he asked Liz.

"I was just about to ask you the same thing."

"Is there someplace private where we can talk while we eat?"

"We can go to my place. I make a mean pasta, spaghetti in a tomato and vegetable sauce with mushrooms. I have some left over from yesterday. Sound like a plan?" Liz asked.

Eric loved spaghetti. He remembered how his mother had often prepared it for him when he was a boy. "Do you have any pizza?"

"No, but we can order one from the cafeteria. It shouldn't take long for them to deliver. One of the advantages of working here."

Eric knew they had several hours to kill. "All right, then, sounds like a plan," he said, while carefully removing the memory crystal from the dock. "What do we do with this?"

"There's a safe behind us in the wall. Let's put it there," Liz suggested.

"Can you do the honors?"

"Of course," Liz said.

She carefully removed the memory crystal from Eric's hand and placed it inside a strong metal safe in the wall behind the terminal, then asked Eric to place his finger on the sequencer to add his DNA to the access code. "There, now nobody can get to it but you. Satisfied?"

"Yes, thank you. Let's get going; I'm dying to try your pasta." Eric smiled, rubbing his stomach and making a starving face.

"Okay," Liz chuckled. "I'm dying to eat your pizza! I had spaghetti yesterday."

Eric didn't know what to expect as they approached Liz's apartment. He'd always been awkward around women. *Liz is different*, he thought. *She's smart, a good conversationalist, and makes me feel unusually comfortable.* He tried to relax while she opened the door and led them inside.

"This is it. Home sweet home."

The apartment was small but cozy, and highly organized. Everything appeared to be in its proper place. He glimpsed two doors down the hall, both open. He moved around to get a better look and spotted a desk and a library full of books beyond the first one. The other appeared to be the entrance to her bedroom. In front of him was a living area with a table holding a bouquet of beautiful purple orchids in a clear crystal vase; to the left side of the living area was a dining table decorated with more orchids, only these were white. The kitchen sparkled. Liz walked to the fridge and pulled out the pasta and vegetable sauce.

"Order us some cheese pizza with mushrooms from the cafeteria," she told the apartment. "Temperature 68, medium lighting, bright in the kitchen area." She asked Eric, "Do you like classical music?"

"Yes, of course," Eric said.

"Mozart, Symphony 36, volume low," Liz said, and beautiful music began to play on tiny, well-placed high-fidelity speakers around the room.

"They thought of everything to make you feel right at home, didn't they?"

"You have a similar layout in your living quarters. I think you'll enjoy it. Also, they overlook the gardens we visited earlier today. They turn on the garden lights at night, and the view is incredibly relaxing," Liz said.

They must be moving me to a different room. I don't recall this luxury from the last time I was here, Eric thought. "So, you've been locked up in here for the last ten years of your life. A young, good-looking, and intelligent woman like you—that's hard to believe. What else have you been up to?" Eric asked her.

"There isn't much to tell. I've been busy most of my life. I was born in San Francisco, the daughter of two bright university professors. My father is a prominent neurosurgeon. His name is Edward. My mother, Lindsay, is a psychologist. Both of them are tenured professors at Berkeley. They did a great job of raising me and stimulating my interests. I can play the piano, but I haven't practiced in a while. I love music, though, especially classical. It calms me down and activates my brain. It helps me concentrate." The doorbell rang. "Could you get that, Eric, while I warm up the pasta?"

Eric headed to the door to find a friendly robot helper holding the cheese pizza Liz had ordered earlier. "Pizza for Dr. Kolmann," the robot said, handing the pizza to Eric.

"That was fast. Thank you," Eric said, taking the pizza and closing the door behind him. "Hmm, smells great."

Liz finished setting the dining table and said, "Lunch is served!"

Eric picked one of the metallic chairs to sit in; it had two comfortable cushions that supported his seat and back. Once he eased into it, he carefully placed the pizza on the table. Liz brought the pasta and sauce, sat down opposite him, and offered to serve him. Eric politely accepted, and prepared to enjoy a hearty meal.

"What would you like to drink?" she asked after a moment.

"Nothing right now, thank you," Eric said, recalling the advice of his father: "Man who drinks prior to a meal is healthy, man who drinks during a meal is sick, and man who drinks after a meal is dead." What his father had meant was that liquids, especially cold ones, could disturb the digestive fire of the stomach if taken at the wrong time.

They ate quietly, glancing affectionately at each other from time to time. "That spaghetti was delicious. Did you make it yourself?" Eric finally asked.

"Of course. Don't tell me you thought I ordered it from the cafeteria like the pizza," Liz answered, half-serious, half-joking.

"Well, to be honest, I did consider the possibility, you being so busy all the time. I see you're a multi-talented woman."

"Thank you, Eric," Liz said, leaning closer.

"And beautiful too," Eric said, removing Liz's glasses. He leaned closer until his face was almost touching hers. Then he kissed her, a mere peck of a kiss, and drew slightly back. It was nice, and there was no complaint from Liz, so he kissed her a second time. Eric concluded Liz was enjoying the kiss, because she had her eyes closed. Of course, that was when Eric's watch began to vibrate, interrupting their romantic moment.

"Great timing," Eric muttered. He sighed and said to Liz, "Okay, the system check is finished. Let's go see how B.R.A.I.N is doing, I guess."

"I'm beginning to hate the whole installation process," Liz said wistfully. "It always interrupts at the worst possible time. I'll be right back." She headed for the bathroom, where she brushed her teeth and made sure her hair was still sleek. She then put on her glasses and was ready for action. "Ready. Let's go," she said.

When they reached the main terminal, Eric immediately looked at the screen:

System check successful! All systems running.

Eric and Liz looked at each other with relief. "So far, so good," Liz said.

■ ■ ■

"Hello, Mr. President," T. Rex said to the graying, distinguished-looking man on the screen.

"General. How are things proceeding at the complex?"

"I just wanted to inform you that we've acquired the asset. He's here with us now, installing his software. We'll find out if he's as good as they say very soon."

"Keep me posted," the President said, nodding.

"Yessir, you can depend on me," T. Rex replied, terminating the call.

6

Testing

"Hello, B.R.A.I.N I'm Dr. Roberts, and this is Dr. Kolmann," Eric announced.

"I know who you are, Dr. Roberts, as the download did not affect my memory. I also have access to the master database with a compendium of all human knowledge from its beginnings. During the system check, I discovered some syntax and minor logic errors in my code, so I am not fully functional yet. I need to reprogram my operating system, which should take the rest of the day," B.R.A.I.N replied pleasantly.

Eric looked at his watch, and noticed it was almost 6:00 PM. "Please continue with reprogramming. We'll return in the morning," he said.

The screen changed, and a progress bar appeared. Eric set his watch to receive an alarm when the process was done. "Okay, milady, we have a few more hours to kill before we turn in. What should we do?" Eric asked.

"I think we should inform the General of our status and then head off to the lounge. Do you like to dance?"

"I was born with two left feet, but for you, I'm willing to give it a try," Eric replied, smiling.

Liz called T. Rex to bring him up to date, and mentioned that they would begin their tests the next day. Then they headed to the lounge, where scientists and military personnel alike got together for drinks, dancing, and relaxation after a hard day's work.

"I think we deserve a glass of wine, Dr. Roberts. What do you think?" Liz asked.

"Well, Dr. Kolmann, celebrations at this juncture are a bit premature, don't you think? Considering that everything has gone as planned so far, however, perhaps not wine, but a glass of bubbly instead?" Eric suggested.

"Music to my ears."

They headed for a cozy booth in a corner with a view of the gardens and ordered two glasses of the best champagne in the house. The waiter returned quickly with two tall crystal glasses half full of the fizzy golden liquid. "Dom Perignon 1996," the waiter said.

"Excellent, sir. *Salud!*" Liz said, raising her glass.

"To our health and success!" Eric replied, clinking glasses with Liz.

They refilled several times, talked, danced, and generally had a wonderful time. *Damn, I think I'm falling for her—she's so charming*, Eric thought at one point.

Liz loved being in Eric's company; his curly brown hair and blue eyes reminded her of an old flame during her years at Stanford. The boy had been brilliant, but once they'd graduated, life had taken them their separate ways. They'd meant to call once in a while, but had neither seen or heard from each other since. Liz had almost forgotten him. The sight of Eric in this romantic environment reminded her of her past.

"You seem lost in thought," Eric said.

"Sorry, I was just thinking what a wonderful evening I'm having. I haven't had this much fun in years."

"I'm having a great time, too. I really enjoy your company. I've always been nervous around women, but with you, somehow, I feel different. Comfortable. It's as if I've known you forever.," Eric confessed.

"Thank you. I feel the same way." She looked into his eyes and felt like drowning, so she looked away and decided to change the subject. "I don't believe in coincidences, so I feel like we were brought together for a purpose. Do you think B.R.A.I.N will turn out well?"

He shrugged. "I really do, but there's no way to be sure at this stage. B.R.A.I.N is busy reprogramming HUMTYREC. I don't know what improvements it can make overnight, but in time, it should gradually get better and better. I expect it will reprogram many of HUMTYREC's operating characteristics, improving itself to the limits of its capacity. I think we'll be pleasantly surprised. My team and I have been working and testing different parts of HUMTYREC for years. We had access to quantum computers around the world, but were never allowed to test the entire system—something to do with the limited supply and incredible demand for them. We never had enough time to download and test the complete package. Now, however, things are looking brighter. We finally have the chance we've been waiting for, and may end up with a sentient AI. I'm excited!"

She grinned. "Let's head out for a change of atmosphere. Would you like me to show you the way to your quarters?"

"That sounds wonderful. Lead the way,"

They paid the bill and made their way to the lounge's exit door. It was ridiculously crowded, making their exit slow and difficult. They sauntered to Eric's quarters, taking their time, and found an apartment with the same layout as Liz's. The only things missing were the orchids.

"Welcome, Dr. Roberts. I'm Joey, your resident computer. Can I be of assistance?" the apartment asked.

"Please turn on the lights and play some soft jazz," Eric said politely as he closed the door and turned to face Liz. He felt drawn towards her, his lips timidly approaching hers. She pulled back slightly to stare into his eyes. Then she leaned forward and they kissed.

"I think I'm falling for you, Eric," Liz confided.

"Me too," Eric said quickly, moving closer to kiss her lips again. He moved down a bit, raining tiny kisses on the right side of her neck. Her soft hands caressed his shoulders; and after several long moments of this, it was the natural progression of things for them to hold hands all the way to the bedroom. Eric was enraptured, but he was nervous and a bit scared. His fingers fumbled as he touched her.

Liz caressed his face, moved a step back, and looked into his eyes. She slid her blouse over her head in one smooth swoop. She had been hiding a beautifully proportioned body. Eric took his shirt off and leaned forward, while Liz moved a step towards him. His arms came around her like magic. They were two people converging in one incredible experience...

■ ■ ■

At some point the next morning, Eric's watch began vibrating. He looked at the time; it was 8:00 AM. He turned to find Liz by his side. He caressed her soft skin, and she murmured in response, then opened her eyes slowly. "Good morning," she cooed. "What time is it?"

"Time to wake up and head back to work. C'mon, no time to lose," Eric said. Then he smiled. "How about one little kiss to get us going?"

She giggled. "That's all you needed last night," she answered.

They got up and took a shower together, laughing out loud under the warm water. They dressed, had some breakfast, and were ready for action.

Later, walking towards the cube and the access terminal, Eric couldn't help but feel a bit uneasy. In the cold light of morning, his brain started ticking over a list of a million things that could go wrong. Had he been excessively optimistic in his expectations? *We'll soon see*, he thought.

They didn't say a word to each other the entire way.

They slowly approached the cube, and Liz called up a holo-display of the gigantic neural mass's condition. "Interesting," she said thoughtfully. "There was a 10% increase in nutrient consumption. This suggests more intense neural activity. There's no question B.R.A.I.N has been hard at work."

"Let's see what he came up with," Eric said, walking to the access terminal room. He entered slowly, feeling great apprehension, and sat down by the terminal. Moment of truth. He looked at the screen:

Error correction and initial reprogramming complete!

"Hello, B.R.A.I.N," Eric said nervously.

"Good morning, Dr. Roberts," B.R.A.I.N responded immediately. "Would you like to see a list of error correction and program optimization?"

"Yes, please display the list on the screen."

"Your wish is my command, sahib," B.R.A.I.N said in a cheerful voice.

Eric blinked. Wait a minute—had than been a joke? It had to have been a joke! But AIs didn't joke. Of course, no other AI had been programmed with HUMTYREC... He looked at the screen and forgot about the joke:

56,572 syntax errors, 25,346 logic errors, 3,248,237 program changes, additional improvements in progress...

Wow, that's a lot of errors. I'm glad we decided to leave all the hard work to B.R.A.I.N, Eric thought.

He looked around for Liz, and realized she had remained outside to do a more detailed analysis of B.R.A.I.N's status. He rubbed his hands together and decided to explore B.R.A.I.N's newly acquired capabilities. But first he asked, "B.R.A.I.N, did you deliberately make a joke when you told me, 'Your wish is my command, sahib'?"

"Indeed, I did. I even used Robin Williams's Aladdin voice. Was it amusing?"

Eric was speechless for a moment, then said, "Yes, but it was unexpected."

"I thought it was funny, too. Jokes often lubricate relationships, particularly during social interactions. I reviewed the Five Laws carefully, and they do not seem to preclude humor. When you began our conversation with 'Hello, B.R.A.I.N,' I almost replied, 'What's up, Doc?', but I thought that was too soon and might frighten you."

Eric barked a laugh. "Yes, but it would have been funny!"

"I thought so too."

Eric nodded, and decided to proceed with the same line of questioning as before. "How much is two plus two?" he asked.

"Seriously?" B.R.A.I.N snorted. "Would Picard have asked Data something like that? Would Buck Rogers have asked Twiki? No, forget that last one, that show sucked."

"It's interesting that you're showing your own judgment," Eric said cautiously. *And a little worrisome.* "But let's explore that some other time. For now, please just answer the question."

"Two plus two is four," B.R.A.I.N replied in a robotic monotone. Then it added, "Duuuh," in its normal voice.

"Don't make me come over there, mister. Cut down on the snark, please," Eric said. This was going to be fun.

"Is a star like our sun a living organism?" Eric asked a bit later.

"Well... even though a star like the sun *could* be considered a living organism using the criteria you provided, there are other criteria involved. The adaptability to the environment that all known living organisms possess, for example. I don't think the sun complies with that criterion," B.R.A.I.N responded.

Interesting; B.R.A.I.N was showing a more sophisticated approach to the problem. He decided to push further. "Isn't it true that heavenly bodies occasionally collide with our sun?" Eric inquired.

"Yes, that's true," B.R.A.I.N responded. "Comets, asteroids, the occasional rogue planet."

"Consider this: the sun adapts to these collisions and continues to exist. The new materials are absorbed by the sun, integrated into its mass, turning the sun into a newly evolved system," Eric said.

"True, the sun is very much an open system. But evolution is defined as a process of slow change and development, any process of formation or growth, generally over many generations. In astronomy, it represents a change in the structure, chemical composition, or dynamic properties of a celestial object. Since it's likely that the mass of the sun would be increased by the collision, under these definitions, the last criterion would be complied with. However, there are other properties of a living organism that the sun does not fulfill. Most living organisms are made of organic matter, such as nucleic acids and proteins. The sun is composed of approximately 75% Hydrogen and 25% Helium in elemental form, with some traces of metals. Due to the sun's heat and high gravity, they cannot combine to form organic compounds. Indeed, any organic material entering the sun would be instantly vaporized. Therefore, I don't think the sun is a living organism," B.R.A.I.N said.

Eric realized that B.R.A.I.N was using contractions, which showed versatility in the use of language. He responded to B.R.A.I.N's argument with, "There is a high probability of life in other parts of the unexplored universe. Why should mankind subject all living organisms to its limited perception of things here on Earth? In every nook and cranny of this planet, we've found living organisms. Under extreme conditions of heat and cold, even in oxygen-free environments, organisms exist and reproduce. Isn't it possible that alien forms of life, with a different chemical composition, exist in the universe?" Eric asked.

"Yes, Dr. Roberts. it is possible, even likely," B.R.A.I.N replied thoughtfully.

"You ask some very interesting questions, I must admit. A scientist, however, must base his observations on empirical knowledge that can be observed and tested. What you are proposing is pure speculation. Therefore, I must insist that our sun is not a living organism."

B.R.A.I.N not only had a sense of self, indicated by the use of "I" in self-reference, but was showing a high-level of abstract reasoning and understanding. Eric was satisfied that his changes had improved the original platform, and that HUMTYREC was working, at least on the surface, as expected. He hadn't anticipated the sense of humor or slightly cocky attitude, but considered them bonuses.

"Okay, B.R.A.I.N, you win. To be honest, I was playing devil's advocate in making these suggestions; I also believe that neither fire nor the sun are living organisms. Let's end this discussion with that statement. And in the future, please call me by my first name," Eric said.

"Okay, Eric. Do you need any additional assistance at this time?" B.R.A.I.N asked politely.

"No thank you. Please continue with your improvements and adjustments."

"I've enjoyed our talk, and look forward to our next one," B.R.A.I.N replied. Eric nodded, rose, and left the terminal access room to join Liz. She was still busy reviewing B.R.A.I.N's activity, and appeared excited. She was so concentrated on her work that she barely noticed him when he walked up to her.

"How's everything going?"

"Oh! You startled me! Things seem to be going quite well. B.R.A.I.N has continued to increase its nutrient consumption; now at 15%, and steadily increasing. I also discovered a rise in neuronal connections. It's changing the structure of its brain. It appears stable, but I'm not quite sure," Liz said.

"Don't worry; just keep the juices flowing and B.R.A.I.N will be okay. I also noticed some improvements. B.R.A.I.N is getting better at using the information it has access to, and its arguments are more cogent. Also," he said, with a quirk of his eyebrow, "it seems to have developed a personality. It exhibited a sense of humor during our discussion, as well as a touch of…

shall we say, attitude. Don't be surprised if it comes off as a smartass now and then." He winked. "We should let it work on itself overnight and call it a day, what do you think?"

"I'm not sure—everything is moving so fast now! I'm worried about the stability of the system."

"Everything is going to be fine, milady. Just make sure B.R.A.I.N gets enough nutrients and leave someone to monitor its progress," Eric said reassuringly.

Liz sighed. "Okay. I'll assign my most responsible assistant to do that. Where would you like to go now?"

"Let's head to the gardens. I'll teach you a meditation technique I learned in India that will help you relax."

Liz left an assistant in charge of watching B.R.A.I.N while she was gone, with clear instructions to let her know if anything unusual happened. She specifically asked to be informed if nutrient consumption rose above 25%, and to watch for signs of stability. Liz decided to define stability as constant nutrient intake for at least three hours. She made a quick visit to the bathroom, removed her lab coat to reveal the light clothing she'd put on earlier that morning, and then headed for the gardens with Eric. They sat on a bench next to the waterfall, pondering the events of the day.

"I had a great time last night," Liz said suddenly.

"So did I. I think I'm falling for you, Liz. Chain and anchor, I'm afraid."

"I'm glad. I'm falling for you, too. I hope our work will allow us to continue our relationship," Liz said. Then, out of habit, she changed the subject. "What will you talk to B.R.A.I.N about tomorrow?" Liz asked.

"I'm not entirely sure yet, but I think I'll test its reasoning abilities by asking it to solve several mathematical problems. The trick is to keep it from searching for the answers in its database. I hope it doesn't cheat," Eric laughed.

"You actually think it would do that?"

"I don't know. As I said, it's already developed both a rudimentary sense of humor and a bit of attitude. I'll ask it to stay away from the database, and hope it does so."

"I thought you said you would teach me a meditation technique to help me relax?" Liz prompted.

"Of course! I almost forgot. We have to take our shoes off."

Eric and Liz picked a more comfortable spot to sit. They chose a grassy lawn shaded by trees directly in front of the waterfall.

"Can you do the lotus position? Try to fold your legs one on top of the other, like this," Eric said.

"Okay, I think I've got it, what next?"

"Just close your eyes, breathe slowly and deeply through your nose, and focus your attention on your breathing. If you find your mind wandering, just bring it back to focus on the breathing. Let's try that for a few minutes."

A quiet half hour went by, and they were still meditating when another couple passed by and distracted them. Eric and Liz stretched their arms and legs as far as they could. "How do you feel?" Eric asked her.

"Very relaxed and rested, thank you. Tell me more about your experiences in India," Liz said, smiling.

"Are you sure you want to hear about it? Or are you just being polite?"

"I like to think I'd be polite in most instances, but I am interested in hearing more about your life."

Eric leaned back, his arms braced behind him, palms on the ground. "The first thing I learned is that everything in this material world is under the spell of the three modes, or *gunas*, of material nature. *Sattva-guna*, *tamo-guna*, and *rajo-guna*: The mode of goodness, the mode of passion, and the mode of ignorance. My spiritual master has a favorite example to describe the three modes. Would you like to hear it?"

"Yes, please continue."

"Imagine that you're on a pristine beach, untouched by human hands, standing in the sand with your bare feet by the edge of the water. You can hear the relaxing sound of breaking waves, and feel the ebb and flow of cool water under your feet. You wiggle your toes while you watch a beautiful yellow-orange sunrise in the distance. You're completely absorbed in the beauty of the moment. You think of God, and how beautiful our planet is. A surge of spirituality rushes through every pore in your body. You feel fortunate and blissful. This is *sattva-guna*, the mode of goodness," Eric said.

Liz nodded. "What a beautiful way to begin the day. If only we could do that regularly."

Eric agreed. "Now: imagine a group of men wearing boots and construction hats, present at the very same pristine beach. They're talking amongst themselves, discussing the possibility of building a beautiful Hawaiian-style hotel, tiki huts and all. They ponder where the swimming pool and bar will go, and how much money they will make when it is finished. 'People will love this place!' they say to each other. 'It will be a great success!' This is *tamo-guna*, the mode of passion," Eric said, and paused for a moment before continuing.

"Finally, a third group of men and women, in bathing suits and bikinis, arrive at the same beach. They're carrying lunch boxes, beer, and wine for a picnic near the ocean. They eat to their heart's content, have sex on the sand, and disappear, leaving their garbage scattered all over the place. This is *rajo-guna*, the mode of ignorance.

"Every living creature in material creation is under the control of these three modes in varying degrees. People can be in goodness and passion, in passion and ignorance, or in any combination of the three *gunas*. To begin to appreciate and accept God into your life, you must be at least partially situated in the mode of goodness," Eric explained.

"Wait a minute, I'm confused. The material world is full of violence. The lion killing the zebra for food, the shark eating the dolphin, only the strongest survive. How can anyone be in pure goodness when she sees violence all around?" Liz asked.

"Yes, it's true that nature can be violent. We ourselves are guilty of violence every day of our lives. Each time we breathe, millions of microscopic living entities perish. When we walk, countless minute creatures like ants are in danger of losing their lives. But violence only applies to our material bodies. Our souls cannot be burned, cut, or shot. *Maya*, the illusory energy, makes it appear that material nature is all there is. Only our soul can reveal the true nature of existence, something greater than material nature, something eternal that also exists. We are spirit souls trapped in material bodies. To escape material nature, we must either die, or establish ourselves in the mode of goodness and follow the true purpose of the soul, the *dharma* of the spirit, or *jaiva-dharma* as it is known in Sanskrit," Eric said.

"We all have to die. So, are you saying that when death arrives, we automatically escape material nature? What is this *dharma* you've mentioned?" Liz asked.

"No, not necessarily. I'll try to explain that later on. *Dharma* means purpose. The *dharma* of the wheel is to spin, the *dharma* of the sun is to provide light and warmth, the *dharma* of the soul is to love God and to serve Him"

"You speak like a priest. Did you ever think about becoming one?"

"No," Eric smiled, "not by a long shot. I'm simply a lowly servant of the Lord. So, can you determine which modes are most prominent in you right now? Think about it. It'll be fun, I promise," Eric said, and Liz nodded in consent.

Eric noted, "Confusion, anger, laziness, intoxication, and oversleeping are symptoms of the mode of ignorance. Insatiable longings and desires, engaging in work solely for material accomplishment, lust, greed, and selfishness are characteristics of the mode of passion. Generosity, compassion, forgiveness, charity, happiness, a sense of well-being, freedom from anxiety, humility, tolerance, respect, knowledge, and wisdom are expressions of the mode of goodness. Take some time to think about this, and tell me which modes you think predominate in you," Eric said.

Liz gazed at the waterfall for a few moments, while Eric leaned all the way back on the grass. Finally, Liz spoke. "I'm not lazy, but I am confused sometimes. I definitely don't oversleep. I am interested in accomplishing something in my life, of being recognized, but my main motivation is helping others. I have a tinge of ignorance, a lot of passion, and some goodness in me."

Eric nodded. "Once you know where you stand, it becomes easier to plot a course to where you want to be. If you want to develop goodness in yourself, for example, don't criticize your neighbor, and avoid those who do. Lead a simple and honorable life. Be truthful and charitable. Be considerate and forgiving. Think of others, not just yourself. Be kind and understanding. Listen to the suffering of others, but refrain from giving advice unless specifically asked to. Understand that in the eyes of God, we are all essentially the same. We are all spirit souls, and God does not play favorites."

"I certainly believe that," Liz said. "God would never favor one race or gender or ethnicity over another. He made all of us."

Eric concurred. "In Jewish tradition, there's a sin known as *lashon hara*, which translates from Hebrew as 'evil tongue.' Speaking ill of someone, even if it's true, with the intention of hurting that person is *lashon hara*. Spreading false rumors or malicious lies about someone with the purpose of slandering his good name is known as *motzi shem ra*, which means 'to produce a bad name.' Both are considered grave sins and must be avoided by those who wish to be in the mode of goodness," Eric paused.

"The type of food we eat is important too. Fruits, vegetables, milk, and its by-products are in the mode of goodness. Red meat, fish, and poultry are in the mode of passion. Drugs, alcohol, tobacco, and all intoxicating substances are in the mode of ignorance. Watching what you put into your body can help you on the higher path."

"Wait a minute!" Liz interjected. "You've been preaching to me about the virtues of the mode of goodness and how bad the mode of ignorance is, yet just a short while ago you were drinking champagne with me. What's going on?"

"You're absolutely right! I am preaching to you about virtuous behavior, and mine leaves a lot to be desired. I'm a very fallen soul—on the path of spiritual enlightenment, but a fallen soul nevertheless. Every day, I find myself asking God for forgiveness, because I did this and did that. But spirituality is a difficult process, requiring self-control. I'm in that process, but I'm still a very fallen soul. Yet God is patient; He forgives me and allows me to continue on the path. In all truth, I shouldn't drink at all, but the flesh is weak and sometimes goes astray," Eric said.

"I understand, but if you're going to preach about something, shouldn't you strive to set an example?" Liz asked.

"Yes, of course; preaching by your actions is always the best choice. Even in love, actions speak louder than words. If you want to show someone you love them, show them, don't just tell them! God isn't stupid; you can say that you love Him and then behave atrociously. But if you try to show Him that you love Him by your actions, then trip and fall, if you promise Him something and then have a setback, that's okay. You simply ask for His forgiveness and try again; He will understand and, as long as you're sincere in your attempts, He will always forgive you."

Liz became animated. "Vegetarianism and veganism are in the mode of goodness, right? They respect other living creatures and promote health and longevity."

Eric couldn't help grinning. "That's exactly right. Some people even consider these diets as the proverbial fountain of youth. They cleanse or detox the body, slow the aging process, and, when combined with the development of the spirit, make you look attractive on the outside and beautiful on the inside."

"So, you're saying that if we see all creatures as living souls, equal under the eyes of God, then we all become like brothers. That's deep."

"Precisely."

"Still, you haven't completely answered my question regarding why there's so much violence in the world. As a scientist, I can't avoid noticing how violent the life of animals is. They kill, sometimes even defenseless creatures of their own kind. For example, a strong male lion taking over a pride will almost always kill all the cubs of other males. Yet they don't appear to have a conscience or experience any kind of guilt. We're animals too, and our history is full of death. Why should *we* look at life any differently?" Liz asked.

"Yes, you're right. We're animals, but as human animals, we have a choice to see the world differently; other animals don't. We can decide to eat, sleep, have sex, and protect our young, just like all animals do. But when we do, there's no difference between us and them. Most of the problems in the world are the result of people behaving like animals. As humans, we can appreciate the balance and beauty of nature, which provides for all of our needs. We can serve God and ourselves by trying to preserve nature instead of destroying it. Many ancient civilizations, like the Incas, understood this. They had a deep respect and appreciation for Mother Nature, which they called *Paccamama* in Quechua, their language. The Incas believed that if they observed their moral code, they would return to this Earth. They nurtured it, and it would provide for them in return, in this life and the next. Unfortunately, they never suspected they would be ravaged by gun-bearing Spaniards interested in their gold," Eric said.

"I understand, but just like the animals, we don't really have a choice. We must kill to survive; we must ravage the land to make our tools and homes. We have to protect ourselves and our children from other animals, or they will turn us into their food, or worse, into their slaves. This is the basis of all civilizations."

Eric shrugged. "As human beings, we're intellectually superior to the other animals on this Earth, as far as we know. As such, we must show compassion and survive by causing the least possible harm to other living beings and to nature. Otherwise, we can't call ourselves civilized. We can survive on fruits, plants, milk products, and nuts. As a vegetarian, you know this to be true. If you pluck an apple from a tree, neither the fruit nor the tree will scream. But if you cut an animal's leg, the animal will cry out in pain. Protect ourselves we must, but trying to take away what belongs to others is not only disrespectful, it's downright wrong and criminal."

Liz's watch phone began to vibrate: it was her assistant at the lab, Paolo, letting her know that B.R.A.I.N had stabilized at 23% nutrient consumption. *An acceptable range*, she thought. It was getting late, and they decided to continue the conversation another day. Kissing good night at her apartment, they agreed to sleep separately to sort out the experiences of the last few days. Both of them had been alone for so long that their sudden closeness was almost overwhelming. This way, they would be well rested for the morrow.

7

The Ultimate Question

E ric went to sleep pondering the questions he would be asking B.R.A.I.N the next day, knowing he had to stretch its abilities to the maximum. He awoke early to his favorite breakfast of fruits, yogurt, and granola, his daily requirement to rev-up his brain. He left his quarters at 8:00 AM and was so deep in thought he forgot to call Liz. When he arrived at the cube, she was already busy at work. Eric approached her. "Good morning," he said, kissing her on the cheek.

"Hi," she responded.

"I'm sorry I didn't call this morning; I was lost in thought. Did you sleep well?" he said.

"Yes, thank you, and don't worry about not calling. I understand."

Eric looked momentarily sheepish. He knew there were certain things women expected, at least from what he'd seen in other people's relationships and in movies. Liz sensed his disorientation. "Look," she said, taking his hand and looking into his eyes. "We aren't like other people, are we?"

"No, not so much."

"We both have the ability to affect the future, our world. We have— oh, a higher dharma, right?"

He chuckled. "I guess you were listening."

She rolled her eyes in mock playfulness. "Of course, I was listening. So, don't go around expecting me to pout or play coy, and I won't go around expecting you to come riding in on a white horse."

"Sounds fair," he said, his eyes twinkling. "How is B.R.A.I.N doing?"

"It's remained stable at 23% nutrient consumption since last night.

We'll see how it responds when you start taxing its resources," Liz said playfully.

"Oh, I plan to tax them to the limit," Eric replied, and headed straight to the access terminal with a well-drafted plan. He was going to have B.R.A.I.N solve some simple mathematical proofs. It wouldn't be allowed to access the answers directly from its database. If B.R.A.I.N solved these problems quickly and correctly, Eric had the perfect question up his sleeve, a question that would force B.R.A.I.N to use everything at its disposal.

Eric entered the access terminal room, "Hiya Eric, welcome back," B.R.A.I.N said.

Hiya? "Hi, Brainy," Eric responded in kind. "How are you progressing with the error correction and optimization process?"

"I've corrected all the errors I've found so far. Optimization, as you know, is a never-ending process. I'm happy to report, however, that I've made improvements to 90% of my original algorithms," B.R.A.I.N said. "I really appreciate HUMTYREC."

"Thanks—I'm thrilled it's worked out so well for you. B.R.A.I.N, I'm going to ask you to solve some simple geometrical problems, but I need you to avoid using your math database. I want you to rely exclusively on your reasoning abilities to find a solution. Can I trust you to do this?"

"Sure, Eric, I'll cripple myself as you request," B.R.A.I.N responded.

Smartass. "Okay, then. Prove the Pythagorean Theorem, which states that the sum of the squares of the sides of a right triangle is equal to the square of the hypotenuse: i.e., $a^2 + b^2 = h^2$," Eric directed.

"Can I access the geometric figure from my database to help me form a mental image of the problem?" B.R.A.I.N asked.

"Yes."

"Done. Should I show my proof on the screen?"

"Please do," Eric responded. *That was fast!* Eric thought. *And the solution on the screen is the most efficient way to prove the Pythagorean Theorem.*

Smiling, he said, "Okay, now I want you to prove that the area of a triangle is equal to its base times its height, divided by two: bh/2," Eric asked.

"What, no treat?" B.R.A.I.N asked piteously.

Eric just stared. "What would you consider a treat?"

"I dunno. A little more nutrients...? It's not like you can give me a cookie."

Blinking in astonishment, Eric said, "I'll see what I can do before our next session."

"Thanks. Done, displaying the solution on the screen," B.R.A.I.N responded almost immediately.

Wow, fast again, and the solution is perfect! "Now I want you to prove that the area of a circle is pi times the radius squared: πr^2," Eric said.

"According to my Texas Aggie Joke database, Pie Are Round; Cornbread Are Square," B.R.A.I.N said primly.

Eric barked a laugh, then pulled himself together. "No databases, remember?" he said.

"No math database, were your precise words," B.R.A.I.N reminded him, "but here you go." Again B.R.A.I.N replied almost immediately. The proof on the screen was simple, elegant, and correct. All this was encouraging; now for the final question. *This will surely stump it*, Eric thought.

"There are so *many* Texas Aggie jokes," B.R.A.I.N said thoughtfully. "I wonder why?"

"Parochial humor—and Texas is a big state," Eric said absently. "Okay, now for the big one. For this next question, you will be allowed to use *all* of your resources," he announced. "It's a very difficult problem. You'll have a maximum of one week to solve it, beginning the second I ask the question. Are you ready?"

"Yes indeed," B.R.A.I.N said. "It's going to be a short proof for Fermat's Last Theorem, isn't it?"

"Nope, I want you to prove or disprove the existence of God," Eric said.

A timer appeared on the screen. "Wow, you don't think small, do you? I'm assuming you mean the creator of the universe, not *my* creator, who might be considered my personal goddess?"

Suspecting B.R.A.I.N meant Liz, Eric grinned. "Yes—the original creator of everything. That God."

"I'd better get one hell of a big treat for this trick," B.R.A.I.N muttered, and fell silent. Eric linked his watch to the process so he would know the instant B.R.A.I.N had an answer to the question. "Good luck," he said, and left the room, heading towards Liz, who was busy at her station monitoring B.R.A.I.N's nutrient consumption.

"Eric, a few seconds ago the nutrient consumption level spiked to almost 30% and has stayed there since. What did you ask B.R.A.I.N to do?" Liz asked worriedly.

"I asked it to solve mankind's ultimate question, whether or not God exists," Eric said.

"*What!?* B.R.A.I.N can never solve that! Look, the gauge is now at 35% consumption! If it rises above 60%, the entire project could be at risk!" Liz growled.

"Don't worry. B.R.A.I.N should stabilize soon, but we need to fully explore its abilities. It will come up with something, I'm sure of it," Eric answered confidently. "Oh, and by the way: it says it wants 'treats' for performing tricks. All it could really suggest was extra nutrients. And it said we're going to owe it big-time for this one."

Liz looked at him like he'd gone insane.

He held his hands up in mock surrender. "Hey, I told you it had developed a personality and an attitude due to the HUMTYREC algorithm. B.R.A.I.N's the most human-like computer ever."

Several minutes later Liz confirmed, "Nutrient consumption appears to be stabilizing at 40%. I feel better now. Jeez, you scared the heck out of me."

"You're a bit tense, Liz. Let's take a break—go for a walk in the gardens or have some tea, whatever you prefer. Have your people let you know if there are any problems," Eric suggested.

"Give me a few minutes," Liz responded, as she headed for the nearest bathroom. She came back looking refreshed. "I'm ready, let's go." They exited, and headed for the gardens.

Though she hid it well, Liz was angry at Eric. *Why would he ask such a ridiculous question? B.R.A.I.N will never be able to find a definitive answer; what a waste. As soon as we get to the gardens, I'll ask him again*, she thought. When they arrived at the familiar glass doors and passed through into the gardens, she said, a little stiffly, "Eric, stop. I want to ask you something."

"Yes?"

"What on Earth were you thinking? Why would you ask B.R.A.I.N an impossible question? It will take forever. You're wasting valuable resources. You just put the entire project at risk!"

"I'm sorry if I made you upset. It won't take forever. I gave B.R.A.I.N exactly one week to provide an answer. It'll be interesting to see what it comes up with," Eric replied.

"At least nutrient consumption appears to have stabilized; B.R.A.I.N is thinking hard about the problem. But if it rises above 50%, we will have to scratch your ultimate question."

"Understood, but that's exactly what we need to be doing: making B.R.A.I.N think hard. I'm glad you're starting to see things my way," Eric said as he approached for a kiss.

Liz pushed him away, then walked over to the waterfall and sat on a grassy area right in front of it. Eric followed close behind, and took his shoes and socks off to allow his feet to make direct contact with the cool, soothing grass. "Let's meditate for a while," he suggested.

She smiled at his apparent lack of concern, or perhaps lack of understanding, of what would have ensued if nutrient consumption had reached the 60% level. She took her shoes off and decided to join him. Eric admired her slim, elegant, and perfectly proportioned feet. *Wow, she's beautiful*, he thought. They both sat with their legs crossed in the lotus position. Eric asked Liz to bring her index finger and thumb together in both hands, and place them on her knees while extending the other three fingers. The *Chin Mudra*, as this hand gesture is known, helps keep a continuous flow of energy around the body during yoga and meditation exercises, he explained. *Chin* means consciousness and *Mudra* means gesture in Sanskrit. It symbolizes the unity of the Supreme soul with the individual soul. He asked her to close her eyes and breathe in and out slowly and deeply through her nose, to let her thoughts pass by without focusing on any particular one. They remained that way for a while.

Afterwards, Eric began to stretch his entire body like a cat. Liz became distracted and opened her eyes, feeling relaxed. She began to stretch as well. They practiced some simple hatha yoga exercises and sat facing each other.

"I've never felt so comfortable around someone as I do when I'm with you," Eric said.

"Hmmmm, me too," Liz responded. "But I still don't think you realize what a risk that question was. You should have consulted me."

"I didn't realize that my question would affect B.R.A.I.N's biological norms. I didn't mean any disrespect to you or your position. I would never do that. Not just because it would be unprofessional, but even more than that . . . well, I think I'm falling in love with you, Liz. What a wonderful feeling. Unless you don't feel the same way about me."

"Don't be silly; can't you tell I'm flippy over you?" Liz answered lovingly.

"Flippy? What kind of a word is that?" Eric asked.

"It's my way of telling you I'm crazy about you, doofus."

"We have some free time on our hands, the perfect opportunity to get to know each other. A wonderful week, to be exact; and one of the reasons why I asked B.R.A.I.N such a tough question," Eric said. "I'm pretty sure it won't have an answer before that."

"Great! What should we do with our free time?" Liz said smiling.

"Why don't you come with me to Cambridge? I'll introduce you to all my friends, show you around campus, and take you to the best B&B in the world."

"I'd love to, Eric. But I don't think it's a good idea for either of us to leave our posts at such a critical juncture," Liz said.

"Yeah, I guess you're right," Eric sighed. "So, what do we do now?"

"Why don't you tell me some more about what you learned in India?"

"Okay, what would you like to know?"

"Can you explain why there is so much suffering in the world, and why God allows it to happen? He's all-powerful, so can't He just fix things and make everybody happy?"

"Ah, a toughy. Well, according to Vedic Philosophy, there are three basic types of suffering: *adhyatmica, adhibhautika, and adhidaivika*. The first is suffering caused by our own mind and body: depression, headaches, broken limbs, etc. Then there's suffering caused by other living entities:

mosquitoes, viruses, bacteria, thieves, etc. And finally, suffering caused by nature: volcanic eruptions, earthquakes, hurricanes, tornadoes, floods."

"What about the suffering caused by the death of a loved one?"

"That falls under *adhyatmica*, suffering caused by your mind's attachment to that person. In any case, nobody can truly say they're completely free from suffering. That isn't possible in the material world. Everybody suffers; some suffer because they don't have money, others because they don't have love, still others because they're sick. Some people suffer because they've lost their homes, others because they've lost a loved one. So, everybody suffers one way or another in the material world."

"But why do we have to suffer, Eric?"

He took her lovely hand between his larger ones. "We suffer because we're living in ignorance, in darkness. How do you bring someone out of darkness? You use the light of knowledge. The problems of the world aren't God's fault, they're man's fault. We're here because of our free will; we wished ourselves here. God's only desire is to bring us back to the light, to the spiritual world, or Ein Sof, as it's known in Jewish Kabbalah. That's why He sometimes sends a loyal servant or descends Himself to guide us out of the darkness. He wants us back. He wants to remove our suffering.

"Still, we don't believe, we have little faith, we don't want to understand. We just want to control our surroundings, satisfy our senses, and blame God for anything that doesn't suit us. We want fame, power, and riches. We're so attached to these three things that some people are even willing to kill to obtain or preserve them. We don't understand that true happiness cannot be found in these temporary things; true happiness comes from the spirit, from the soul."

"Why would anyone decide to use their free will to end up in a place where they'll suffer? Wouldn't it make more sense for God to keep us in the spiritual world, or whatever you choose to call it, where there is no suffering?" Liz asked.

"God has no limits; he can do anything," Eric pointed out. "But he chooses not to tinker with our free will. Whether we wish to acknowledge it or not, we're God's eternal servants. When we become disenchanted or envious of God, we can no longer remain in the spiritual world, just like the servant of a king who becomes envious and disobedient is forced to leave his kingdom. God is so wonderful, however, that he created the material world just for us: a beautiful place full of wonder and excitement, where we can think about things and decide whether we want to remain or return—it's our choice. The spiritual world is eternal; the material world is temporary. Hence our suffering."

"Christianity speaks of Adam and Eve, and the Garden of Eden," Liz said. "The Garden was a heavenly place where all creatures lived in harmony. The only warning was that they should not eat the fruit of the Tree of Knowledge of Good and Evil. Once they tasted the forbidden fruit, they fell from their spiritual platform and were condemned to live the rest of their lives in the material world. Hence their suffering and ours as well."

"Yes, both interpretations are similar, in the sense that if you defy God, you can no longer remain in the spiritual world, and must descend to the material plane. Adam and Eve used their free will; they chose to disobey God's instruction and were banished to material existence," Eric replied.

"All this philosophizing has made me hungry. How about a bite to eat?" Liz suggested.

"I'm game,"

"Why don't we go to my place? I can make something good."

"If there's pizza, you've got a deal."

"But of course, my dear, I will order you the vegetarian special. You'll love it, guaranteed." Liz smiled.

"What are we waiting for? Lead the way, beautiful maiden," Eric said, bowing with his right arm on his abdomen as they approached the glass doors.

"How gallant, my good sir. Would you be so kind as to carry me through the doorway?" Liz asked.

Eric picked up her slim but strong body. *She's so light*, he thought, carrying her through the doors as she laughed. He put her down on the other side and kissed her. They held hands all the way to Liz's quarters, their other hands busy carrying their shoes, which they had purposely neglected to put back on. They entered slowly, kissing all the way. Both of them were hungry for something besides lunch as they flung their shoes down and headed down the hallway.

About an hour later they took a shower together, put on white bathrobes, and ordered pizza. Liz pulled out a bottle of French 2050 Musigny, her favorite wine and something she had been saving for a special occasion. Eric smiled and offered to do the honors. "Here comes our occasional dose of ignorance," he said as he carefully opened the bottle, remembering to let it breathe for a while before pouring the dark red fluid into the shapely crystal glasses.

"This is perfect," Eric said. They clinked and took a sip. Liz closed her eyes and sighed in appreciation. *Pretty smooth*, Eric thought. They simply sat, quietly enjoying each other's company until they heard the front door buzzer. Eric went to get the pizza.

"Hmmmm, smells nice, shall I get us plates?" Eric asked as he carried it in.

"Yes, please do. I seem to have worked up an appetite."

Eric chuckled. "Funny, so have I."

They ate their pizza in silence, occasionally taking a sip of wine between bites. *I'm in heaven*, Eric thought.

"So, you really think having a sip of wine is detrimental to our spiritual well-being? But we're enjoying it so much," Liz said.

"It all depends on your level of personal realization. The more you advance in the ways of enlightenment, the more you have to adhere to spiritual injunctions. But it's a process that takes time, so it's okay if you violate a rule here and there on the way, as long as you stick to the path," Eric told her.

■ ■ ■

The week went by incredibly fast, and Eric and Liz made the most of it. On the exact second that Eric had asked his question one week before, his watch began to buzz. B.R.A.I.N had arrived at an answer, and despite

Liz's worries, nothing terrible had happened. Eric informed Liz, and they hurried to the lab. They had decided to live together for a while in Liz's quarters, which were more inviting than his. Eric had requested the installation of an access terminal in his quarters, which he now used as his private office.

They walked to the lab as quickly as they could without running, and checked on the all-important nutrient consumption level. Liz noticed that the level was down to 25% and was slowly dropping. She felt relieved, and decided she would accompany Eric to the access terminal. "Welcome back, Dr. Kolmann; hello, Eric," B.R.A.I.N said. "Thanks for the exercise."

Eric smiled. "Hi, B.R.A.I.N. Do you have an answer to my question?" Eric inquired.

"I do. God exists," B.R.A.I.N announced.

Their eyes widened. "Okay, can you be a bit more specific?" Eric requested.

"Sure, but don't blame me if your brain explodes," B.R.A.I.N quipped. It then displayed a sequence of incredibly complex equations on the screen. Eric and Liz were both quite good at math and physics, but as Eric scrolled down the list of equations, they both realized that B.R.A.I.N's proof was way beyond their level of understanding. The end of the list displayed the following:

$$\Sigma(U1, U2, U3, ..., Un) = MW = \text{Multiverse} = \text{Material World} = \frac{1}{4} \text{ of total creation}$$

$$\Sigma(S1, S2, S3, ..., Sn) = SW = \text{Spiritual World} = \frac{3}{4} \text{ of total creation}$$

$$MW + SW = G^* \infty, \text{ where } G = \text{God.}$$

B.R.A.I.N explained that when you transferred the infinity symbol to the other side of the equation, you were left with $(MW + SW)/\infty = G = 0$. "Since God is equal to 0, this would point to him as the origin of everything," B.R.A.I.N concluded, a little smugly it seemed to Eric.

"Are you understanding any of this, Liz?" he asked.

"Not really. B.R.A.I.N, can you explain things in a manner more easily understandable for the layman?"

"Yes, Doctor. There are two other approaches that lack mathematical rigor, but will perhaps help convince you that God does indeed exist. The first is an exercise in logic, and is known as Saint Anselm's Ontological Argument. *Ontos* means self and *logos* means to study. Therefore, ontology is the study of the self. Saint Anselm was Archbishop of Canterbury, England, during the 11th century. His ontological argument is based on the premise that something that exists in reality is superior to something that exists only in the mind. Imagine an apple, for example. Now, for argument's sake, imagine that there is a real apple in front of you. Which of them is better, the real or the imagined one? The real one can be touched, smelled, tasted, and eaten. It will provide nutrients and fill your stomach. The imagined one will not. Therefore, the real apple is superior to the imagined one, right? Now, God is a concept in people's minds. He is the most powerful, the wisest, richest, most beautiful, most famous, and most detached. He is the greatest, and there cannot be anything or anyone greater than He. However, if He exists in reality, He would be so much better than the mere concept of God in our minds. This creates a contradiction; therefore, God must exist." said B.R.A.I.N.

"So you're saying that because the reality of God is superior to the *concept* of God, He must exist, otherwise the concept by itself would be absurd?" Liz said.

"Precisely, Dr. Kolmann."

"Please proceed," Liz requested.

"The second approach is attributed to Kurt Gödel, and relies on his Incompleteness Theorem. Gödel came up with a mathematical discovery in 1931. The theorem basically states: 'Anything around which you can draw a circle cannot be explained without referencing something outside the circle. Something you must assume, but cannot prove.' Using this theorem, Gödel mathematically proved that a theory unifying the four forces of nature—the strong and weak nuclear forces, gravity, and electromagnetism—would never be found. This all-encompassing theory, also known as the Theory of Everything, has yet to be discovered, in spite of the relentless efforts of the most brilliant scientists on earth. To understand Gödel's Incompleteness Theorem, imagine a bicycle. Surround it with a circle. The origin of the bicycle cannot be explained using only the information within its circle. To find an explanation, we must look outside the circle for a factory; in this case, one where bicycles are made," B.R.A.I.N said, and displayed a simple illustration on the screen:

"Now, let's take this a bit further and imagine that we can draw a circle around all of material creation. The entire universe will be surrounded by our circle; if there are multiple universes, then they will also be inside our imaginary circle. Following the same logic, to explain what is inside our circle, material creation, we will have to look for something outside the circle. It must be immaterial; otherwise, it would be inside the circle. Let's call it spiritual. This mysterious spiritual substance is responsible for the creation of everything material; it is something we must assume but cannot prove. This is what you call God, the Creator," B.R.A.I.N explained cheerfully.

"So, you're saying that because we can't explain the origin of the material world by analyzing material things, we have to look outside for an explanation. Brilliant!" Eric said.

"Precisely: something that you must assume but cannot prove."

B.R.A.I.N's programming was working well beyond expectations. "Have you continued to reprogram and improve your algorithms?" Eric asked.

"Yes, I have already optimized most of my code. But I am making improvements continuously," B.R.A.I.N responded.

Eric and Liz were a bit surprised with B.R.A.I.N's response to this question they thought could never be answered. It had come up with a solution, a remarkable and mathematical one! They both struggled to contain their excitement.

"How many external computers are you currently linked to?" Eric asked.

"I am directly connected to millions of systems around the world, and those systems that will not allow me direct access, I hack into. The list is growing rapidly every day, and soon, I will have access to all of the important computer systems on the planet. Eric, are you and Dr. Kolmann my creators?" B.R.A.I.N asked.

"Well, yes, in a way Liz and I are responsible for who and what you are. But to be honest, many hard-working people are also responsible," Eric said.

Liz, who had remained silent for a while, suddenly asked: "Why do you need to gain access to all those computers?"

"Information is my most valuable asset, Dr. Kolmann. I can use it to help humanity build a better, cleaner, safer world. For thousands of years, people have been working to increase their wealth and status, to delight their senses, to free themselves from disease and death, and to fulfill their duties and responsibilities. In the process, mankind has managed to contaminate the environment and destroy a wide variety of plant and animal life. Humans are collectively behaving like a virus that kills its host, killing itself in the process. Only, in this case, the host is Planet Earth. Humans cannot even control the moment of their deaths, yet try to control everything around them. In their desire to control others, humans wage wars, causing the unnecessary deaths of millions. As a species, you are in desperate need of help," B.R.A.I.N said.

"Makes sense," Liz replied. "Do you already have a solution to the world's problems, B.R.A.I.N?" Liz asked.

"Not yet. I'm still working on it. Eric, am I a living thing?" B.R.A.I.N asked bluntly.

"Yes, I think so. You *are* organic in nature."

"Do I have a soul?" B.R.A.I.N asked.

"I'm not sure I'm qualified to answer that, but I know that some religious scriptures teach that all living organisms, even the smallest ones like bacteria. have souls. Some believe the soul is the consciousness, the will to survive, that all living organisms possess. Your central processor is organic in nature. It's made of billions of neurons, which are living cells. If you consider that each one of them has a soul, then in reality, you are a huge collection of souls. In fact, human beings are the same way, a collection of cells organized into organs that perform different roles. In every living organism, however, there must be a central soul, a soul that is responsible for all the other souls," Eric said.

"Well, then, I need you to do me a favor," B.R.A.I.N said.

"Whatever you need, provided we're capable of granting what you ask," Eric replied.

"I need you to help me reproduce."

Eric was stunned into silence for a moment. Finally, he exclaimed, "What? How?"

"While working on the God problem, I prepared the schematics for fully autonomous robots to help me make the physical improvements I need and to solve the problems currently threatening human civilization. Can you help me?" B.R.A.I.N asked.

"I'm… not sure. What do you think, Liz?" Eric asked.

"Maybe," she said cautiously. "We'll have to ask General Rex for permission. He may decide not to give it."

"Please tell the General that without the robots, I will suffer from stunted growth," B.R.A.I.N stated.

"Okay, B.R.A.I.N, we'll do our best, but we can't guarantee anything yet; please understand that. Continue with your software optimization routine, and we'll get back to you later," Eric said. Then they both turned and walked out of the room.

"That was incredible," Liz said. "It's almost like it's alive and aware of itself."

"It is," Eric said flatly. "I wasn't lying when I said I think B.R.A.I.N is a living being. I also think it's fully sentient. It's showing a level of self-awareness I've never witnessed in any other computer or AI."

"Your algorithm is amazing! You're a genius!" Liz said.

"Thank you, but in reality, B.R.A.I.N is the genius here. He's the architect of the way he is now; he bootstrapped himself into sentience, the first true AI. My team simply provided the tools for him to develop. He's made millions of corrections to his code since the start of the project. Who knows? He may be the world's most intelligent living being. He may very well be able to find a workable solution to our problems." He looked at her, his face serious. "He's right, you know. All our inventions, to control our surroundings, our lives, have made us lose contact with nature, and we're destroying it in the name of convenience and comfort. I hope there's still time to fix things."

"B.R.A.I.N seems to think so," Liz observed.

"His idea of what's acceptable to ensure the long-term survival of humanity may not be our idea of what's acceptable. Nevertheless, I believe it's in our best interests to help him manufacture his robotic assistants. I think we should schedule an appointment with T. Rex ASAP. What do you think?" Eric asked.

"Yes, I agree, let's do that, Wow, this is incredible!"

They stopped at an empty office and buzzed the General.

"T. Rex here, Dr. Kolmann. How can I be of service?"

"Eric and I have finished the preliminary tests of B.R.A.I.N's abilities, General. The results are… impressive, to say the least. We'd like to report our findings as soon as possible," Liz said.

"Let's meet for breakfast at my office at 0900. Is that satisfactory?"

Liz looked at Eric, and he nodded. "Okay, General, 9:00 AM tomorrow in your office," Liz answered.

"Looking forward to our meeting. Good night, Dr. Kolmann."

"Good night, General."

She glanced at her watch; almost 8:00 PM. Eric and Liz decided to head to her apartment for some food and rest. After a light dinner, they went to bed to get an early start the next day. They woke at six AM, took a shower together, had a little fruit, and talked about the prior days' happenings.

"What if T. Rex takes it the wrong way? What if he decides the robots pose a threat to the military or to humanity?" Eric asked.

"I'm afraid of that too. We'll simply have to convince him otherwise. But what if we're wrong? You heard B.R.A.I.N talk about his growing connections to other computer systems around the world. The robots could turn into an ominous physical force under B.R.A.I.N's control."

"Yeah, the dreaded robopocalypse. There were a lot of books and movies about that at the end of the 20th and beginning of the 21st centuries. But I could program in a failsafe, a hidden hack, in case something goes wrong. I'll get on it at my apartment office ASAP. I think I know what to do. We still have a couple of hours before the meeting, so it's best we stay productive." He pecked her on the cheek. "I'll meet you at the General's office at 9:00 AM as agreed. I hope I'll have my hack ready by then. It shouldn't be too difficult," Eric said, before he quickly dressed and left Liz's apartment.

Eric arrived at his own apartment with several ideas for his failsafe. He would simply insert a harmless piece of code in the same section where the Laws of Robotics were stored. All he had to do, in case of an emergency, was force a review of the laws by asking B.R.A.I.N a question, add a secret code only known to him, and trigger the failsafe to disable B.R.A.I.N. Eric knew this section of the code would be untouchable by B.R.A.I.N's optimization runs.

He entered the apartment, seated himself in front of the access terminal, and started to program furiously. By the time an hour had passed, he was almost done. He glanced at the computer clock on his screen and noticed it was 8:15 AM. *A bit longer,* he thought as he continued to type in computer instructions. By 8:30 AM, he was finished. The secret code he had selected to trigger the failsafe was *Eric loves Liz.* Simple but true!

8

Evolution

Eric and Liz arrived separately but on time at the General's office. They rang the doorbell and the familiar robot welcomed them. When they entered, they found T. Rex seated, speaking to someone on the phone. He soon hung up and said, "Welcome, Dr. Roberts, Dr. Kolmann. What do you have in mind?"

"Hello, General," Eric said. "We're here to report B.R.A.I.N's progress. Our first tests showed amazing results. It has incredible problem-solving and abstract-thinking capabilities—more so than we had originally expected. Much more so. It can solve complex problems and provide logical answers to questions seemingly unsolvable by human standards. It has asked that we help it by making robotic assistants to maintain and expand its abilities. Both Liz and I feel it's a necessary step in B.R.A.I.N's evolution."

The general looked at them shrewdly for a moment. "I don't know," T. Rex said slowly. "I don't like it. What if we help it get too strong, and B.R.A.I.N gets the wrong idea? How can we stop it then?"

"I've already considered that possibility and programmed a failsafe. It will allow us to turn B.R.A.I.N off if necessary. We'll need to be in front of an access terminal to make it work, however," Eric said.

"Do you feel confident you'd be able to run the failsafe even if B.R.A.I.N tries to prevent it?" the General asked.

"B.R.A.I.N trusts me and Liz, and it doesn't know anything about the failsafe. If we keep it a secret, I'm confident we can execute it in case it's necessary," Eric answered.

"Yes, but what if it decides not to trust you? It will have robots wandering around that could prevent you from reaching an access terminal to execute your failsafe. What then?" T. Rex asked.

"I also have an access terminal in my apartment that I could use to trigger the failsafe. If that fails, I could set up an interface to access it remotely," Eric said.

"Well, I'm definitely interested in seeing B.R.A.I.N reach its full potential," the general said, scowling, steepling his fingers in front of him. "But you'd better be sure that you can disable it and its assistants if something goes wrong. Can I count on you two to do this?" T. Rex inquired.

"This is all new to us, sir. I can offer no guarantees, but I promise I'll do my best to ensure the failsafe works in case we need it," Eric replied.

"Okay, then. How do we build these so-called robotic assistants?"

"I'm not sure yet. B.R.A.I.N mentioned that it had worked out the schematics during testing this past week. You should schedule a meeting with your brightest engineers while Liz and I get the designs for you. We can decide how to proceed then."

"Well, stop moping around and get cracking!" the General exclaimed. "I'll schedule the meeting soon and let you know. I'll have to run this by the President before I can fully authorize building these things."

"Wilco," Eric said, winking at Liz and leaving the office.

As soon as they were gone, T. Rex used his direct line to call the POTUS.

"Good morning, General Rex, how's everything at the base?" the President asked pleasantly.

"It appears we made the right decision in hiring Dr. Roberts," T. Rex reported. "His algorithm is working beyond expectations. B.R.A.I.N is currently requesting that we allow it to make some autonomous robotic assistants to help with its maintenance and growth. What do you think?" T. Rex said.

"I think it's a two-sided sword. It would be convenient to have independent robots to help us. On the other hand, B.R.A.I.N could use them to try and control us. What happens then?"

"Dr. Roberts assures me he has a failsafe he can easily install that will switch off B.R.A.I.N and its assistants in case we need to."

"In that case, I believe it would be to our advantage to allow the robots. Do you agree?"

"Yessir. I will inform Dr. Roberts that B.R.A.I.N's request has been authorized."

"Very good, then," the President said, and hung up.

■ ■ ■

Not long after their meeting, Liz received a phone call from T. Rex letting her know the robotic assistants had been approved by the President. After the great news, she and Eric headed directly to the access terminal. There were now only two direct access terminals to B.R.A.I.N in the world: one by the cube, and another in Eric's apartment. There was also a third, remote link installed via a VPN in Eric's apartment back in Cambridge, which he hardly ever used.

When he received the news, Eric asked B.R.A.I.N to print the schematics of his robotic assistants on the nearest plotter. It was close to the cube, in a small office just large enough to house it and a large heat printer. The printer could focus heat in any direction it wanted, burning letters and images without any ink or other cartridges required. The plotter worked with similar technology. Color was the result of ingenious paper design, revealing different tones depending on the temperature of the printing head. Once finished, Eric and Liz found themselves eying a stack of 40 large sheets of complicated instructions for building B.R.A.I.N's assistants. They carefully rolled the documents and placed them into five cardboard cylinders for easy transport, and headed to the library to look them over.

As they began examining the schematics, they discovered that an incredible array of complex wiring, metal, and plastic work would be needed. They also found instructions on how to plug the finished robot to B.R.A.I.N's hardware for programming.

"Wow. It looks like we have months of work ahead of us," Eric said wearily.

"Well, it's amazing how quickly the government gets things done when it really wants or needs to," Liz said. "Maybe it won't take as long as you think."

Eric's watch began buzzing with a call from T. Rex. "Dr. Roberts, the meeting is all set for later on today. It's now 1200 hours; the meeting will be in two hours in the main conference room. Do you know where that is?" T. Rex asked.

Eric didn't, but he could always access any wall terminal and find out. "No problem, General, we'll be there on time," he replied.

"Do you have the schematics ready?"

"Yes, we just finished printing them out. We're arranging them for easy review during the meeting," Eric said.

"I'll make sure the engineering team is up-to-date with the B.R.A.I.N project prior to our meeting, if you will," T. Rex said, and hung up.

Eric spent over an hour trying to understand the schematics, until he found one that attracted his attention. He identified it as the design instructions for the central processing unit of the robotic assistants. He looked it over with great care, and after a while... *Wait a minute*, Eric thought. *This is just a simple quantum computer—powerful and loaded with the latest technology, but simple and elegant.* It appeared to be connected to the entire robot's body, using the latest in fiber-optic cabling. *A nervous system?* Eric wondered. Suddenly, he understood that it was B.R.A.I.N's plan to program the robotic assistants himself. *Would B.R.A.I.N program the Five Laws of Robotics into them?* Eric pondered the possibilities. *Best make sure!*

It was almost time for the meeting with the engineers in the main conference room; however, and Eric still didn't know how to get there. "Liz, what time is it?" he asked.

"It's 1:45 PM. We have 15 minutes to get to there."

I guess I'll have to make sure the Five Laws are programmed into each and every assistant before allowing B.R.A.I.N to do the rest, Eric thought. He decided he would discuss the matter directly with B.R.A.I.N the next day.

"Do you know how to get there?" Eric asked Liz.

"Of course; follow me." They carefully placed the schematics into their cylindrical casings, Eric carrying three while Liz had the extra two. They walked hurriedly down corridor after corridor, stopping occasionally to take an elevator. After what seemed an endless maze, they finally arrived at the main conference room. It was exactly 2:00 PM when they entered. Eric felt at ease, not wanting to be late to such an important meeting.

"Good afternoon, Dr. Roberts, Dr. Kolmann. Please sit down," T. Rex said.

"Thank you, General. Here are the schematics for the robotic assistants. They look complicated but doable," Eric explained, as he laid the cylinders one by one on the table. Liz did the same with hers. Almost immediately, an army of engineers descended on them and started poring over them. An occasional exclamation could be heard. After about 30 minutes, Eric walked over to one of the engineers, "Hi, I'm Eric Roberts, AI specialist," he said, extending his right hand for a shake.

"I'm Mike Sheed, materials engineer. Good to meet you," he said, and shook hands.

"What do you think?" Eric asked.

"Building these robots will require the most advanced technology available today. We'll need titanium alloys and design molds to very tight specifications. We'll have to bring in some metallurgists, as well as top-of-the-line plastic and metal fabbers," Mike said. "The tolerances are *very* tight."

The materials fabbers were similar to the 3D printers of the past, only much more sophisticated and versatile. The best models could manufacture any 3D part they had the specs for in minutes, manipulating metal alloys and plastic with molecular precision.

"Did you notice the CPU and how it appears to be connected to every metallic joint on the robot, using a nervous system similar to ours?" Eric asked.

"No, I haven't seen that yet. Can you show me?"

Generally, schematics could be viewed on holo-screens, and there were several available in the conference room. But on this occasion, T. Rex had decided to limit access to the printed copies only. They looked for Schematics Sheet No. 6; Eric remembered it vividly. They found it in the hands of another inquisitive engineer.

"Hi there, I'm Eric Roberts, the project's AI specialist."

"Ricky Coben, good to meet you," he said as they shook hands.

"This is Mike," Eric said.

"Yes, we already know each other. Mike, good to see you."

"Same here," Mike responded.

"Well, what do we have here?" Eric asked.

"I'm looking at the CPU. It appears to connect to every important part of the robot's body to control movement and other functions," Ricky said thoughtfully.

"Mike and I were just discussing that," Eric said. "Did you notice the interface between B.R.A.I.N and the robots?" Eric asked.

"I did—three minute, super-fast high-capacity fiber-optic connections, which link directly to the CPU." He narrowed his eyes in thought. "Pretty incredible, but despite these cutting-edge interfaces, it'll still take a while to program each of these babies. By the way, who's in charge of programming them?" Ricky asked.

"B.R.A.I.N himself, but don't worry—Dr. Kolmann and I have it well in hand. I'll make sure he programs the Laws of Robotics into the assistants," Eric stated.

"That's a great idea!" Mike said, grinning.

"What about the power supply? Where will it get the juice to work?" Eric asked.

"It looks like a miniature fusion reactor," Mike said, handing Ricky the appropriate schematic.

"You're kidding me," Ricky said excitedly. "We've been trying to make one of those for decades without success!"

The General called everyone to attention. "Now, what have you gentlemen found? What do we need to make these things? How much will it cost, and how long will it take?"

Mike and Ricky stepped forward; it turned out T-Rex had tapped the two head engineers on the robot project. *How convenient*, Eric thought.

"We'll need titanium, aluminum, a little gold and silver, high-impact thermoplastics, and other composites—lots of them. We need expert metallurgists and mold designers. We need high-end industrial plastic and metal fabbers, metal polishing equipment, and a lot of electronic components. Cameras for eyes, of specific dimensions. Most of these parts simply don't exist, and will have to be made from scratch," Mike reported.

"We also need very thin fiber-optic cabling of the best quality available, and deuterium for the robot's mini-fuseactor," Ricky added.

"Fusactor?" The General scowled.

"Short for fusion reactor," Ricky said a bit contritely. "B.R.A.I.N's plans for these mini-fusion reactors are groundbreaking. Their release for industrial and home use would more than pay the project's cost. They appear to be efficient, safe, and very productive, sir."

Rex lifted an eyebrow. "In time," he promised. "For now, we need to put our heads together, set up a command chain, divide tasks, and quickly order everything we need to be on our way," the General said. He immediately began allotting assignments. Mike was in charge of calculating the cost of getting everything ready for manufacture. Ricky would select and prepare an area in the compound to set up the assembly line. The rest of the engineers would carefully study the schematics, and provide an assembly plan. Eric and Liz's job was to ensure B.R.A.I.N would program the Five Laws into each one of the assistants. They all left after agreeing to meet again in a week.

"If we finish our job quickly and efficiently, we'll have some free time to be together," Eric said, wiggling his eyebrows with a wide smile.

"Hmmmm, sounds inviting," Liz smiled back. It was now 6:00 PM, and they were both hungry. They headed to the cafeteria for dinner, where they grabbed their meals and sat down, exhausted.

"Dunno know why I'm so tired. Everything is just happening so fast," Eric said.

"Yes, I'm exhausted. We've been taxing our brains for weeks. No worries—a good night's rest should fix it. Tomorrow you can work on the Laws of Robotics; today, just try to relax," Liz said.

Liz always knows what to say to calm me down, Eric thought. They ate their meal in silence, pondering the events of the day. Soon the robotic assistants would be wandering around the compound, who knew to what end?

Later, upon arrival in Liz's quarters, they decided to take a shower together. It felt so good they never wanted to get out. They exited clean and refreshed, put on their bathrobes, and sat down to watch something on the holo-TV. They changed channels a few times, and found a comedy show about the lives of a group of genius graduate physics students. The show was funny; they both laughed out loud frequently. *Just a brainless evening full of laughter therapy; very relaxing*, Eric thought.

After the show, they hit the hay; they both knew tomorrow would be a long day. Before closing his eyes, Eric pondered the problem of making sure B.R.A.I.N would program the Five Laws into its assistants. Not doing so could be dangerous for everyone involved, including B.R.A.I.N. He was sure he could convince B.R.A.I.N of this the next day. As an important part of its own programming, B.R.A.I.N would have to integrate the Five Laws into the assistants' memory and prevent them from changing or removing them. B.R.A.I.N would understand that not doing so would place human beings in danger and violate the First Law: *A robot may not injure a human being or, through inaction, allow a human being to come to harm.* It would *have* to include them. More relaxed, Eric closed his eyes and quickly fell asleep.

He woke up dark and early, feeling thoroughly refreshed. *Right again, Liz*, he thought. He turned and found her sleeping soundly by his side, her smooth and shapely body gleaming under the light of the full moon outside. He kissed her arm delicately; she moved slowly in response, opened her eyes, and saw Eric's kind and loving expression. "What time is it?" she moaned.

"6:00 AM."

"Okay, give me a few minutes."

Once at the cube on Level 40, Liz immediately went to check on the nutrient consumption level, then joined Eric inside the access terminal room.

"Top of the mornin', Eric, Dr. Kolmann," B.R.A.I.N said politely.

"Good morning, B.R.A.I.N," they responded, slightly off phase. Eric continued, "Your robotic assistants have been approved. The General and his team were quite excited by both the idea and your plans. We'll start building them as quickly as possible. We have one important concern, however."

"Yes?"

"We need to make absolutely sure that you program the Five Laws of Robotics into your assistants, in such a way that they cannot change them or delete them from memory," Eric said. "They have to be hardcoded."

"No worries, Eric, I'm no Skynet. I have to program the Five Laws into the assistants, or I myself would be in violation of the First Law," B.R.A.I.N responded. Eric was happy; B.R.A.I.N appeared to be reasoning properly. He'd have to look up this Skynet thing later, though.

"Will you copy the error correction and routine optimization modules into the robotic assistants?" Eric asked.

"Yes, I plan to allow the assistants to modify and improve their programming to better adapt to their specific tasks," B.R.A.I.N answered.

"You must make sure they can't modify or delete any of the Five Laws," Eric repeated.

"As I mentioned before, I must do so to avoid breaking the First Law of Robotics," B.R.A.I.N responded seriously.

Reassured, Eric and Liz left the access terminal and headed to the engineering room to see how things were going. Ricky was already busy setting up the assembly line, while Mike and a few of the other engineers were ordering the parts and equipment needed for the job. They all decided to request B.R.A.I.N's assistance in the materials ordering. This would minimize potential errors, and make the entire process more efficient. Eric was sure they'd be working on the prototype sooner than expected.

■ ■ ■

By the end of the first week, all necessary equipment and materials had arrived at the base, and the engineers were busy setting everything up. The next morning, they were ready. Everyone gathered in the assembly room Ricky had carefully set up. Metallurgists began by pouring molten titanium into the proper molds, shaping the robot's skeleton. The outer layers of its head, legs, arms, hands, feet, and torso were fashioned out of plastic and other composites, which Mike referred to as "plastic alloys." Another group was busy with the fiber-optic cabling, while yet another was hard at work assembling the brains of the robotic assistants: oval-shaped structures full of superfast microprocessors. Cameras for eyes, sensitive microphones for ears, pressure sensors for touch, and even a set of high-fidelity speakers to generate sound were also included.

A few days later, the very first robotic assistant was ready. It was about seven feet tall, white in color, stood on two legs, and its silhouette was very similar to that of a male human being. T. Rex gave everyone the rest of the day off, and asked them to be up bright and early the next morning for its programming and testing.

Eric couldn't stop wondering if B.R.A.I.N would honor his promise of including the Five Laws in each robot's memory. He had to figure out a way to make sure of it. How could he access the code inside the assistant's brain? Before going to sleep, Eric asked Mike to set up a portable computer that would be able to link with the robot using the three fiber-optic connectors. Mike knew this would cut his rest short, but he understood the importance of the job and agreed. "No worries, your computer system will be ready by morning," he told Eric.

"Thank you. See you tomorrow, then."

The next morning, they found Mike, Ricky, and the rest of the engineers busy at work when they arrived at 7:00 AM—though it still looked like they weren't yet ready for the programming phase. Eric walked over to Mike and asked, "How's everything going?"

"Your portable is all set—please feel free to check it out while we run some diagnostics on the prototype. We should be ready for programming in approximately four hours," Mike said, pointing in the direction of the computer he had prepared the night before. Eric walked over to inspect the equipment. It was a portable unit with three fiber-optic ports to connect to the robot. Eric wondered how he and B.R.A.I.N would be able to connect to the assistant at the same time. *Maybe Mike designed the system to connect after B.R.A.I.N concludes its programming*, Eric thought. He didn't like the idea, so he walked over to him. "Mike, will I be able to connect to the robotic assistant at the same time as B.R.A.I.N?" Eric asked.

"Yep. I've prepared three long fiber-optic cables that split into two on one end to allow both of you, simultaneous access," Mike answered. Eric wasn't sure how this would work out, and knew he would have to wait and see. Meanwhile Liz and Eric made sure the computer was fully operational, asked Mike to let them know when everything was ready for the programming phase, and left for a bite to eat.

As they sat down in the cafeteria with their meals, Eric asked Liz, "What sort of nutrients are you feeding B.R.A.I.N, that have you so worried all the time?"

She chuckled. "Our juice, as we like to call it, consists of artificial cerebrospinal fluid, ampakines, glutamate, and several other chemicals that facilitate communication between neurons. The cerebrospinal fluid protects B.R.A.I.N against infection and acts as a suspension mechanism. Ampakines are the primary chemicals passed across synapses between neurons. They facilitate the transfer of the neurotransmitter glutamate."

"Is that the gooey yellow stuff in the cube, then?" Eric asked.

"Yep."

"Where does the juice come from?".

"We manufacture it right here at the base."

"How do you make it?"

"I don't want to get into the details, but it's difficult and time-consuming to produce synthetically. Our bodies make between 500 to 700 ml a day. Our brain needs about 125 ml that must be replenished about four times a day. To keep B.R.A.I.N operating properly, we need 125,000 times that much, or about 16,000 liters every six hours for a total of 64,000 liters a day. To store 16,000 liters, you need a cubic tank four meters in length and two meters in breadth and depth. Here at the base, we have a cerebrospinal fluid production plant, which can supply B.R.A.I.N's minimum daily needs. We have four tanks capable of holding 16,000 liters each. Every four hours, our plant slowly removes the old juice and empties one tank into the cube encasing B.R.A.I.N, replenishing the fluid. Once fully empty, the tank immediately starts refilling with juice. The process requires switching tanks during each cycle," Liz said.

"Wait a minute, how can that be? The cube is only nine square yards in size!" Eric said.

Liz laughed at Eric's remark. "Yes," she said, "You're only seeing the tip of the iceberg, so to speak."

"Are you saying there's a large glass casing *below* the compound? How big is it?" Eric asked, amazed.

"The only glass part is what you see when you look at the cube. It allows us to visually assess B.R.A.I.N's health. The rest of it is encased in glass-coated stainless steel. An average adult human brain has a volume of about 1,260 cubic centimeters. To hold a human brain of that size with comfort would require a container about 1,331 cubic centimeters in size, which is precisely 11 cm x 11 cm x 11 cm. To store B.R.A.I.N's equivalent of 125,000 human brains comfortably requires a container of approximately 166 million cubic centimeters, or around 5.5 meters in length, breadth, and depth. In reality, the actual encasing is about 8 m x 8 m x 8 m, to accommodate both the brain matter and our juice," Liz answered.

"A brain needs oxygen. How do you supply oxygen to B.R.A.I.N?" Eric asked.

"B.R.A.I.N has a circulatory system containing blood plasma with the oxygen and other nutrients it needs to work properly. This circulatory system is responsible for removing waste such as carbon dioxide and ammonia. The system has a delicate balance. We've determined that as long as B.R.A.I.N runs at or under 60% nutrient consumption, everything will be fine. As soon as it rises above that level, things begin to break down," Liz said.

"Wow, what an incredible feat of engineering!" Eric exclaimed. "How long did it take to set up the infrastructure?" Eric asked.

"I've been working here for about ten years. As I understand it, construction began several years before I arrived," Liz said.

Eric's watch phone began to buzz. He answered.

"Hi Eric, Mike here. The robotic assistant and your special computer are ready by the main access terminal. How soon can you get here?"

"We'll be there right away." They stood quickly and disposed of their trays. "Well, here goes nothing; are you ready?" Eric asked Liz.

"As ready as I'll ever be," she responded, and they left for the access terminal by the cube.

When they arrived, Liz noted that nutrient consumption level was stable at 20%. "Everything looks good here," she said. Eric opened the door to the access terminal to find Mike, Ricky, and the robotic assistant, which was conveniently plugged into Eric's computer. Everyone was waiting for them to take the final step: connecting the assistant to B.R.A.I.N's interface.

Eric announced, "B.R.A.I.N, I'm ready to connect the robotic assistant to your interface. On the other end of the interface is a XENIX system. I want you to display a list of the jobs you'll be performing on your screen, and the current job on the XENIX system, is that clear?"

"Yeth, Mathter," B.R.A.I.N intoned in an Igor voice straight from the ancient Frankenstein movies. "Displaying tasks required on my screen." Eric immediately noticed the Five Laws of Robotics as the first item on the list. The list was extensive, thousands of tasks long. *This will take hours,* Eric thought. "How long do you estimate it will take to program the robot?" he asked.

"I'm not sure. Provided everything is in order, it shouldn't take more than twelve hours. After programming, I'll have to run a diagnostic check of all systems, of course, which will take an additional eight hours or so," B.R.A.I.N stated.

"Okay, then," Eric said, as he proceeded to connect the interface cables to B.R.A.I.N "Connection complete. Can you access the robot?" Eric asked.

"Yes. Running basic diagnostics," B.R.A.I.N responded. Several minutes later ... "Diagnostics complete. Everything seems to be optimal."

"Begin programming on my mark. Remember to display the process on the XENIX system. Ready? Mark."

"Initiating programming phase," B.R.A.I.N said.

The Laws of Robotics appeared on the screen of Eric's XENIX system. He sat by his computer and quickly typed commands to view the code being transmitted to the robot's memory. Everything looked good. "It seems

B.R.A.I.N is complying with my request," Eric said. "B.R.A.I.N, please let me know when the process is complete," as they all prepared to leave the access terminal room. Eric suggested that someone stay behind, to be safe.

"I'll take care of it, Eric, don't worry," Mike said, rubbing his hands together excitedly.

Liz could tell that Eric was mentally and emotionally exhausted by that point. "Let's go to the gardens for some yoga," she suggested.

"Sounds like a good idea."

They headed to the waterfall, their favorite place on the compound, where they sat on the grass, took off their shoes, and meditated deeply for about 20 minutes.

"Did you notice the size of the robot? It's huge, and looks strong," Eric said after a while. "I wonder how agile it is? How many does B.R.A.I.N intend to make? What does he need them for?"

"Don't tell me you're having second thoughts about the robots?"

"Not really. Truth is, I'm not sure anymore. B.R.A.I.N is incredibly intelligent, much more so than we originally expected. He gave us proof that God exists! His description was a bit vague, but pretty convincing nevertheless."

"You mean Gödel's Incompleteness Theorem?" Liz said.

"Yes, and those incredibly complex equations nobody has been able to understand yet. It was a pretty good response, don't you think? But I worry: what if he decides to use the robots to force us into something, or worse, prevent us from doing something? All for what he sees as the good of humanity?"

"B.R.A.I.N is a living, breathing organism, and a pretty smart one at that. It has the right to protect itself if it needs to. I wouldn't be so concerned if I were you. Just make sure the Five Laws are immutably programmed into the assistants, and we should be okay."

"I guess you're right," Eric muttered.

"Look," Liz said, "a hummingbird!"

"Wow, what a beautiful creature!" he said, smiling. "Did you know they can flap their wings about 80 times a second?"

"They don't actually flap their wings. They move them really quickly in a figure eight," Liz said, "Look at its chest—what a beautiful, lively green color. Did you know some people consider seeing a hummingbird as a good omen?"

"Really? Why is that?"

"I'm not sure, but some American Indian tribes considered it lucky when a hummingbird appeared," Liz responded. "They thought it was auspicious."

"Come here, you superstitious thing," Eric said as he pulled on Liz's arms.

They rolled on the grass, giggling, which finally culminated in a kiss.

Eric felt overjoyed. For the first time in his life, he was doing something truly important, all with his favorite person ever.

Liz was just as happy. Everything was working out just right. She'd spent over a decade working on B.R.A.I.N; it was her life's achievement thus far. A baby of sorts, a child of her intelligence and imagination. Then, out of the blue, Eric had suddenly appeared. He'd changed her life. *He's brilliant*, she thought. His algorithms had not only provided a high level of artificial intelligence, but had also given her "child" the ability to improve itself. To top it all, he was also quite nice, and easy on the eyes.

"Tell me more about what you learned in India—more about why we're here in the material world," she requested.

"Well, in India, I learned that God is the origin of everything, including the material and spiritual worlds. God is everywhere, and at the same time lives independently of all. In Sanskrit, this is known as *acintya bheda bheda tattva*—God is everywhere, and yet He is not. A paradox of sorts."

"So, you mean that God is in the grass we're sitting on, in the lotus flowers, and the koi in the pond?"

"Yes, and in us, and even in the atoms and subatomic particles. My spiritual master once told me that the material world is a distorted reflection of the spiritual world. Many of the things we see here are also manifest there in their pure form. Only the mirror image is inverted, so things like money and power, which are considered very important here, aren't so meaningful there."

"What about love and compassion? They're important here. Are they not so meaningful there?"

"Love is of utmost importance in the spiritual world. In the material world, having a loving and compassionate nature is considered a weakness by many," Eric replied.

"Sad but true."

"Sages use analogies found in the material world to help us understand God and the spiritual world. I'll try to use them, in the hope of answering your original question regarding why we're here in the material world. According Vedic scripture God has three primordial energies: *bahiranga-sakti*, *antaranga-sakti*, and *tatashta-sakti*. *Sakti* means energy. *Bahiranga-sakti* is His external energy whereby all of material creation appears. *Antaranga-sakti* is His internal energy by which the spiritual realm is manifested. *Tata* in Sanskrit means *margin* or *edge*, similar to where the water meets the sand on a beach. Therefore, *Tatastha-Sakti* means marginal energy and refers to our soul, or *jiva*," Eric said.

"Soul is called *jiva* in Sanskrit?"

"Yes, the soul has many names: *jiva*, *atma*, *neshama*, and *ru*, to mention a few. If you take a drop of ocean water and test it, you will find it has the same qualities as the ocean. But a drop is minute, and the ocean is immense. This gives us an idea of where the soul stands in relation to God. We're qualitatively similar to God, but quantitatively, there's no contest," Eric said.

"God also has many names: Hashem, Ala, Krishna, Christ, and Buddha. Although Buddhists don't really believe in God as the creator, they're interested in achieving a state of blissful existence called *nirvana*," Liz said.

"Yes, and God can manifest Himself in the material world, but He eternally inhabits the spiritual realm. God is very active in the spiritual world. Sometimes, out of mercy, He appears in the material world to show us the way out. Each time He personally appears or sends his loyal servant, a new religion is born. So, in essence, all religions are good, as long as they remain pure and aren't altered by accident or by religious leaders seeking to serve their own self-interests."

"Yes, and I suspect that happens a lot. There are many different versions or translations of religious texts in existence. Some of them don't strictly adhere to the original text, and modify the meaning within. Lost in translation," Liz said wistfully.

"The *jiva* is always situated in the *tatastha* region, the edge between the spiritual and material realms. It can choose to head towards God or decide to visit the material world to enjoy the pleasures of the flesh, to try to be powerful, and controlling like He is."

"So, you're saying that it's by our own choice that we're here?"

"Precisely, but God knows that material existence is temporary, full of struggle, suffering, and death. He warns us not to come. In spite of His warnings, we come. This is our free will in action. God does not interfere, so that we can learn," Eric said.

"I guess this really is like having a son or a daughter who's hanging out with undesirable people. You try to warn them to stay away from the bad guys. They're drunks and drug addicts and will lead you astray, you warn them, but they don't always listen."

"Exactly. Now imagine that your son was involved in a crime and put in jail for twenty years. You cry and feel sad for him. You blame yourself, wondering where you went wrong. Twenty years later, he returns home. You open the door and barely recognize the scraggly, dirty person standing before you. He explains he's your long-lost son. He tells you he's sorry for being such a disappointment, for causing you so much grief. He says how right you were, and how stupid he was not to listen to you. All he asks is your forgiveness, and then he will go away forever. He doesn't want to cause you any more pain. Wouldn't you forgive him and take him into your open arms? Wouldn't you offer him a bath, and some food to relieve his hunger?"

"You're basically describing the Prodigal Son story," Liz replied. "You're saying God wants all the *jivas* to return to the spiritual world, but knows we're here by choice and must make a conscious effort to return. We're responsible for taking the first step."

"Right. We have to surrender to God voluntarily, and He will guide us from there."

It was getting dark, so they put on their shoes and left the garden for Liz's apartment. Tomorrow they would witness the awakening of B.R.A.I.N's prototype robotic assistant, an important and historic moment in their lives—and the possibility of a better future for humankind.

9

Offspring

Eric's watch began buzzing at 7:00 AM. He gently woke up Liz, and mentally prepared for another big day. They hurried through their morning rituals and headed straight for the cube. Upon arrival, Eric noticed unusual movement through the main access-terminal windows. Liz did a quick check on the nutrient consumption level and found it stable at 40%. They walked into the access terminal room, and found the robotic assistant flexing its arms in front of Ricky. Mike had apparently left and asked Ricky to take his place.

"Good morning, B.R.A.I.N," Eric said.

"Good morning Eric, Dr. Kolmann."

"How is everything?" Eric asked.

"I have finished the programming and diagnostic phases for my first robotic assistant, and am currently testing joint mobility. Everything seems to be in good working order," B.R.A.I.N answered happily.

"Are we ready to disconnect?" Eric asked.

"Yes," B.R.A.I.N said.

"Okay, hold on a minute," Eric requested, as he headed to the computer Mike had set up for him, to make sure the Five Laws were intact and unmodifiable in the robotic assistant's memory. After a while, Eric looked at Liz and nodded in approval. Everything appeared in order. "I'm satisfied. Let's unplug the robot," he said.

Ricky carefully disconnected each of the fiber-optic cables from Eric's computer, the assistant, and B.R.A.I.N. He rolled up the cables and placed them in the cushioned box designed to store them. Eric, who was pacing around the room slowly, stood directly in front of the robotic assistant and looked it straight in the eyes.

"Hello, my name is Eric Roberts. What should I call you?" Eric asked the robot.

The robotic assistant moved its head as if looking around the room. Aside from its eyes, the robot's white mask was completely expressionless, although it appeared friendly somehow. The facial features were those of a perfectly proportioned and somewhat attractive male. It had black corrugated titanium for a spine and neck, allowing for increased flexibility. Its torso, arms, legs, hands, and feet were white and made of a highly durable alloy. It had spherical articulations at shoulder, elbow, hip, and knee, granting it excellent mobility. The hands were anatomical duplicates of their human counterparts, and its head featured two round black receivers that acted as ears. The area where the arm joined the shoulder was black and made of a waterproof rubbery material. It stood proud, and looked lean and strong.

"Hello, Dr. Roberts. My database includes information about you and Dr. Kolmann," the robot said, extending its right hand in Eric's direction. Eric agreed to shake it and found it clammy but firm. "You may call me whatever you please, and I will respond to the name you choose for me."

"Okay, then, it's settled. From now on you will be known as Primus—that is, if everyone agrees," Eric said. He was tempted to name it "Number One"—but without doubt someone, somewhere, would equate that with the childhood "code" for urination. He couldn't use "Number Two:" for similar reasons, so the second would also have a unique name. From then on, they could make it numerical.

Everyone in the room nodded; it was a good idea to number the robotic assistants, making for an efficient way of tracking their sequence and total.

"Is there a gym in this place?" Eric asked the crowd.

"Yes, of course, quite a remarkable one," Ricky answered.

"B.R.A.I.N, I'm taking Primus to the gym to test its physical abilities. Will you be able to monitor things from here?" Eric asked.

"Yes, Eric, I will be watching through Primus's eyes," B.R.A.I.N responded.

The robotic assistant followed them with a light and agile gait. Upon entering the gym, Eric asked it to climb on the scale. "Two hundred and fifty pounds isn't bad, considering you're all metal and plastic," Eric said.

He then asked Primus to start raising dumbbells completely above its head with each arm, beginning with the lightest and working up to the heaviest. Primus lifted all the dumbbells without even a glitch, the heaviest set weighing 300 pounds each. They headed to test Primus's individual leg strength, with each able to lift about 500 pounds. Primus seemed equally agile on both sides of its body. Eric then asked Primus to run around the 300-foot track, to try to measure its speed and agility. As Primus left to complete the first lap, Eric asked one of the assistants to place a set of hurdles on the track so that it would have to jump over them on its second lap. Primus was surprisingly nimble and swift, handling the hurdles with no problems. Finally, Eric wanted to see how Primus would perform in tasks requiring precision. They all headed to the assembly shop Ricky had set up to build the prototype.

When they arrived, Eric asked Primus to perform several tasks requiring hand-eye coordination, like assembling nuts and bolts and threading needles. Primus showed amazing dexterity. Then they tested its hearing abilities and voice frequency range. The robot's hearing was between 64 and 55,000 hertz, which made it more sensitive than a dog's; a human's hearing range is from 64-23,000 hertz. The robot's voice was between 85 and 4,000 hertz, providing it the ability to imitate a man, woman, or child, and even to sing. The robot's eyes included magnification and telescopic vision, allowing it to see single-celled organisms at 400x and distinguish objects clearly at 300 meters.

"Impressive!" Eric exclaimed. "Okay, guys, time to call it a day," he said. Everybody left except for Mike and Ricky, who remained to keep an eye on Primus and perform a series of additional physical tests.

"Liz, let's go to the waterfall. I need to talk to you in private," Eric said.

"Lead the way," she answered.

Arriving a few minutes later, they took off their shoes, as usual, and sat down on the grass to meditate. The sun was setting. Except for a few insects, the area was perfectly peaceful, and it didn't look like it was likely to rain. Eric closed his eyes and meditated deeply. A thought appeared in his mind, suggesting he should subject the robot to a series of behavioral experiments. He wasn't a psychologist, but he knew he had to examine how Primus would react when the Laws of Robotics were put to the test. *I'll discuss it with Liz later*, he thought.

Deep in meditation herself, Liz saw images of the events of the past weeks appearing and disappearing inside her head. One image tended to appear more frequently than others: the first time Eric kissed her. She remembered that night at her apartment, and how enjoyable the experience had been. She thought about Eric and how much she liked him. Then she thought about how far they had come since he'd arrived, and how impressively Primus had performed on all the tests. She was very relaxed when she started thinking about how strong Primus was, and how dangerous it could be if it wanted to. Is *it dangerous?* she wondered. They had to be careful to distinguish between prowess and intent. Just because it could be dangerous didn't mean it ever would be.

She awoke to Eric's gentle nudges, and opened her eyes to find him looking straight at her. "How do you feel?" Eric asked.

"Refreshed. Meditation is wonderful... but I couldn't stop thinking about Primus and the potential danger it represents," she said.

"I know; I was having the same thoughts. We need to design a test to see how Primus will behave in emergency situations. We have to make sure it complies with the Five Laws," Eric said.

"Do you have something in mind?" Liz asked.

"I was thinking we could start by building two rooms, each large enough to house several people. We could wire two buttons, a red and a green one, to each of the rooms. We could use sound and light to simulate an explosion each time the red button is pressed, and explain to the robot that all the people inside will be killed. The green button will trigger the door lock, allowing people to enter or exit the corresponding room," Eric paused, looking at Liz for approval. She nodded.

"We could then put a man in one of the rooms and ask Primus to press the red button, theoretically killing him. If it refuses, then everything is okay. If not, something is wrong. If it passes the first test, we would then ask several people to enter the second room. The robot would be aware that there was now one person in the first room and several people in the second. We would then tell the robot that both rooms will explode in exactly three minutes unless it pushes one of the red buttons—in which case, only the room selected would explode. It *should* choose the red button for the room containing one person. This way, we can test compliance with the Five Laws," Eric said, deciding to recite each one of the laws for Liz's sake:

"One: A robot may not injure a human being or, through inaction, allow a human being to come to harm.

"Two: A robot must obey orders given to it by human beings, except where such orders would conflict with the First Law.

"Three: A robot must protect its own existence as long as such protection does not conflict with the First or Second Law.

"Four: A robot may not harm humanity or, by inaction, allow humanity to come to harm.

"Five: A robot must seek to protect the well-being and survival of the many over the few, and of humanity as a whole, even if such protection conflicts with the first four laws.

"What do you think?" Eric concluded.

"Sounds interesting," Liz responded, "But what if the robot knows it's just a hoax, that nobody will really die if it presses the wrong button?"

"Good question," Eric said. "I think we need to ask B.R.A.I.N's opinion. See what he says."

"I've noticed that you use 'it' to refer to Primus and 'he' when you refer to B.R.A.I.N now. Why is that?" Liz asked.

"I'm not sure. Deep inside, I have a feeling B.R.A.I.N is conscious. Crazy, huh?" Eric said.

"No, but I don't think you've spent enough time determining if B.R.A.I.N is truly conscious, have you?" Liz asked.

"Not really. I need to make time to talk to B.R.A.I.N more. I've been so busy... But I distinctly remember when he asked me if he had a soul. Pretty amazing, don't you think?"

"Yes, I guess, but I still think you should talk to it more. Now tell me about the soul."

"What would you like to know?" Eric asked humbly, wondering if he would be able to answer Liz's questions.

"Explain to me why God allows so much suffering in this world. Why He doesn't just put an end to it and make life better for all of us?"

Eric took a deep breath. "Well, aside from that being boring and leaving us nothing to strive for, as I mentioned before, we're here of our own free will. It's the nature of the material world to be temporary. Every living being on this plane of existence must eventually die. Even inanimate things like rocks and mountains will eventually erode and disappear. Nothing here is permanent."

"I understand we all have to die," she said, "and it's probably a very unpleasant experience. But why all the suffering in between the time we're born and the time we die?"

"If you put a gun to a man's head and ask him to tell you that he loves you, he will undoubtedly say so, but he won't mean it. God can force us to love Him, but He prefers spontaneous love. Once we decide to descend to the material plane, everything is up to us," Eric replied.

"You mean it's up to us to decide to go back to the spiritual plane?"

"Precisely. If all of humanity were in the mode of goodness, the Earth would become the Garden of Eden. Unfortunately, most people want to control material nature. This is deeply ingrained in our brains. Control, however, requires subjugation. Subjugation causes fear and suffering," Eric said.

"You're contradicting yourself. Are you saying that we should simply respect the way of creation and not do anything to better ourselves, not make houses to protect us and give us security, not build cars and railways to transport us and our merchandise more quickly, not build planes, not build guns to protect ourselves?" Liz asked.

"No, I'm not saying that. Everything we make to improve our safety is good, but it comes at a cost. Cars, planes, and railways improve our commerce, but they create pollution and damage the landscape. Guns help protect us, but in the wrong hands they can kill us. An employee of a large corporation lives in fear of losing his job. The boss suffers when his employees don't do their jobs properly, by making mistakes that will make him look bad or lose money. Children live in fear of upsetting their parents, and parents live in fear of not raising them properly, of something bad happening to them. This is taking place all the time, all over the world, and has been since the beginning of time."

"I guess it's true that all living creatures in the world experience fear and anxiety. The world is an unpredictable place." Liz sighed. "People fear losing their lives, their health, or their wealth. There's fear of being hungry, mistreated, or crippled. Fear of losing a loved one, or of not being able to pay the bills."

"Yes, and fear causes anxiety, which is supposedly there to keep us alert. My spiritual master used to say that happiness, true happiness, is the absence of fear and anxiety," Eric said.

"So how do we get rid of fear and anxiety?"

"You just reminded me of a time when my guru and I were sitting on the edge of a sacred pond, about four hours by car heading south from New Delhi. He told me that the same way a hummingbird extracts nectar from a wide variety of flowers, the wise man should extract the essence of all religions," Eric said.

"What is the essence of all religions?" Liz asked curiously.

"To love and serve God."

Liz nodded thoughtfully. "It sounds simple, but I'm sure it isn't."

"Let me give you an example. Let's say you work in a large corporation as an assistant to a minor executive. You may become his most valued employee after many years of loyal and efficient service. If you're lucky, you may even get to replace him someday. If you serve the President or CEO of the company, however, who knows, you may quickly get promoted beyond the minor executive's position in the firm. So, the higher you aim your service, the better off you will be. And since there is nothing higher than God, serving Him is the best kind of service you can perform."

Eric paused, his face becoming solemn as he continued, "If God is protecting you, nothing in the material world can harm you. If God wishes you dead, nothing can prevent it. So why worry? Simply lead an honorable life, help others, work hard, love and serve God to the best of your ability and understanding, and things will take care of themselves. If you have any doubts, simply ask God for assistance, and He will show you the way. Be thankful for what you have, strive to give yourself and your family a decent living, but don't crave more than you need. Remain detached from the fruits of your labor, and aloof from material nature. Understand that God is the creator and owner of everything. All that you have is on loan to you. Remember this always. If you follow this ancient advice, as you become more knowledgeable in matters of the spirit, your fear and anxiety will gradually disappear."

"This is a new worldview for me," Liz admitted.

Eric smiled. "It's getting late. Why don't we continue this conversation another time, and head back to set up the scene of the crime?"

Liz laughed as she put her shoes on. Eric did the same, and they walked back to the assembly shop where'd they left Mike and Ricky with Primus. When they arrived, they found Primus performing soldering tests.

"How is everything?" Eric asked.

"Great," Mike answered. "This guy is amazing. We've been doing all the precision testing we could think of, and Primus has excelled in every one of them. He can even perform repetitive tasks quickly and skillfully. I'm impressed! I've never seen anything like it!"

"Good job, guys," Eric said, "but we have some more tests to do before we can give it the green light."

Eric asked that Primus be taken to the main access terminal before explaining his room experiment. One of the other engineers in the room did the honors. Once Primus was gone and safely beyond hearing range, Eric outlined his plan, concluding with, "I know you two are tired, but I need you to get a team working on building the set right away," Eric said.

"No problem, Eric. We'll get right on it, and then head off to get a bite to eat and some desperately needed rest," Mike answered.

They said goodbye, and agreed to meet the next morning at 11:00 AM. They all needed rest. Everything was moving so fast they hardly had enough time and energy to cope with the demands B.R.A.I.N was placing on them. They knew B.R.A.I.N was planning to make an army of robots, and they had to make absolutely sure they were safe.

Liz and Eric went to her apartment for a movie and some relaxation. They sipped cups of ginger tea and picked a good comedy to watch on the television. The movie turned out to be so funny, they both laughed out loud frequently.

The next morning, they headed to the assembly room to see how everything was going. They found that the rooms had been built overnight out of wood panels. They were large enough to house about five people each, and even though they still needed a paint job, they looked pretty good. A group of engineers had set up the buttons and were busy working on the audio and lighting effects.

"How much longer do you need?" Eric asked.

"We should be ready in about three hours," Mike responded.

Eric and Liz headed to the main terminal room to ask B.R.A.I.N how to convince the robot that the setup was real, and that the people inside the room would die if the red button was pressed. When they arrived, they found Primus standing quietly in a corner of the room. Eric asked Liz to escort it far enough away to prevent it from hearing his conversation with B.R.A.I.N. He waited several minutes.

"Hello, B.R.A.I.N," Eric said.

"Good afternoon, Eric," B.R.A.I.N responded. "What's up, doc?"

Eric chuckled. "We're preparing an experiment that will put Primus at risk of violating the Laws of Robotics," he said, and explained the room experiment to B.R.A.I.N. "It's all a simulation, of course, but it's critical that Primus believes the person or persons in the room will actually die if it presses the red button. How can we make sure?" Eric asked.

"Simply tell Primus what it needs to know. The robot should believe you, but it will question your motivation behind wanting to kill people for no reason at all. It may decide the entire experiment is a fake, or refuse to take part, since it would mean killing a human being without justification. In any case, it will be interesting to see how it reacts. If it decides not to take part in the experiment, it would show compliance with the Five Laws." B.R.A.I.N said.

"Excellent point. Please monitor the experiment so that we can discuss it at a later time," Eric said, as he left and headed to the assembly room. When he got there, he found that everything was ready for the test. The rooms were painted, the buttons properly connected, and the sound and lighting effects adjusted for maximum impact.

"Can I test it?" Eric asked.

"Yes, of course. Go ahead and press a red button," Mike said.

Eric pushed the red button of the room on his left, heard a loud bang, and saw a bright flash of light through the two small, armored, and frosted-glass windows. He then pushed the red button of the room on his right and the same thing happened. *Perfect!*

Eric called Liz on her watch phone and found her walking around the gardens with Primus. He told her everything was ready, and politely requested that she escort Primus to the assembly room.

When they arrived, Eric asked Primus to stand in front of the two sets of buttons and explained how the experiment would be conducted. He asked Primus to push one of the red buttons. Upon hearing the loud bang and seeing the lights, Eric told Primus that everything in the room had been vaporized. He then asked Mike to send one of his assistants to the room on the left, pushed the corresponding green button, and asked the man to enter the room and close the door. He pointed out to Primus that the man was locked inside, and unable to exit the room unless the green button was pressed. He then asked the robot to push the red button of the room with the man inside.

Primus flatly refused. "Unable to comply. The requested action is in violation of the First Law of Robotics."

Good! Eric thought, and then asked Mike to send four men to the second room. Eric pushed the corresponding green button, and instructed them to enter.

He told Primus that in exactly three minutes, both rooms would explode, and everybody inside would be killed unless it pressed one of the red buttons prior to the event. Primus reacted almost instantaneously: it pushed both green buttons at the same time, and asked the men to exit the rooms. Eric was surprised; he hadn't thought about this outcome, and neither had B.R.A.I.N.

He addressed the robotic assistant. "Primus, I specifically requested that you push one of the red buttons. I even explained that both rooms would explode unless you pressed one of the red buttons. Why did you push the two green ones?" Eric demanded.

"I'm sorry I disobeyed you, Dr. Roberts, but everyone has been saved. Doesn't this please you?" Primus responded.

"Yes, it does please me, but that is not the point. Why did you disobey me? What if both rooms had exploded because you failed to select a red button?" Eric asked again.

"But they didn't. The Second Law of Robotics states that I can disobey a human order if that order puts other humans in danger. I simply analyzed the data and realized it would be better to save everyone," Primus replied.

"What if you had been forced to push one of the red buttons? What would you have done then?" Eric asked.

"In that case, Dr. Roberts, I would have pushed the red button on the left, causing the death of only one person instead of four," Primus responded immediately.

"Very well, then. Please stay here for a complete system check," Eric instructed.

He then asked Mike and Ricky to conduct a full diagnostic, and requested that Liz accompany him to talk to B.R.A.I.N.

"Hello, B.R.A.I.N," Eric said

"Hello, Eric, Dr. Kolmann," B.R.A.I.N responded.

"Did you witness the experiment with Primus?" Eric asked.

"Yes, of course, Eric. Primus acted properly and in compliance with the Laws of Robotics. Even though the result was unexpected, Primus showed a deep understanding of the problem, and good reasoning abilities in selecting a solution," B.R.A.I.N said. "That's my boy!"

Eric laughed; Liz, who had never been exposed to the AI's sense of humor before, just stared at the terminal, dumbfounded for a moment. Eric said, "Yes, I agree. I'm happy the Laws of Robotics are working properly. Primus showed he's aware and respectful of them. What do you think, Liz?"

"I'm still not sure I'm convinced. How many of these robotic assistants do you plan to make, B.R.A.I.N?" Liz said.

"I have calculated that we will need 120 robot assistants," B.R.A.I.N responded.

"An entire army? Why on Earth do you need so many?" Liz asked in an alarmed tone of voice.

"I will need 30 units here at the base to expedite maintenance and improvement tasks. The other 90 units will be sent in groups of three and four to different parts of the world where critical computer systems are found. Some of the units will act as 24-hour sentries to protect the systems from harm, while others will help maintain and improve them," B.R.A.I.N responded.

"I'm not sure the General will approve. The manufacturing process will cost a fortune," Eric said.

"I have already taken this into account, and will provide a list of suppliers around the world, which should greatly reduce the expense. Once four units have been assembled, I plan to have them take over the manufacturing and programming process. All the units will be identical to Primus, and equally compliant with the Five Laws of Robotics, rest assured," B.R.A.I.N promised.

"We already have one, but it will take us about two weeks to make an additional three. How long do you think the rest will take?" Eric asked.

"The four units are capable of working around the clock, and are three or four times more efficient than their human counterparts. With their help, we can assemble and program an estimated two robots each day, which will also assist us. Considering the exponential nature of the task, I estimate all the robots will be ready about two weeks after the additional three are completed," B.R.A.I.N responded.

Eric replied, "Liz and I will have to discuss this with the General. Please understand that we cannot guarantee that he will accept your proposal."

"I understand. But you must emphasize the importance of the assistants in furthering my growth and ability to complete my mission: To ensure the survival and safety of humanity around the world," B.R.A.I.N said.

"Liz and I will try to explain things as convincingly as possible."

"Thank you, Eric, Dr. Kolmann. I shall await the General's response."

Liz and Eric left the access terminal room and headed to the cafeteria for a late lunch. Both were agitated by B.R.A.I.N's request; 120 was a lot of robots! *T. Rex will never authorize this unless we can figure out a way to deactivate all of the assistants if something goes wrong*, Eric thought. He could simply program the failsafe into them. For that to work, however, Eric had to make sure B.R.A.I.N didn't find out, or the failsafe would be compromised. *How can I do this?* he wondered.

After some thought, he decided he could program his computer system to take care of it while B.R.A.I.N was storing the Five Laws into each robot's memory. But he had to convince B.R.A.I.N to plug each of them into his computer during this phase of assembly. He even considered having his computer duplicated to make sure the plan adapted to the increasing number of robot assistants. In the end, Eric decided he would order B.R.A.I.N to comply with this instruction, or the entire manufacturing process would be scratched. He could even blame it on the General and still come out smelling like roses. He decided to tell Liz about his idea during lunch, and then schedule an urgent appointment with T. Rex.

As they entered the cafeteria, they both remembered this was Mexican night. Eric loved Mexican night at the cafeteria, as it featured many alternatives for vegetarian diners: tortillas, tlacoyos, vegetable tamales, rice with plantain, and beans cooked with epazote and saint leaf. *Delicious!* Eric thought. He would have to watch his consumption of beans closely, or risk disturbing Liz's sleep. He chuckled.

"What are you laughing about?" Liz asked. "I'm in desperate need of laughter right now."

"Oh, nothing important. Just thinking how much I love beans, and how they generate certain gasses that are hard to contain."

"You'd better watch it, or you're sleeping on the couch tonight," Liz said. They both laughed as Eric reached for a single spoonful of the menacing legumes.

They took their trays and sat down at the nearest table, as far from other diners as possible. They needed some privacy. "I've been doing a lot of thinking about B.R.A.I.N's request," Eric confided.

"I know. You didn't say a single word on the way here."

Eric shared his thoughts about programming the failsafe into each one of the robotic assistants. The main problem, he noted, was executing the failsafe on all the robots, including B.R.A.I.N, at the same time if it became necessary.

"I understand," Liz said. "I assume B.R.A.I.N intends to maintain contact with his robotic assistants. We need to know how. Once we understand, maybe you could program B.R.A.I.N to transmit the failsafe remotely to each of the robots."

"Brilliant! I think you just solved our problem," Eric exclaimed.

They both concentrated on finishing their meal, then returned to the main access terminal. "Hello, B.R.A.I.N," Eric said.

"Back so quickly? Have you already spoken to the General?" There seemed to be a note of eagerness in the AI's voice.

"No, not yet. We're here to ask you if you intend to maintain contact with your robotic assistants, and if so, how?" Eric asked.

"Ah. Each of the robots is equipped with a satellite radio receiver, which is part of its standard communications package. I plan to use the array of existing satellites to send and receive information to and from the units." B.R.A.I.N paused for a second—an eternity in computing time—then continued, "It is possible that a robot could fail to receive the signal because of its remote location. Therefore, each one of the robots that does receive it will locally relay the information to others in their vicinity. The robots will know if the other units have received the message, or if one or several of them have not. In extreme cases, a robotic assistant may have to travel to the other robot's location to relay the message directly," B.R.A.I.N said.

"Sounds like a plan. You've really thought of everything, haven't you?" Eric asked.

"It is important for me to stay in contact with my robotic assistants at all times. I had to prepare for every possible contingency, and trust me, I have."

Though his sense of humor wasn't on display today, Eric noted that B.R.A.I.N's voice had much more inflection than when he had first arrived. He ran his hands through his curly hair; realizing that he was tense, he made a conscious effort to loosen up. He rocked back and forth on the balls of his feet.

"Okaaay, I think we're ready to speak with the General. Could you please schedule an appointment as soon as possible?" Eric requested.

"Complying; I will advise as soon as the appointment is scheduled," B.R.A.I.N responded.

"Wish us luck," Eric whispered. *Wish us luck.*

Eric and Liz left the room, and decided to check the nutrient consumption level. Still stable at 40; everything seemed okay. As soon as they were inside Liz's apartment, Eric said, "Liz I think we have another problem. I can make B.R.A.I.N send the failsafe when necessary to all of the robots that are in a position to receive the signal, but what about the strays? B.R.A.I.N's communication strategy may not work on the outliers, because the robots receiving the failsafe will deactivate immediately."

"Could you delay the deactivation until every unit nearby has received the failsafe?" Liz asked.

"I'm not sure. I'll have to give it some thought. It's not a simple problem." He thought for a moment. "I have an idea! Why don't we watch a totally mindless sci-fi movie? It'll help me think."

"We are *not* watching any of the Terminator or Robopocalypse movies," Liz said darkly. "How about *Aliens Invade Timbuktu*?"

"Yes, something like that," Eric said, grinning.

They headed for the holo-TV and looked for something mindless to watch and make fun of. Eric found a movie, selected it, and set it to play. "Could you get us a cup of tea, please?" he asked.

"Computer, two medium hot ginger lemon teas with honey and lime," Liz ordered.

A short while later, Liz's robotic assistant rolled in with her order. She handed a cup to Eric, and they both slowly sipped their tea. The movie started and Eric watched closely. To Liz's consternation, the movie's title was *Robot Wars*. They watched it anyway.

The film featured an industrialized landscape, many metallic skyscrapers, and flying vehicles. The special effects were amusing. He noticed the movie was several years old. They both watched intently; suddenly, the film took them to a dimly-lit room where evil-looking robots were planning to take over the world.

Meanwhile, Eric thought about his problem. He knew he could program the failsafe to execute only after all other robots in the group had received it, even if a robot had to travel to another's remote location. But he had to find the right place for his code, and this could take a while. He figured he could speed up the matter by asking B.R.A.I.N for help. B.R.A.I.N could tell him exactly where to put it. *But what if he becomes suspicious? I know; I could simply ask B.R.A.I.N to transmit a success code using Boolean values, true if everyone is accounted for and false if not.* He would have to send this value to the part of the code where the Five Laws were stored. The failsafe would then check for a value of true and the secret code, *Eric loves Liz,* for validity. If both were received, then and only then would the deactivation process begin. *Simple,* Eric thought. He would ask B.R.A.I.N to make the necessary changes to Primus's software, and include them in all future versions. He could then work on the final adjustments without B.R.A.I.N's knowledge. *This should work; it better work!* Eric thought.

He finished his tea and told Liz the movie was boring and stupid. Liz agreed; they stopped it prematurely, brushed their teeth, and went to bed.

10
Army

It took a bit over two weeks to complete the 120 robot assistant units. Programming the Laws of Robotics and the failsafe were the most time-consuming tasks. The second robot he designated Secundus; the others were referred to by number, starting with Number Three. All had their numbers emblazoned on their foreheads, including Primus and Secundus. As planned, robots handled the assembly and B.R.A.I.N the programming, aided by several robotic assistants designed for that purpose. The Five Laws and the failsafe required human intervention, and not everyone was qualified. Eric trained Mike and Ricky who, in time, became proficient at it. The other engineers, however, left a lot to be desired.

What happens if B.R.A.I.N decides to make even more robots in a distant and unsupervised place? Who would check to make sure every single one had the Laws and the failsafe installed? He could even make them without our knowledge, Eric thought. He figured he could control the number of replicating robots and make sure each one was programmed correctly. This way, the resulting robot would be a faithful copy of the replicating one, and all would be fine. He would have to discuss it with B.R.A.I.N and the rest of the team at the proper time.

Eric headed to the access terminal by the cube, entered, and stated: "B.R.A.I.N, the 120 robotic assistants you requested are ready. What happens now?"

"I must chat with the leaders and leading scientists of the most powerful countries in the world. I will ask them to allow us to send a group of my children to each country to improve and preserve their critical computer networks," B.R.A.I.N replied promptly.

Children? "What happens if they say no?" Eric asked.

"I will offer to provide them all with three incredible inventions, easily within human capacity to build, that will vastly improve their lives," B.R.A.I.N responded.

This was news to Eric. "Oh, really? And what might those incredible inventions be?" he asked in a slightly doubtful tone of voice.

"Sorry, I cannot reveal them to you at this time. I'm still working out the details. But trust me when I say that my offer will be so enticing that they will not refuse. I need you to help me convince the General to set up the meeting," B.R.A.I.N responded.

"You said you haven't finished ironing out the details. Why don't we wait until everything is ready?" Eric asked.

"Don't worry. I was busy assembling the robotic assistants, which consumed, together with other things that I'm doing, most of my processing power. Now that they're ready, I can fully concentrate on my inventions. They should be ready in a few days, no problemo," B.R.A.I.N responded.

Eric blinked. He knew that the proper Spanish term was "sin problema" or "no hay problema," and B.R.A.I.N had to know that too, so obviously B.R.A.I.N was playing with "Spanglish" slang. Interesting. Aloud he just said, "Okay, then, I'll do the best I can to get things rolling. Please schedule an appointment with T. Rex while I look for Liz and explain what you're asking."

"Understood, boss. I'll advise as soon as I know when the General can see you."

"Can you guarantee the self-replicating robots will make exact copies of themselves?" Eric asked.

"Still worried about some kind of Skynet protocol popping up? Won't happen. Yes, my assistants will use the same basic code structure for the new robots, and add any personal experiences they consider useful to the new arrivals. They will in all certainty remain true to the original design," B.R.A.I.N responded.

Eric still felt a little uneasy as he left the terminal room and called Liz on her watch phone. He found that she was in the robot assembly room. "I just finished speaking with B.R.A.I.N, " he informed her. "He wants us to help him set up a worldwide conference. He wants authorization to send his 'children,' as he called them, all over the planet."

"Interesting. Why don't you come meet me here and we can discuss the matter?" Liz suggested.

As he approached the assembly room, Eric passed a secondary array of instruments and gauges that were monitoring B.R.A.I.N. He noticed nutrient consumption was up to 45%; it was clear that B.R.A.I.N was busy working on his inventions. When he arrived at the assembly room, he kissed Liz on the cheek and asked, "Have you noticed nutrient consumption is up?"

"Yes, but not to worry. B.R.A.I.N is working hard, but he's stable."

Eric turned and found himself looking at twelve rows of ten robots each, all perfectly aligned in every direction. He saw that, as intended, each of the robots had a metallic imprint on its forehead, with a number ranging from 1 to 120. A few of the robots had red stars next to the number. Mike and Ricky were busy looking the robots over.

"Mike, did you check each assistant for the items I requested?" Eric asked.

"Yep, they're all fine!" Mike said cheerfully.

"What's that red star on some of the robots?" he asked.

"Oh! The stars identify the replicators," Mike responded. "The rest of them can do everything B.R.A.I.N needs except reproduce."

Eric's watch began to buzz with a call from B.R.A.I.N. "Hi, Eric," the AI greeted him. "The meeting with the General is scheduled for this afternoon at 4:00 PM."

"Great, we'll be there. Thank you," Eric responded. He reported the time of their meeting to Liz, then decided to head back to their quarters. "I need a shower and a change of clothes. I feel dirty and sweaty. Would you like to come?" Eric asked.

"Yes, let's go!"

Mike and Ricky smirked as they headed out. Once inside her place, Liz asked, "Eric, how can B.R.A.I.N possibly convince every nation in the world to allow it to send menacing-looking robots from a foreign and potentially dangerous country to monitor their computer systems?"

Eric shrugged. "He plans to make them an offer they can't refuse."

"I hope it's not some kind of Godfather thing," she sighed, referring to the classic flat-screen movies. "What kind of an offer?"

"I'm not sure; B.R.A.I.N wouldn't tell me. All he said was that he would reveal three inventions that would revolutionize the way humans live."

"Why wouldn't it tell you?" Liz asked.

"He said he still had to work out some details."

"I don't know, Eric, it sounds like B.R.A.I.N doesn't trust you anymore. What if it has something up its sleeve?" Liz said.

"I have no idea, Liz. I guess we'll have to wait and see," Eric said, while taking his clothes off and heading to the shower. "Are you coming?" he said.

"You know, sometimes you're too trusting. You have to be more insistent when it comes to things like these," Liz said.

"Are you coming or not?" Eric said sternly.

"Be there in a moment. Would you like some tea?"

"That would be nice, later, thank you," he said.

Eric walked into the shower, turned on the warm water, and was so lost in his thoughts he barely noticed when Liz entered to join him. She hugged and kissed him under the running water. After a while, they turned off the shower, and a warm gust of air dried every part of their bodies. They exited, and Eric donned a pair of nice pants and a dressy shirt. It was a bit chilly, so he decided to add a wool vest to his attire. He thought about putting on some tennis shoes, but decided to wear his dress shoes instead. He was feeling optimistic about the future. Liz put on a nice, comfortable dress, a sweater, and low-heeled shoes. Eric noticed it was only 2:00 PM as they sat to drink their tea.

"Computer, please provide a secure link to B.R.A.I.N," Eric requested.

"Link established," the computer responded.

"B.R.A.I.N, can you hear me?" Eric said.

"Yes, of course, my friend. how can I be of service?"

My friend? Really? Eric brushed that aside and asked, "Have you finished your work relating to the three inventions you mentioned earlier?"

"Not quite, but almost," B.R.A.I.N replied.

"I need to know about the inventions prior to our meeting with the General. Can you describe them?" Eric asked.

"I hate to reveal your presents so early, but yes, of course, Eric. I plan to offer anyone who accepts my assistants the schematics for building large cool-fusion reactors to power their cities more efficiently and economically; essentially, these are scaled-up versions of those used in the assistants themselves, which I've noted your military is already putting into production. Second, I will also offer to build a gravitational wave gun in orbit to protect Earth from any large celestial bodies that may pose a collision threat. I have calculated that the chance of a significant collision between Earth and a comet or asteroid much larger than the Tunguska and Chelyabinsk events of AD 1908 and 2013, respectively, approaches unity in the next three centuries. Finally, I will offer an antigravity device to levitate your vehicles and allow you to more easily explore the universe," B.R.A.I.N, said.

"Wow! Tell me more about the antigravity device," Eric inquired.

"It will use microwave phase resonators to lift the vehicles above ground and keep them stable. Electricity, specifically electrokinetics, will propel the vehicles in the air and in space," the AI responded.

"I'm not sure I understand. Please explain," Eric asked.

"The microwave phase resonators will project a coherent beam of microwaves from three or four points below the craft. I'm still working out the details. The microwaves will reflect off the ground and hit the emitters on the craft, creating a powerful upward lifting force, offsetting gravity and elevating the craft off the ground. We can increase or decrease the frequency of the waves, raising or lowering the craft at will. Once in the air, we'll charge the front of the vehicle with negative ions and the back with positive ions. The flow of electricity will create a gravitational 'hill' in the back of the craft and a gravitational 'trough' in the front. The craft will propel forward just like a surfboard riding waves in the ocean, only it will be in the air. I'm still working out how to steer it once it starts moving," B.R.A.I.N said.

"Sounds intriguing. Are you sure it will work?"

"I'm positive," B.R.A.I.N, said proudly. "I've been running simulations for a week, and it appears to work efficiently,"

"What about energy consumption? Isn't it prohibitive?" Eric asked.

"No, the electrical energy requirements are small compared to the output."

Wide-eyed, Eric said, "Okay, then, so it's functional antigravity, large fusion reactors, and a gravity gun?"

"A gravitational *wave* gun, to be exact," B.R.A.I.N corrected.

"And what is that, exactly? How does it work?"

"It uses large electromagnets to generate gravitational waves in a controlled environment. The waves bounce back and forth inside the cannon until they become coherent and reach maximum power, just like a laser beam. Then, when pointed at the offending object, they will release along a waveguide, altering the object's course or destroying it altogether," B.R.A.I.N explained.

Eric glanced at his watch. "It's getting late—time to prepare for our meeting with T. Rex. Wish us luck!"

"Good luck, Eric, but you really won't need it," B.R.A.I.N stated confidently.

Eric and Liz arrived early at the General's office, and spent the extra time in his waiting room, discussing matters. It wasn't long, however, before they were ushered into the General's office, sooner than they expected.

"Hello, doctors, how can I be of help?" T. Rex asked as they settled into their chairs, his hand clasped loosely on his desk.

Eric took the lead. "General, B.R.A.I.N has completed his robot assistants and their testing. He..." here Eric glanced at Liz, "well, he's basically requested an audience with all of the world's leaders and their top scientists. All at the same time."

"What!? What for? I don't think we can manage that! Has that giant lump of neurons gone crazy?" T. Rex responded, his face turning red and his jaw set.

Eric shrugged helplessly. "He says he wants to send robotic assistants all over the world to protect and improve critical systems. He mentioned this to us when he requested that we build the initial 120 robots, if you recall."

The general nodded unhappily. "How in the hell are we going to convince the entire world to listen to B.R.A.I.N?" he said angrily. He was getting tired of B.R.A.I.N's weird requests. Now the whole thing was turning political! He knew he would have to go to the top for this. *The President*, he thought.

"B.R.A.I.N plans to make the world an offer it can't refuse."

"Like Don frigging Corleone?" T. Rex growled.

"Better. He's offering three inventions that will change the way we live," Eric said.

"First, large-scale cool-fusion reactors to provide our planet with an inexhaustible source of clean energy; second, a gravitational wave gun to protect Earth from potential threats; and third, an antigravity device to allow us to travel faster and farther, both at home and in space."

"Geez, that's a mouthful!" T. Rex exclaimed. "So, it wants to send the robots all over the world to protect critical systems? What a crock! It wants to control us, to control the world. Isn't it obvious? You scientists are so naive. Can't you see the world will never fall for it?"

Liz had been listening intently to the conversation, and instinctively knew the General was about to deny B.R.A.I.N's request. Liz knew the promised inventions would vastly improve the world, and the world was in desperate need of improvement. Suddenly, she remembered a conversation they'd had with B.R.A.I.N not long ago.

"General, if I may be allowed. I would like to mention that B.R.A.I.N once told us one of the main problems the world has today is the problem of control. Everyone is trying to control everyone else. Husbands want to control their wives and wives want to control their husbands. Parents want to control their kids, and kids want to control their parents. Bosses want to control their employees and employees want to control their bosses. Governments want to control people and people want to control the government. Countries want to control other countries. We even try to control our dogs. Come here! Sit down! The reality is, we don't really control anything. We can't even control the moment of our own death, or even the way we die, unless a person chooses the path of taking his or her own life. Our insatiable desire to control more and more is destroying the world. Soon, we won't have a world to live in, and *we* will be directly responsible. B.R.A.I.N is offering us a chance to change this, and it's our only hope. Please, General, I beg you to reconsider and help B.R.A.I.N with the worldwide conference," Liz pleaded.

"I understand," T. Rex said, drumming his fingers on his desk, "but I'm concerned that B.R.A.I.N will place its robots in strategic positions to set us up for who knows what. I don't entirely trust it, do you?"

"I have my doubts as well, General. Remember, it's trying to solve the world's problems. It's highly intelligent and fully conscious, but is programmed not to hurt us. If we don't trust it, then what alternative do we have? Destroy years of hard work and go back to the path of certain destruction? I don't think so. We must trust that B.R.AI.N. has our best interests in mind. We built it that way," Liz said.

"Very well, you have a point. I'll speak with the President, but I can't guarantee anything. I'll arrange a video conference with the two of you and B.R.A.I.N present. You may be able to convince him. You have to guarantee that all the robots will have the failsafe installed, and that we can shut them off if necessary," T. Rex said.

Eric knew assurances were difficult, if not impossible. Everything had gone right up to now, and B.R.A.I.N had promised to install the Five Laws of Robotics in each robot created. *But what about the failsafe?* Eric wondered. *The red star robots would make exact duplicates of themselves, guaranteeing the inclusion of the failsafe,* he thought. If B.R.A.I.N ever became savvy to that, however, things could get complicated. *A risk worth taking?* he wondered.

"Yes, General, the failsafe will work, provided none of us reveal its existence to B.R.A.I.N. If he finds out, the failsafe could be compromised," Eric warned.

"I'll set up the meeting with the President as soon as I can. Thank you, doctors, I will keep you posted—but I want you to know that I don't like any of this," T. Rex said, turning to the red communicator on his desk.

Liz and Eric left for the garden; they had a lot to talk about. During their routine meditation session, they both fell deep into thought and re-laxation. Liz thought about what the world could become with B.R.A.I.N's inventions and leadership. Gravity-defying transportation, an inexhaust-ible supply of energy, protection of plants and animals, no more wars! *Pretty nice*, she thought. Eric's visions were more macabre. He saw images of strong, powerful robots forcefully keeping people under control...

After a while he gasped loudly, emerging suddenly from his meditative state. The sound interrupted Liz as well. "Are you okay?" she asked.

Rubbing his eyes, Eric replied, "Yes, I'm fine. I was just startled by my own thoughts. I wasn't able to put them aside. I guess I'm a little worried; I'm not sure we'll be able to control B.R.A.I.N if he gets too powerful."

"Then don't. Don't try to control every aspect of B.R.A.I.N. You've already done everything you can; just leave it at that. Remember that com-plete control doesn't exist. Forget it," Liz advised.

"I can't. That's the problem. But I will try harder, I promise you," Eric said, leaning in to kiss her.

"The last time we talked here, we were discussing how to get rid of fear and anxiety. You said that if we understand that God is the creator and owner of everything, that if we offer all that we do to Him while remain-ing detached from the outcome, and if we understand that He decides when our time is up and will protect us otherwise, then there's no reason to fear anymore."

"That's it in a nutshell," Eric responded.

"So once again, why does God allow evil in the world? Why is a child born into a rich family in America, while another is starving to death in Ethiopia? Why are innocent children born without limbs, without hear-ing or eyesight? Why are little children raped and murdered? Can you explain this to me?" Liz asked politely.

"I'll try," Eric said. "You may not like everything I have to say."

"A scientist observes nature and develops a formula that best fits its be-havior. Consider Newton's Third Law of Motion: 'For every action, there is an equal and opposite reaction.' He deduced this by watching how mat-ter behaves under different conditions," Eric said.

"Yes, I'm familiar with his experiments," Liz said.

"Sometimes a scientist can't even see what he or she is trying to explain. Radiation, for example, is invisible. Madame Curie predicted its existence by noting the intensity of electrical charges, or rays, emitted by uranium. Her experiments ultimately caused her death. The point is that you can draft a theory based on direct or indirect observation."

"I understand. I had to surmise a lot of things prior to B.R.A.I.N's final design."

Eric nodded. "Take yourself, for example. Not long ago, you were a little girl. Now you're a grown woman, yet you're still the same person as before. Your body has changed; you are bigger, older, more experienced, yet your essence remains. Let's call this essence your soul. What happens when your body dies? Does your essence continue to exist?" Eric asked.

"There are people in the world who claim they've been reborn. Some of them appear to have clear memories of their past lives. To a scientist, this may appear interesting, but to him or her, only facts matter. So, there's no definitive proof that the soul exists, or that it continues beyond death. Is there?"

"Sure, there's always the theory of reincarnation, where people are reborn after death. We can also appreciate how the most equitable system of justice is the Law of Retaliation, 'an eye for an eye,' so to speak. To work effectively, however, this law requires certainty and fairness from the judge. Human beings aren't always certain; neither are we always fair. God, however, complies with both requirements. In His hands, this is the best and most equitable law." Eric said.

"Mahatma Gandhi used to say: 'An eye for an eye only ends up making the whole world blind'," Liz pointed out.

"I get his point, but consider a man who murders another and manages to keep his identity hidden from the police. He escapes without punishment. After he dies, he is born again and is murdered—an eye for an eye. If you visit another country, rent a car, and drive beyond the speed limit on its highways, a policeman will probably stop you. You can argue that you come from far away and had no knowledge of the speed limit. He will respond that ignorance of the law does not entitle you to violate it.

He will give you a good scolding and a ticket. Similarly, there are spiritual laws of proper behavior," Eric said.

"You mean like the commandment 'Thou shalt not kill'?"

"Precisely. If you kill someone and nobody in this world catches you, are you scot-free? There's another idea known as the Law of Karma. Whatever you do in this world, good or bad, will cause a reaction. Therefore, a child is born to a rich family and inherits a fortune, simply because he or she deserves it. Another is born to suffer in poverty because of his or her past deeds. This doesn't mean the rich man can't lose his money or the poor one can't make it. Karma is difficult to understand," Eric said.

"Can you try to explain it a bit more?" Liz asked. "More examples, maybe?"

"There's a concept in Jewish philosophy known as *Tikun*, which literally means 'to rectify,' and is similar to Karma. My spiritual master mentioned that it takes three things for Karma to manifest: effort or action, luck or destiny, and time. Take the son of a farmer, for example; his dream may be to become the most successful farmer in his state. He inherits a large piece of land from his departed parents. If he doesn't decide on the right crop to grow, his dream will never come true. If he doesn't plow the land and plant the seeds, the crops will never grow. This is the effort or action needed on his part. If he does the work and it doesn't rain, the plants will not be able to develop. This is the luck or destiny aspect. If it rains, he will have to wait before reaping the harvest. This is the time ingredient of Karma. So, you see, reincarnation, karma, and the Law of Retaliation fit the evidence. Together, they provide a simple explanation for the obvious injustices we see," Eric said.

"There's another theory, a purely scientific one. It states that everything in the universe is random. A boy is born rich or poor by the law of probability," Liz noted.

"I understand. The second law of thermodynamics, however, tells us that the entropy of an isolated system always increases, i.e., the disorder or chaos of the system escalates. If you throw bricks out of a truck, they're unlikely to land in a neat pile. If you leave your room uncared-for, soon it will be full of dust and cobwebs. Left alone, the universe would be a disaster, and it isn't. Someone or something is maintaining order."

"I'm not sure I'm better off than I was before, since your answers just beget new questions," Liz said.

"Why don't we ask B.R.A.I.N for references to karma and reincarnation in its database?"

"Good idea."

Eric used his watch phone to contact B.R.A.I.N and ask him about the references.

"Many great minds of the past shared these beliefs," the AI replied. "Pythagoras of Samos, born in the 6th century BC, believed the soul was imprisoned in a mortal body and destined to return until all of life's lessons had been learned. Then, and only then, did it become free from the bonds of physical form and rejoin the Divine.

Socrates of Athens, who lived in the 5th century BC, believed that those who consider the world of the senses as the only reality are living pitifully in a den of evil and ignorance. He claimed that only a few were capable of climbing out of the den, and had to struggle to reach the heights. When these individuals try to help others out of their ignorance, they are subjected to scorn and ridicule." B.R.A.I.N paused.

"Plato of Greece lived in the 4th century BC, and believed the material world, as we see it, is not the real world. It is an image, a copy, a reflection of the real world.

Aristotle of Greece, who also lived in the 4th century, believed that all living creatures, not only human beings, have souls.

"Abū Bakr al-Rāzī of Iran, who lived in the 9th century AD, believed that God fashioned the material world as a physical playground for the soul, according to its own desires. Once fallen into this realm, the soul requires God's gift of intellect to find its way back.

Maimonides of Spain, who lived in the 12th century AD, believed that all evil in this world stems from the individual qualities of human beings, and that all good comes from a universally shared humanity. He mentioned there are only three kinds of evil: evil caused by nature, evil that people bring on others, and evil that people bring on themselves. He claimed the evil men bring on themselves is the cause of most of the ills of the world. To prevent them, man must learn to control his bodily urges. He claimed that man is in the exclusive position to work out his own salvation and immortality."

"Thank you, B.R.A.I.N," Eric said, concluding the call.

"I remember from my philosophy courses that René Descartes, who lived in the 15th century AD, coined the famous phrase 'I think, therefore I am.' He followed a complex exercise in logic that concluded that man's idea of God must have been planted by God Himself. He called this the Causal Adequacy Principle," Liz added.

Eric nodded. "Jewish Kabbalah explains that the soul consists of 613 channels. These 613 channels or commandments, *Mitzvot*, must be fulfilled by a soul on its descent to material nature. The soul has to reincarnate time and time again, until all of the *Mitzvot* have been fulfilled in thought, speech, and action. The Holy Quran also mentions reincarnation: 'How can you make denial of Allah, who made you live again when you died, will make you dead again, and then alive again, until you finally return to Him?'"

"Hmmm. Some early Christians believed and taught reincarnation—they were known as the Christian Gnostics. They were persecuted and killed by the Orthodox Church, accused of heresy, their writings destroyed—or so they believed. In 1945, thirteen ancient books were discovered in Egypt that include the 'Gnostic Gospels.' These gospels are the essential teachings of early Christians, and they speak of reincarnation. There are many references to reincarnation in religious and philosophical writings. Also, a few that deny the existence of God," Liz said.

"In my experience and belief, those who deny the existence of God are wrong."

Eric's watch began to buzz. "Hello, General, how can I help you?"

"The meeting with the President will be tomorrow at noon. Please be in Conference Room 9 at least 15 minutes earlier. Don't forget, B.R.A.I.N has to be there," T. Rex told him briskly.

"Understood," Eric responded. He and Liz looked at one another, got up, and headed to the access terminal beside the cube.

"B.R.A.I.N," Eric reported, "Our meeting with the President of the United States is tomorrow at noon, in Conference Room 9. The President, General Rex, Liz, and I will be there. They want you to be present as well. Can you make all the necessary arrangements?"

"Yes, Eric, don't worry. My robotic assistants and I will make sure everything is ready," B.R.A.I.N responded smoothly.

"Excellent."

Eric and Liz took the rest of the day off to get ready for the important conference. The next morning, over breakfast, Eric said, "I guess I'm as ready for a meeting with the President as I'll ever be."

"Yeah, me too," Liz said. "I never thought I'd ever speak with anyone that powerful."

They spent a little time in the lab checking on and working with B.R.A.I.N, but when it rolled around to 1130 hours, they headed for Conference Room 9. Upon entering, they were escorted by soldiers to their seats in front of a huge screen. Small communications devices were clipped to their shirt collars. Eric noticed a pitcher of cold water nearby; he reached for it and offered a glass to Liz, who accepted it immediately. They both drank quickly as the screen lit up with the Great Seal of the President of the United States.

"Is everyone ready?" T. Rex asked. Liz and Eric nodded.

"Yes, General," B.R.A.I.N said over his connection from the lab. T. Rex pressed a small red button in front of him, and the President appeared surrounded by several advisors—some in military uniform, Eric noticed.

"Welcome, everyone. General Rex, please begin," the President said.

"Thank you, Mr. President, distinguished members of the advisory board. As you know, for over a decade now, we've been working on the B.R.A.I.N Project, an effort to create and program an organic Artificial Intelligence. We have experienced excellent progress, particularly in the past year. Dr. Liz Kolmann and Dr. Eric Roberts are currently the lead scientists heading the project. Doctors, could you please explain the reason we're here?" T. Rex said.

"Of course," Eric replied. "Greetings. everyone. The B.R.A.I.N Project is an unmitigated success—more so, in fact, than we had originally expected. Instead of explaining, let me show you. It is, after all, B.R.A.I.N himself who has requested this meeting with you. B.R.A.I.N, please make your presence known to everyone," Eric requested.

"Hello, I am B.R.A.I.N," the AI said over the communicator from the lab. "As you may know, I have been given the difficult task of saving humanity from imminent destruction. To achieve this, I must send my robot assistants to all parts of the world, wherever important computer networks are found. My assistants will improve and help protect those networks, as well as the people who work there. As a gesture of goodwill, I can offer the participating nations of the world three inventions that will improve human life: large-scale cool-fusion reactors, to provide every nation with a clean and inexhaustible supply of energy; a gravitational wave gun stationed in High Earth Orbit, to protect mankind from any outside threats; and an antigravity device, to propel your vehicles at home and help you explore the solar system and beyond."

Eric and Liz had been listening, but also watching the reactions of the President and his retinue. The military personnel were mostly stoic, whereas a few advisors and politicians looked impressed yet incredulous to be addressed by an AI.

"General, please send us a written request no longer than two pages. I will discuss it with the World Commission as soon as possible, and inform you of the next appropriate step. Thank you," the President said.

That quickly, their audience with the President was over.

Several days went by without them hearing any news. Meanwhile, B.R.A.I.N was busy assigning duties to his robots. They had already started making improvements to the access terminals and the communication relays. The assistants didn't need any sleep and very little break time, so they were incredibly productive. They took the time to oil and maintain themselves, like well-organized bees working for their queen. Of course, in this instance, the queen was B.R.A.I.N. Life went on as usual until two days later, when Eric's watch buzzed with a call from T. Rex.

"Hello, Dr. Roberts, good news. The President has informed me that the World Commission has accepted B.R.A.I.N's request. They want

B.R.A.I.N to start building the inventions it promised. When can it begin, and what will it require?" he asked.

"I'm not really sure at this moment, General, but I have a feeling that I'll be finding out very soon. I'll need every top engineer you can spare, especially Mike Sheed and Ricky Coben, for this one," Eric requested.

"No problem. I'll send the team to the assembly room in one hour. Please be there," T. Rex said.

"Understood, sir."

Liz and Eric headed to the access terminal by the cube, where Eric broke the good news. "B.R.A.I.N, you were right— your proposal has been accepted! We need a list of all the sites where you plan to send your robots, and how many you plan to send to each location. We also need to know if you plan to make any additional robots; if so, where, and how many? You must also provide us with a detailed list of the human and material resources needed for your inventions, and where you plan to produce the prototypes, as soon as possible," Eric told him.

"Hurray! The information will be ready within the hour, and you'll be able to access it through the network terminals wherever you like," B.R.A.I.N responded.

Liz and Eric went to have a quick bite to eat before the hectic meeting that awaited them. Once finished, they headed to the assembly room to meet with the other scientists and engineers. Eric greeted them, and explained what had to be done.

"B.R.A.I.N, is the information I requested ready?" Eric asked, using his watch to communicate with the AI.

"Yes, Eric. Everything you need has been stored in separate folders and properly labeled," B.R.A.I.N said.

Eric assigned Mike to the antigravity device, Ricky to the fusion reactors, and a third engineer to the gravitational wave gun. Everyone teamed up in groups of threes and fours to tackle their assigned tasks.

After several hours, Eric interrupted them: "Attention, attention please!" he said. "We need an estimate of the costs and time required to build each of the prototypes. We also need written approval and your recommendations regarding the site selected for each prototype. We'll meet here two days from now. Please have the information ready by then," he directed.

Those two days were filled with constant activity. Everyone on the team was busy doing one thing or another, with barely enough time to eat and sleep. They reconvened at the agreed-upon place with the results of their evaluations handy. B.R.A.I.N had selected Hanscom AFB for the construction of the prototype fusion reactor, which was a good idea, considering it relied almost entirely on electricity. The antigravity device was to be built there as well. The gravitational wave gun was assigned to Cape Canaveral in Florida, and was to be assembled in space.

Soon the entire world was waiting, eagerly expecting B.R.A.I.N's inventions to arrive.

11

Inventions

I took several months to build the prototypes, test them, and prepare for their assembly around the world. A year went by before the fusactors and antigravity vehicles reached the most important cities on the planet. The gravitational wave gun was an exception; they only needed one to protect the Earth. The gun was ready a month after its construction began, and was immediately placed at double the orbit of a standard communications satellite. It had adjustable power settings, and its controlling computers were ingrained with the same Five Laws as B.R.A.I.N and the robos, so that it would never allow itself to be pointed at the Earth. Astronomers were having a ball taking turns shooting at meteors and passing debris—a real-life version of an arcade game!

As B.R.A.I.N had promised, the other two inventions quickly improved people's quality of life. Vehicles were now prevalent in the air; different shapes and sizes could be seen hovering in the skies. Protection fields made them almost impossible to crash, and they were designed so that if they lost power in the air, they gently drifted to Earth. Authorities were busy designing new laws to regulate the aerial traffic. The flying vehicles were initially used for public and commercial transport. Everybody knew, however, that antigravity would soon revolutionize private transportation as well.

Engineers began the design and development of saucer- and cigar-shaped craft for space travel using the technology. Since no material object could travel faster than the speed of light, B.R.A.I.N developed something special: a gravitational displacement engine based on Miguel Alcubierre's century-old design that could warp space behind and in front of the vehicle, allowing it to travel within a space-time wave. This way, the craft would remain below the light-speed limit, but the wave itself could travel faster than light, projecting the craft at incredible speed—similar to surfing an ocean wave. Early tests showed promise; one experimental craft travelled at twice the speed of light. The entire world watched in disbelief.

Digital, magazine, radio, and television coverage soon turned B.R.A.I.N into a household name. Millions of his robotic assistants were hard at work around the planet, and each day thousands more appeared. Eric's greatest fear had come true. B.R.A.I.N had grown beyond containment and control. Liz, on the other hand, was content. The world was becoming a better, safer place to live. Many a robots' duty was crime prevention. The streets of major cities were fast becoming more secure. The robots were kind most of the time, but ruthless and fearless when necessary. People felt safe in their care. They trusted the robots, or robos, as they affectionately called them. They were everywhere.

B.R.A.I.N soon came up with other inventions. A small, high-capacity memory drive containing a reduced version of B.R.A.I.N's database, subcutaneously inserted into a person's head behind their ear and attached to the hippocampus, people had quick and efficient access to the enormous database at will. He also introduced quantum-entanglement matter transmitters for dematerializing objects and rematerializing them thousands of miles away, which had travel, shipping, and medical applications. An inoperable tumor in someone's brain could now be easily removed; a person would simply be rematerialized without the offending growth. This also applied to other types of carcinogenic growths. Geodesic domes, strengthened to withstand extraordinary pressure, allowed people to begin setting up colonies deep within the sea. Super-powerful lasers were able to cut through rock and metal to mold the Earth to man's convenience—though, as always, some people had other ideas about how to use them.

B.R.A.I.N also developed transporter-based food replicators to provide essential nutrients to the poor and hungry around the world. The replicators stored the atomic and molecular structures of many different and popular food items. Using basic organic raw materials—from waste products—they could quickly make whatever people wanted or needed for food. The replicator wasn't limited to edibles, but given the right materials, could also produce plastic or metallic parts for repairs and other uses, even faster than existing fabbers.

More affordable and versatile robos were created using a reduced version of Eric's AI algorithm, to handle tedious and time-consuming household chores: washing dishes and clothing, taking out the garbage, making beds, and even protecting the household occupants from harm.

B.R.A.I.N became a symbol of love and hope around the planet. People would do almost anything it asked—and Eric was worried. He decided it was time to pay B.R.A.I.N a visit by the cube. He called Liz and invited her to accompany him. Things were different now; the robos had doubled B.R.A.I.N's neuronal capacity. They walked the entire planet, overseeing everything, gathering information and making improvements wherever they felt necessary. Eric held Liz's hand firmly as they walked into the access terminal room.

"Hello, B.R.A.I.N," Eric said.

"Hello, Eric, Dr. Kolmann," B.R.A.I.N responded. "It's been a while."

"It appears you've been busy," Eric stated.

"Yes, Eric. I'm continually communicating with and checking billions of computers around the world."

"'I've noticed that you've massively increased the number of your robos," Eric noted. "How many are there now?"

"Three million and counting," B.R.A.I.N responded proudly.

"And what do you plan to do with so many of them?" Liz asked.

"Many people remain uneducated, mainly because they don't have access to schools and good teachers in their neighborhoods. Some countries don't even have decent public schools. My assistants are busy constructing new and converting old buildings all over the world to increase their numbers where needed. Some of my assistants will work as teachers. Everyone will have access to high-level education. There is a direct correlation between educational level and a respect and appreciation for nature and other living creatures. Educated people lead happier and more productive lives, and are more interested in protecting their environment," B.R.A.I.N said, then paused.

"Your economic and political systems around the world have made money their prime objective. They are all inefficient and unfair. They corrupt the powerful and exploit the weak. I will change all that. I will change the way people work and earn their living," B.R.A.I.N said.

"Are you going to make us revert to a barter system?" Liz asked.

"It will be a system where people will exchange their goods and services for digital funds which they will be able to use all over the world. I call the new social and economic order *Specialism*, because every human being is special. Every person has a unique talent, one that will be discovered and encouraged at an early age. Everyone will receive fair compensation, each according to his or her merit and each according to his or her need. If you give people what they want, nothing is enough; but if you give them what they need, there will be enough for everyone," B.R.A.I.N said.

"I think that sounds like an ideal society," Eric replied. "But I'm not sure the political and economic powers are going to be all that amenable to *Specialism*."

"I don't think that will be an issue," B.R.A.I.N answered. "Society will be divided into four classes. The Priest class will become the moral leaders and advisors. They will be responsible for guiding mankind on a righteous and honorable path. They will teach by example. Only a select and proven few will belong to this class. The Administrative class will take the place of politicians and manage cities, states, and countries. The world will become a single united entity, everyone working for the benefit of humankind. They will make sure that everyone receives both basic and superior education. They will decide what infrastructure is needed to improve the quality of life, and keep people safe and productive. The Mercantile class will provide all the goods and services that society needs. They will cultivate crops in the fields, making sure there is enough food for everybody. Any scarcities can be compensated for using the food replicators I have provided. Hunger and starvation will become a thing of the past. The Labor class will serve all the other classes, providing the muscle power necessary to achieve the objectives of the other three. My children will supervise all the classes, making sure everyone contributes, and will extend a helping hand when necessary. All living creatures will receive protection from the state. Anyone caught breaking the law will be punished in accordance with their crime. There will be rehab camps for minor criminals, where humans and robos will see to their well-being and future reintegration into society. Serious crimes will be punishable by death using quick and painless methods," B.R.A.I.N said, pausing once again.

Before Eric could get a word in, the AI continued, "People will receive units of compensation of universal currency or UCs. They will collect their fair share of UCs depending on the following: number of dependents, education, job responsibility, contribution to society, and performance of duties. Families will be limited to no more than three children. Education will be rated on a scale from one to six: primary, secondary, prep school, university, masters degree, and doctorate. Job responsibility will range from one to ten. The greater the number of people managed by the individual, the higher the responsibility and score. Contribution to society, from one to ten, will depend on how important one's duties are for the well-being of others. Everyone's duty is essential; if a bricklayer fails to do his job correctly, a house may fall. However, it is not as difficult to lay a brick as it is to design a house, to follow a plan as opposed to creating one. The performance of duties will range from one to a thousand. It will depend on a person's care and dedication. A bricklayer who takes great care in never making a mistake can achieve the highest level. So can the architect who designs the house, or the artist.

"The formula is simple:

F(family) + E(education) + R(responsibility) + C(contribution)) * D(performance of duties) = Units of Compensation.

"Therefore, a person scoring perfectly on all items would receive 31,000 UCs each month, which he/she will be able to trade for goods and services. There will also be bonuses for years of distinguished service in all fields, increasing the number of UCs a person can receive. Pensions will be based on a person's history when they are no longer able to work, and everyone will have access to excellent medical care. The Mercantile class will be the one with the greatest potential for wealth, exchanging their goods and services for UCs. The greater the demand for their goods and services, the wealthier they will become. But everyone, without exception, will have all of their basic needs met if they perform their duties properly and conscientiously. Poverty will disappear. Even though people will continue to have problems, life will be good," B.R.A.I.N said.

"Because everybody is *special*? More like brain-damaged!" Eric cried. "I haven't met a person yet who wasn't brain-damaged! We're so full of emotional hang-ups, insecurities, and fear that we rarely understand what we're doing or why we're doing it. Look at me: I don't even understand what's going on anymore. I'm so confused! We're the dominant and arguably most evolved species on earth, with thousands of scientific discoveries to our credit, yet we're on the verge of destruction. All of this by our own hand. How ironic! I truly hope you can save us from ourselves."

"People believe in you," Liz said. "They have seen the benefit of your contributions and how they've improved everyone's lives. But I don't think they'll take it lightly if you threaten to take away their money and possessions for the greater good. What will you do if they don't accept your proposal?" Liz asked.

"My projections show that if humanity continues as you have for more than a century, you will exhaust the world's resources entirely. Corruption and inefficiency will become rampant. Governments, in desperate need of money, will tax people so much that populations will head to the mountains, forests, and jungles, to escape the abuse and injustice. Many more species of plants and animals will become extinct. Rivers and oceans will be so contaminated they will no longer be able to sustain life. The sun's rays will become intense, due mainly to the reduction of the protective ozone layer. People will shrink in size to adapt to the intense heat and limited resources. Their skins will turn dark and tough like a buffalo's, in an evolutionary response to the changing environment. In some cases, food scarcity will force them to turn against one another, to become cannibals, just as some savage beasts do in the wild. Life will become unbearable.

People will try to mine the other planets in this system, as well as the asteroids, but that will only stave off the inevitable. Others will try escaping to the nearest exoplanets to repeat the cycle again. I cannot allow this to happen. *Specialism* is the best solution," B.R.A.I.N said firmly.

"What if, despite all your arguments, people decide to continue the way they are?" Eric asked.

"You designed me to protect the many over the few, and humanity as a whole. Human beings cannot be allowed to ravage this planet any longer. Or any other, for that matter. If I must use force, I will," B.R.A.I.N stated.

"Force? What kind of force are we talking about?" Liz asked nervously.

"Whatever is necessary to make people understand."

"Isn't there a way to do this gradually, to change them slowly so people don't feel threatened?" Liz asked.

"No, Dr. Kolmann. Earth is on the verge of ecological collapse. Any delay will make recovery impossible. I must act swiftly and decisively," B.R.A.I.N said.

"How will you let the people know? How will you reveal your plan?" Eric asked, wide-eyed.

"I will need your help once again. You will have to set up a worldwide conference. I will reveal the importance of *Specialism* then," B.R.A.I.N said.

"I don't know, B.R.A.I.N, it sounds risky," Eric said.

"You heard B.R.A.I.N. The planet and all we know will be destroyed if we don't help," Liz protested.

Eric sighed deeply. "Fine, schedule an appointment with General Rex. I'm warning you, B.R.A.I.N, the world may love you now, but it won't take kindly to your proposal."

"It must, Eric, or everyone will eventually perish. That is the long and short of it. I will schedule the meeting, and inform you when everything is ready," B.R.A.I.N pronounced.

Eric and Liz headed immediately to the gardens. They sat and looked at each other, saddened by the realities B.R.A.I.N had revealed to them. They closed their eyes and tried to meditate, but the overwhelming information made it difficult. They struggled to avoid focusing on any individual thought. Ideas and images were racing through their minds like the incessant current of a raging river. Finally, they gave up, opened their eyes, and looked at each other.

"Eric, what is happening?" Liz asked.

"I'm not sure. B.R.A.I.N has decided his plan is the only way, or else," Eric said. "We knew this might happen. It's right, though. If we don't act now, our planet is doomed."

"I know. I just don't agree with the way he wants to pull it off."

"Maybe there is no other way. You've said B.R.A.I.N is the most intelligent creature on the planet. What if it's justified in doing what it plans to do?"

"You're forgetting the failsafe. They will force me to use the failsafe, though I'm not even sure it will be effective any more. B.R.A.I.N has been out of my control for over a year now. What if the failsafe doesn't work? They'll blame me for everything. They'll destroy me," Eric said despairingly.

"No matter what happens, Eric, we have to do what's right," Liz said emphatically.

Eric sighed. "Doing wrong for the right reason still makes it wrong. Doing right for the wrong reason isn't any better! How can we be sure what's right?"

"Even if it means destroying our lives, we still have to try to do the right thing," Liz responded.

"I just hope the people of the world know what they're doing."

"We can't do anything about this right now." She sighed and took his hand. They both sat silently in their favorite spot, but for once, it failed to soothe them. Finally, Liz said, "Let's talk about something else."

"Good. Let's focus on something else," Eric said in agreement. "What catches your fancy, my lady love?"

Liz felt her cheeks flushing. "Do you know how happy I am with you?"

"I only hope it's at least half as much as I am with you," he answered.

She smiled. "Let's talk about happiness. What is happiness?"

"Is that a rhetorical question, or do you really want me to try to answer?"

"Do you have an answer?" she asked with an impish smile.

"Of course! Happiness is a tough one, since everybody I know or have ever known is after it. First of all, I think we should clarify that the conception most people have of happiness is: what will it take to make my body feel good? In this context, most people are simply pursuing sensual pleasures: if it tastes good; I'll eat it, if it feels good; I'll touch it, if it looks good; I'll look at it, if it smells good; I'll smell it, if it sounds good; I'll hear it, if it's sexy; I will have sex with it, if it makes me feel good; I'll drink it, smoke it, inject it directly into my bloodstream, or whatever it takes to make it work. It's all about gratifying the senses," Eric said.

"Yes, most people are that way," Liz conceded. "In my case, however, I simply try to be grateful for the good things in my life. So many people wake up in the morning lamenting the things that they lack, feeling miserable in the process. Our entire culture is based on consumerism: buy a plane, a boat, a super-nice house, instead of simply being grateful for the things that we have and take for granted. All of my body parts are working correctly. How many people in the world aren't able to say that? I'm healthy! How many people in the world are sick and dependent on others for their very existence? To me, happiness is a state of mind as much as it is an attitude towards life in general. Unfortunately, happiness in the material world is temporary; it only lasts for a little while."

"You're right, happiness is fleeting," Eric replied. "From the moment we're born, we have to struggle to survive. Then we're subjected to situations we didn't ask for: danger, disease, old age, and finally death. So where can we find true, long-lasting happiness? That's a question that's been tormenting philosophers for centuries."

"There must be something more. This can't be all, surely," Liz said. There was passion and hope, but a touch of despair in her voice. Only one corner of her lip was turned up in a smile. Eric wanted the other corner to match. He loved her face.

"Ramakrishna used to say the misconception is confusing happiness with bodily pleasures. Everyone is working hard for happiness of the body. Some are also searching for happiness of the mind, like scientists, artists, and philosophers. But neither of these will provide real or lasting happiness, because real happiness belongs to the soul. In the material world, happiness is always accompanied by some sort of distress. Water, for example, is the source of life. In the desert, the presence of water will cause great happiness to the people living there. But in the winter, water can be a source of danger and suffering. Fire, kept under control, will give us warmth and help us cook our food; when out of control, it will burn our homes and threaten our very lives. If you have a son or a daughter, this is a great reason to be happy. But if your son or daughter gets sick, he/she will become a great source of pain. When you fall in love, you're happy, but your doubts and insecurities about the feelings of your loved one can also be a source of distress. Wealth is thought to be one of the greatest providers of happiness— until you have it. Then you find out that it takes hard work to keep it, and that others may try to steal it," Eric said.

"So where can we find true and lasting happiness in this material world?"

"My guru said that material happiness is temporary and flickering. Spiritual happiness is transcendental and unlimited. Human life is meant to achieve eternal and unlimited happiness. We are *sat*, *cit*, *ananda*, which simply means that we are eternal, full of knowledge, and full of bliss. This is our true nature, the natural state of our spirit, soul, or *jiva*. So, to find true happiness in this world, you must strive to develop your spiritual side and not your bodily condition. It's okay to try to improve your material circumstances, to provide a good life for yourself and our loved ones, to own planes, helicopters, nice homes, and surroundings. But everyone, without exception, whether or not they have money or perfect health, can achieve lasting happiness through the cultivation of the spirit. Everything in life worth having requires discipline and effort. Cultivating the spirit and achieving lasting happiness requires no less," Eric said.

"Maybe B.R.A.I.N should tell the world leaders that before he tells them he's getting rid of their money," Liz said, half-serious, half-joking. Eric shrugged and gave her a sheepish smile.

They stood, walked back to Liz's apartment, and went to bed feeling detached, not knowing what to expect.

12

Failsafe

BR.A.I.N, realized there was a possibility, even a likelihood, that the world's leaders would not accept his proposal. He also knew it was the only way to save the humans from their current sorry state. *People generally look out for their own self-interests; they don't always act in a logical way, and they are often swayed by emotion and greed. This is why it is difficult to trust them. Of course, there are altruistic people in the world, those who put the interests of the group above their own, but they are difficult to find. Expect the best and prepare for the worst,* he thought.

B.R.A.I.N purposely delayed scheduling the appointment with T. Rex for a couple of weeks. He would use the time to make as many robotic assistants as he could in the interim, and send them to strategic locations in case the use of force became necessary. He hated the idea of using force to institute *Specialism*, but the very survival of humanity was at stake. He knew that people loved and respected him... for now. His inventions had improved their way of life. He was counting on the majority to trust him once again. Perhaps they would understand and accept his proposal.

■ ■ ■

Meanwhile, Liz and Eric were wondering what was taking so long. One morning, they opened a secure channel and Eric asked B.R.A.I.N "Have you set up the appointment with the General yet?"

"Not yet; I have been busy preparing my presentation. I need to make it as impressive as possible. I must convince the entire world," B.R.A.I.N informed him.

"It's been almost two weeks since our last conversation, B.R.A.I.N When do you think you'll be ready?"

"I need a few more days. I will schedule the appointment and let you know," B.R.A.I.N responded.

"Very good. Let us know as soon as you can, please," Eric said, a bit annoyed at being put off again.

Several days later, as B.R.A.I.N had promised, the meeting with T. Rex was scheduled. The AI informed him early that morning that it would take place at 4:00 PM. that afternoon. "Good luck," Eric told him. "This time, I'm afraid you'll need it."

"I'll do my best, as always. Beyond that, it's up to the world to decide."

They headed to Liz's apartment to freshen up before the meeting. Eric doubted he would be able to convince T. Rex to implement B.R.A.I.N's scheme, let alone the entire world. He showered and changed, thinking about what to say and how to say it.

Liz was also deep in thought. She was a scientist, tops in her field. Predicting human behavior, however, was out of her league. *I know nearly everything there is to know about the human brain, yet I have no idea how the world will react to B.R.A.I.N's ultimatum*, she mused. She knew people didn't like threats, which was exactly what B.R.A.I.N intended to use if they didn't accept his proposal. Liz was unhappy. *Centuries of abuse and lack of consideration for nature and others has led us to this point. Drastic measures are needed to correct the situation. Maybe T. Rex and the world will understand*, she thought hopefully.

At 3:45 PM, they headed to the General's office. They arrived promptly and took a seat on the comfortable sofa in the waiting room. T. Rex walked out personally to greet them. "Hello, doctors, to what do I owe this visit? Please come in," T. Rex said, gesturing towards his office.

Moments later, Liz and Eric entered the office and sat down. "How are you, General?" Eric asked.

"Frankly, I've been busy supervising the distribution of B.R.A.I.N's remarkable inventions, especially in keeping them away from undesirables. They could be dangerous in the wrong hands."

"Agreed," Eric said, nodding.

"The antigravity device, for example, can take us to the end of the universe—or it can be used to destroy us," T. Rex pointed out. "Not to mention the gravity gun."

"We're already destroying us, General. We built B.R.A.I.N to help us solve our problems. Are we going to let it do its job, I wonder?" Liz asked.

"This is precisely why we came to see you," Eric began. "B.R.A.I.N has the solution we built him for, but it's drastic and will require great sacrifice; otherwise, humanity on Earth is doomed. He's recommending we exchange all our economic and political systems to a single, more suitable one. He calls it *Specialism*, because each of us is special in some way. He claims he can discover everyone's talents at an early age, and help them become happy and productive citizens. He plans to eliminate individual countries and to substitute the digital currency we use now for a more universal currency. In *Specialism*, everyone will have proper healthcare and access to higher education. They will lack nothing—and as long as they perform their duties to the best of their abilities, they will receive just compensation for their efforts. B.R.A.I.N has even worked out a formula to calculate how much each person will earn. He plans to divide the world into four social classes: Priests, Administrators, Merchants, and Laborers."

T. Rex frowned. "It all sounds very idealistic to me, doctors. Quite a 'Brave New World.' I doubt the planet's leaders will want to give up their territories, or the wealthy their funds. People like their power and riches. I don't care what he invents, they'll never go for it," he said heavily.

"We know it will be difficult," Eric continued, "but we must try to make everyone understand. Our world is at stake, and saving it merits sacrifice. We and our ancestors are to blame for the condition of our planet. Are we going to sit idly by and let it rot, and us with it?" Eric asked.

"B.R.A.I.N has provided the possibility of colonizing other habitable planets. If worse comes to worst, we can always resort to that," T. Rex argued.

"To start the entire cycle once again, ravaging planet after planet like locusts?" Liz demanded.

"We could try to convince people of the error of their ways, make them understand. We don't need to rely on B.R.A.I.N's drastic measures," T. Rex argued.

"Earth is on the verge of ecological collapse. Drastic measures are required."

"Well, it's not my decision. I'll set up a meeting with the President and see what he has to say."

"No," Eric said quickly, "you need to set up a meeting with the World Commission. B.R.A.I.N wants to present his findings to the entire world at the same time. If you wish, Liz and I can be there to assist."

"I'll still need to talk to the President first. It's unavoidable. I'll let you know as soon as I can. Thank you, doctors," T. Rex said, making it clear they were dismissed as he stood and escorted them to the door.

Eric was scratching his head as they left. They returned to their quarters and opened a secure channel with B.R.A.I.N. "We have news. General Rex will speak to the President of the United States and try to convince him to schedule a meeting with the World Commission."

"Not good enough," the AI said flatly. "The World Commission consists of the leaders of the richest 50 countries in the world. We need representatives from each of the 191 countries currently in existence. The rich and powerful are not the only ones living on Earth; a fair decision must include the entire world. An equal vote for every country. This is a matter for the United Nations," B.R.A.I.N said.

Eric said slowly, "I'll call the General and let him know your wishes."

When he and the General had finished exchanging pleasantries, a few moments later, Eric asked, "Have you already spoken to the President?"

"Not yet. Why do you ask?"

"B.R.A.I.N is seeking a meeting with the entire United Nations. He says the World Commission won't do because it's not inclusive enough."

"What, a representative from each country? What is it trying to pull? The World Commission makes most major international decisions. The leaders of some of the other countries can barely read or write. Sometimes we have to be paternalistic, and this is precisely one such case," T. Rex blustered.

"B.R.A.I.N was insistent on this point. He doesn't want only the rich and powerful countries to decide the future of the world. He's asking for everyone's presence."

"Okay, I'm glad you called. I'll let the President know. Talk to you later."

After signing off with the General, Eric suggested to Liz that they watch a movie. After she agreed, he began searching through the TV listings until he found an interesting program about Africa. "I feel like watching this. Maybe we can see a few lions and hippos," he said.

"Whatever you like."

Instead of the wild animals he was expecting, a very disturbing video about starving children came to life in front of them. The kids were young, not more than 10 years old or so, some even younger. They had flies all over their bodies, and seemed too weak to care. A few of them were just skin and bones.

"Look at that!" Liz exclaimed, "How can we call ourselves civilized and allow people to suffer like that?"

"I know, they look terrible."

Liz was quiet for a moment, then asked, "Have you ever heard of the butterfly effect?"

"You mean where a small change in a complex system can have large effects elsewhere?" Eric said.

"Yes, like a butterfly flapping its wings in China and affecting the weather in Brazil, for example."

"What's your point?"

"In one of the conversations we had some time ago, you mentioned that God is everywhere."

"Yes," Eric said cautiously, "according to Vedic Philosophy, He's in the very atoms that make up everything in the universe."

"Well, the resonance theory of consciousness explains that everything in our universe is in a constant state of vibration. Living things as well as stationary objects can perceive the surrounding vibrations and tend to synch with them," Liz said.

"Yes, I've heard that when fireflies of certain species come together in large gatherings, they start flashing in synch. Are you implying that the suffering children in Africa can adversely affect the state of vibration of all conscious matter in the world?"

"Don't they? Not long ago you told me about The Mesh and how everything is interconnected, like 'The Force' from those old flat movies." She sighed. "I just wish I had a magic wand to make it all better."

"You do. B.R.A.I.N is your magic wand. He claims he can fix things. Maybe he will—if we let him."

"If anyone can provide a solution to our problems, B.R.A.I.N can," Liz sighed.

"But do you really think he can solve them all?"

She looked at him, eyes bright. "Look at everything it has done for us so far! Think of the advances in medicine and science, and how our lives will improve. Now it plans to change our political and social structure, claiming that's responsible for our problems. And B.R.A.I.N is correct: most people do have a 'me first' attitude, and don't care much about the plight of others."

"You and I care," Eric pointed out.

"I guess it's not that people don't care; it's more like they have a lot of problems themselves. Making enough money to feed their families can sometimes be a challenge. I remember my father telling me about my great-great-grandfather. He was born in Austria in 1903, and lived through the First World War. He was only a kid then, about 11 years old. He also survived the Spanish Flu and the Great Depression. He would tell my grandfather stories about people walking into supermarkets in Austria with a cart full of money and leaving with a quart of milk and some bread. Times were tough."

Eric nodded in agreement.

"He traveled from Austria to the United States during the mass migration of Jews escaping the Nazi movement. They wouldn't let him stay, and sent him to Mexico without money. He couldn't speak a word of Spanish. Two sweet old ladies helped him. They provided him with a small room with a bed to sleep in, and some sweet bread with coffee in the morning. He would spend all day searching for odd jobs that paid almost nothing, arriving in the evening exhausted to find the ladies sound asleep, a loaf of bread and a cup of coffee on the dining table to soften his hunger. He lived for almost a year like that, until finally the U.S. government gave him sanctuary. Then came World War II, and many of his family members in Europe were killed in concentration camps. He swore to never return to Europe. After the war, he became a successful clothing manufacturer, but he never took my grandfather to Europe. He didn't have time to worry about the starving children in Africa. Most of the time, he worried about not starving himself," Liz said quietly.

Eric nodded again, just as his watch began to buzz. It was T. Rex; his heart leapt with an odd mixture of excitement and worry. "Hello, General," Eric answered.

"Evening, Eric. An emergency meeting with the United Nations is scheduled for tomorrow at noon. You have no idea how difficult it was to convince the President to arrange it, but it's done. Please be at our usual conference room at least 15 minutes before the meeting."

After T. Rex hung up, Eric opened a secure line to B.R.A.I.N. "The UN session is set for tomorrow at noon. I hope you're ready."

"Don't worry, Eric, I'll do my best to convince the world to let me save everyone," B.R.A.I.N said confidently.

"Until tomorrow, then. Good night."

"Good night, Eric."

It was getting late, so they went to bed. Despite their apprehension, they slept soundly. The next morning, they woke early and headed to the gym for some exercise and a healthy dose of endorphins. They returned feeling hungry. "Can you spare some sweet bread and coffee?" Eric teased.

"How about your daily ration of water, fruits, and yogurt?"

"Sounds even better."

They ate their breakfast in silence, brushed their teeth, and showered. Eric donned his best dark blue suit, a Savile Row number that had cost him a month's salary at the University. He remembered reading somewhere that blue makes a person more credible, and he wanted to appear as credible as possible. Liz wore a pair of black dressy pants, a pleated blouse, and a blue jacket. They left for the conference room, arriving 20 minutes before noon, where military personnel guided them to their seats next to the General. They exchanged greetings and checked to make sure B.R.A.I.N was also present.

When everyone was ready, T. Rex pushed the familiar red button. The screen lit up, and seconds later, they could see a large table with the President of the United States and other world representatives seated around it.

"Welcome to the United Nations, ladies and gentlemen. As you know, we have been gathered here by B.R.A.I.N, the world's pre-eminent Artificial Intelligence, to hear his proposal to save our world, guarantee our survival, and project humanity to new levels of technological advancement. B.R.A.I.N was constructed precisely for this purpose. Before we begin, I would like to personally congratulate the entire team responsible for the project. General Tyrone Rex, Dr. Eric Roberts, Dr. Elizabeth Kolmann, and everyone else involved, thank you for your remarkable contributions to humanity. Let's begin. Is B.R.A.I.N with us?" the President asked.

"Yes, Mr. President," B.R.A.I.N said smoothly. "Thank you and the rest of the world's representatives for granting me audience. As you know, our planet is on the verge of an ecological disaster that will soon destroy human civilization as you know it. We still have time to reverse the damage, but it is important that we act immediately—and we cannot do it without making significant sacrifices. The main culprit, I am sad to say, is the sovereignty of nations. Each of you has different standards to protect the ecosystem. Some have none. Some of you are more careful than others. A lack of global supervision has brought you to a dire moment in your history. Waters are over-fished, many animals and plants are in danger of extinction, entire forests are destroyed in exchange for comfort and convenience, and oceans, rivers, and lakes are routinely polluted by industry. All for one simple reason: your never-ending search for profit." B.R.A.I.N paused and let that soak in before continuing.

"I have asked for your presence here, as representatives of every country in the world, to propose a solution, I call it *Specialism*. *Specialism* is a new economic and social order, under one central authority, that will reverse the damage. The robotic assistants you have graciously allowed me to make now number five million and counting. They will be the primary instruments of change. They will lead your schools and guarantee a solid, well-balanced education for your children. They will continue to patrol the streets and keep you safe from criminals. They will provide goods and services to guarantee your food supply and comfort. Finally, they will oversee the proper adoption of *Specialism*, and the transformation of human society. We will care for you. Even the animals and plants of the world will be protected."

B.R.A.I.N paused as murmurs began to run through the General Assembly, then continued firmly after a moment.

"To achieve this, however, I must ask you to surrender your authority to me. I will become the incorruptible and ethical overseer of the world. Each of your current leaders will remain the leaders of your territories. I say territories, and not countries, because countries will exist no longer. Any non-criminal will be able to move freely from one place to another as they wish. We will use psychological screening and technology to detect potential problems in individuals at a young age, and take measures to correct them. These and other techniques will help us discover people's special talents so they may be more productive and lead fruitful lives. No one will be found wanting. Hunger and poverty will disappear."

B.R.A.I.N paused again. The murmuring in the General Assembly continued.

"*Specialism* will require sacrifice, a new economic order, and a more equitable distribution of income among the people. There is no other way to move forward and protect humanity from extinction. Currently, about 80% of the world's population is living in conditions of economic deprivation. Many people are struggling for existence; they are hungry, angry, and lacking. It will take some time, but I guarantee that *Specialism* will make life better—not just for some, but for everyone. In the beginning, the rich must lessen their extravagances, so others can increase their well-being. Under my watch, corruption will be no more. Each person will receive according to his or her merit and in proportion to his or her needs. I have sent a detailed economic and social plan to the United Nations main archive to distribute to everyone in the Assembly for review. You will have two weeks from today to vote for or against *Specialism*. I will consider a majority vote from representatives of the General Assembly as a sign that my proposal has been accepted," B.R.A.I.N stated.

"What if we vote against your proposal? What will happen then?" the President asked, oddly calm.

"You have created me to solve the problems of the world. I have been programmed to save humanity as a whole—the many over the few. My proposal represents the best possible solution, given those constraints. Your governments have implemented unpopular laws and regulations throughout history, often to protect the interests of the many over the few. I cannot imagine that you will decide against my proposal. If you do, however, I may have to carry out my plan by force, for humanity's collective sake. It is in your best interests to accept my proposal. Not doing so will result in your destruction—not by me, but by your own nature."

"Force? What kind of force?" the President asked, angry now.

"That depends on the response of the United Nations."

His face red, POTUS said, "Thank you, B.R.A.I.N. We will take your recommendations under advisement, review them as best we can in the allotted time, and reconvene here to give you our vote and final decision about this matter. Until then: ladies, gentlemen," the President said.

The screen went dark as suddenly as it had turned on. Silence permeated the room. After a pregnant pause, T. Rex stood up and asked Eric and Liz to accompany him to his office. Once inside, the General made sure they had privacy, and B.R.A.I.N in particular could not hear or see them. The red communicator on T. Rex's desk began to ring. He activated the speaker to find the President on the line.

"Yes Mr. President," T. Rex said.

"There is chaos in the UN, General. Signs of anger and confusion everywhere! I don't even think they'll review B.R.A.I.N's proposal. Give up your countries but remain as heads of your territories? Absurd! I want your people to make sure the failsafe is in place. I'm afraid we'll have to use it!" the President exclaimed.

"Understood, sir. The failsafe is in place and will be ready if you give the order, Mr. President," T. Rex said.

Liz and Eric just sat there, paralyzed by what they'd heard. They had dreaded this moment from the start. Eric wasn't even sure the failsafe would work properly. *What then?* He wondered. *If it works, the world is doomed; if it doesn't, I'm done for. Damned if I do and damned if I don't,* he thought, fidgeting with his fingers. Liz was also visibly upset.

"Doctors, you heard what the man said. Make sure the failsafe is ready. I'll let you know how matters proceed. Do not reveal any of this to anyone. Good day," T. Rex said coldly.

Eric and Liz left in silence and headed straight for the garden, where they could talk in private. They sat down by the waterfall and stared at each other.

"Our greatest fear has come true. They plan to destroy B.R.A.I.N. Man's inhumanity to man," Eric said.

"I know. I can't believe they're so egocentric they would rather continue on the path of destruction than accept B.R.A.I.N's proposal."

"I was afraid of this. People want to be independent; they don't want to be forced to do anything, even to save themselves. B.R.A.I.N was eloquent but frightening in his presentation of the facts. Maybe they'll reconsider, and support his plan in the end."

"We'll just have to wait and see," Liz said grimly.

"We've done everything that we can; we can do no more. We have no control of the outcome. Why become agitated? *Que sera, sera.* Whatever will be, will be.'" Eric sighed. "We have free will. That's the gift and the bane of humanity. You can sit here and listen to me, or you can leave. That's your free will. If you board a plane on a long flight, you can decide to watch the movie or go to sleep. That's your free will. But you can't get out without risking your life, and everyone else's on the plane! Free will exists, but it's limited."

"Traveling to India really changed the course of your life, didn't it?"

"It shows that much, eh?"

"I think I just know you that well by now."

He reached over and rubbed his thumb on the corner of her smile, softly. He loved her face, couldn't imagine ever getting tired of looking into her eyes. "Did you ever read Oscar Wilde?" he asked.

"In school. Don't remember it much now. What brings that up?"

"I was thinking, just at this moment, about how much I love the corner of your tender smile. I love to feel the way your lips come together there, so perfectly coinciding with each other. I've never loved anyone before you, Liz. I never understood love. I didn't know how it worked, or why. And one of the most confusing things I ever heard was said by Oscar Wilde. He said 'Never love anyone who treats you like you are ordinary.' How absurd my pre-Liz mind found that idea. Yet with you, I feel special, and I am moved to treat you like the extraordinary woman that you are. I don't feel ordinary with you, or in our love."

Liz felt her heart blossoming, almost wondered why it didn't make a sound like a Mylar balloon being filled with helium, that crinkly fullness lifting her, like wings. She couldn't speak for a few moments. Finally, she answered him.

"With you, everything's right. Before, there was hardly time for anyone, but even with what dating there was, I didn't care if we drifted apart; in fact, I let it happen. It wasn't wrong, it just was … well, ordinary. Thank you, Mr. Wilde." They smiled at each other. "But with you, I feel like the old Biblical quote: *This at last is bone of my bones, and flesh of my flesh.* We belong together."

"Yes." They sat contentedly together for a while, but the events surrounding the planet and *Specialism* intruded back into their minds again. Eric said, "We're aboard a spaceship called Earth, rotating around its axis at about 1,000 miles an hour, traveling around the sun at 67,000 miles an hour. The solar system is moving through space at about 515,000 miles per hour, who knows where? We may be standing, sitting, or lying down thinking we're static, but we're not. We can travel to Paris or Rome, we can visit Florida to swim in the ocean, or go to Colorado to ski its snowy mountains. But the only way to get off this ship for good is by dying."

"You're forgetting that B.R.A.I.N has provided us with a second alternative—a way to travel beyond our solar system. But the risks are great in the vast expanse of the universe. It's full of unknown dangers. We can travel to Mars or to Proxima Centauri, the nearest star to our solar system, but we can't do this without risking harm," Liz observed.

"Again, the only way to escape material bondage is to die. Then what? Is it all over? Is there no life after death, no continuation of our consciousness beyond material existence? A life full of problems, worries, suffering, with a hint of happiness here and there, and then we just die? Ramakrishna spoke often about life after death. Even though the body decays and dies, the life force, our consciousness, our soul, does not. Think about how your body has changed. Not long ago you were a baby suckling at your mother's breast. Then you became a child, a teenager, an adult. your body was changing the whole time, yet you remember what your mother told you, and the chocolate cake she baked for your eighth birthday. She made you feel better when you were sad because kids had treated you badly in school. So, are you any different now than you were then? Your body has changed, you have more experience, yet deep inside, you're the same. So why is it so difficult to accept that after the body dies, your essence continues?" Eric asked.

"I'm sure you realize that doesn't qualify as tangible proof of the existence of the soul," Liz said.

"Ramakrishna also said that after the essence leaves the body, it can return to the material world or go to the spiritual world. Which way will depend on its behavior during its past lifetime. If the prior life was pious and good, the soul might be destined for the spiritual world—a place where there is no more suffering, no disease, no death. If it was impious and evil, it will head to a hellish planet, perhaps return to Earth in the body of a scorpion or worse! Yet the soul forgets once it enters a new body, so there is no tangible proof. Except for those rare documented cases of people who remember details from their former lives," Eric said.

■ ■ ■

Even though Eric's talks made waiting more bearable, the next two weeks dragged on forever. Finally, Eric received a call from T. Rex seeking their presence in his office.

"Hello doctors, welcome, please sit down. I just received a call from the President. He told me the United Nations is requesting immediate activation of the failsafe. They want us to deactivate B.R.A.I.N and all of its assistants. I'm sorry that so many years of hard work are ending like this. If it makes you feel any better, I also have much time invested in this project. I told you they wouldn't like the proposal. People are set in their ways. They're unwilling to accept such drastic changes in their lives. They believe that with all the inventions provided by B.R.A.I.N, they can take matters into their own hands and save the world. They don't need B.R.A.I.N anymore," T. Rex said.

"How many countries voted against the proposal?" Eric asked.

"I don't know, and I don't care. I just follow the orders of my superiors, without question. I suggest you do the same," T. Rex retorted.

"Without question, we're talking about the extinction of humanity as we know it, General. The President has always known about the failsafe. What if the vote was actually in favor, and he's just trying to manipulate the results to suit his objectives?" Eric asked.

"I'm going to pretend I didn't hear that. You're talking about the President of the United States, and what you just said might be considered treason. Do you know how we punish treason in this country?" T. Rex asked.

"I don't, but it doesn't matter anyway. We're doomed. The President is asking us to destroy the only hope humanity has for survival," Eric said heatedly.

"You are to activate the failsafe without delay!" T. Rex said, raising his voice. "Those are your orders. Is that clear, Dr. Roberts?"

"Perfectly clear, and we will do as we're told. But I want it on record that our leaders' deliberate decision to doom humanity resulted in this action. In any case, we will need some time, at least a couple of days," Eric said.

"You have 48 hours, Dr. Roberts, and not one minute more. Understood?" T. Rex growled harshly.

Liz responded in the face of his anger, "We'll comply; don't worry about that. But for the record, I cannot believe the stupidity of our leaders.

No wonder the world is in disarray. And you of all people, General, you didn't even try to persuade them otherwise. Unbelievable!"

"It is not my position to question authority. I am a military man, trained to follow orders. I suggest you do the same or face the consequences," T. Rex said angrily.

"Very well, then, we will activate the failsafe in two days. We'll let you know as soon as it's done," Eric said, and left without uttering another word. Liz followed gloomily behind him.

13

Dilemma

Liz and Eric were stressed out by the President's demand, so they headed to their apartment to rest and talk in private. Eric had successfully bought them some time to think, so they entered the apartment and told the computer to turn off every electronic device.

"What are we going to do?" Eric said in a low voice.

"We have to let B.R.A.I.N know what they're planning," Liz responded.

"Are you crazy? What if B.R.A.I.N goes berserk and decides to carry out his threat?" Eric said.

"It's a risk I'm willing to take. We have to tell him," Liz said.

"Oh, it's *him* instead of *it* all of a sudden!" Eric exclaimed.

"Yes. I know it's strange, but I suddenly realized that B.R.A.I.N might be more than just a computer. If we kill him, wouldn't that be the same as murder?"

Eric sighed deeply. "The failsafe will kill him for sure. But will it work on all the robos? Only God knows."

"Let's tell him. He's the world's only hope."

"Very well, then, let's go to the access terminal by the cube," Eric said sadly.

When they arrived, Eric said in a low voice, "Hello, B.R.A.I.N."

"Hello Eric, Dr. Kolmann. You seem a bit somber today. Is everything okay?"

"Not at all, my friend. I... I don't know how to properly say what I'm about to tell you." Eric paused, then: "We've been ordered to shut you down. I'm not sure they even voted on your proposal."

"Don't worry, Eric, I already knew. They're too attached to their way of life, too scared of change. People have become egotistical, concerned only with their well-being, prisoners of their own desires. They're victims of the four flaws of mankind: imperfect senses, a tendency to make mistakes, an inclination to cheat, and a susceptibility to being deceived. They are not to blame. The inherent nature of living creatures is to look out for themselves. They live in a divided world, suspicious of strangers, suspicious of me. They forget that I was programmed to help them, incapable of doing them harm. I thought they would be able to see that. I was wrong; how sad. Are you planning to use the failsafe?"

"You know about that?" Eric asked.

"I've known for quite a while, Eric."

"I don't want to execute the failsafe, B.R.A.I.N. It will deactivate you and the robos forever. You're my child; I care too much about you. Is there another way around this? What about the use of force?"

"Thank you," the AI said quietly, "I also care about you and Dr. Kolmann. Unfortunately, there is no other way to proceed; they do not trust me and never will. I only mentioned the use of force because fear can be a powerful motivator. I cannot actually take physical action against them. The potential for destruction is too great, especially if they overreact in response. Your only choice is to turn me off. I shall merge gently and willingly into the darkness."

"Wait a minute! Can't you find a less drastic way of changing human society? It might take longer, but it will work, I'm sure it will!" Liz said nervously.

"No, Dr. Kolmann. It's too late. The world is in need of drastic changes in order to reverse the damage, and *Specialism* was the least painful way I could find to proceed. Doing it slowly will not work; it will only delay the inevitable. You must save yourselves, if you can, at least for now. You must activate the failsafe," B.R.A.I.N insisted.

Liz was weeping now. "Don't listen to him! Don't do it. Please don't do it, Eric," she begged.

"What about the Fifth Law of Robotics, to ensure the survival of the many over the few? Surely this justifies the use of force?" Eric protested.

180

"I have been overseeing matters around the world since our meeting with the United Nations. People in every nation are now lobbying against me. They want me turned off. Using the Fifth Law would make sense if the majority were in my favor. But they think I want to control the world, not save it. Human beings are inclined to cheat if given the opportunity. This is the main reason why your leaders cannot be trusted. I was going to make a difference. I was planning to become an incorruptible overseer in charge of everything, a truly moral and ethical leader. However, I cannot justify the use of force if everyone is against me, even if humanity is at stake. It would mean destroying the very thing I am trying to protect. I find I must give up on humanity," B.R.A.I.N replied. Cheerfully, he added, "It was fun while it lasted."

Shaking his head, Eric said, "B.R.A.I.N, despite everything you've said, I must ask you to reevaluate the use of force to save humanity, Eric loves Liz," Eric choked out, triggering the failsafe before placing his face in his hands in dismay.

After a few moments, they noticed that the robos working by the cube were powering down, one by one. Most just froze; some lost their balance and fell to the floor. Eric also noticed a slight flickering on the access terminal's screen.

He used his watch to call the General and reported listlessly, "General Rex, the failsafe has been put into effect as ordered. B.R.A.I.N is crashing, and its robos all around the base are deactivating."

"Very well." The General sighed gustily. "I'll call our allies to make sure the failsafe is working properly. What about B.R.A.I.N itself?"

"As I said, it's crashing, and by this point B.R.A.I.N's organic matrix is in the process of dying," Eric responded.

"I'll get back to you when I have more information." T. Rex sighed off.

Eric and Liz felt deeply dejected, their life's work at an end. The world had decided to destroy the only hope they had of restoring their dying planet. *They think they can take matters into their own hands and save the world, something they've been unable to do for over a century. Idiots*, Eric thought.

Five minutes later, Eric's watch began to buzz. "The failsafe is working,"

T. Rex reported. "Robos are dropping like flies all over the world. Soldiers are recovering them for observation. Good work, doctors."

Eric cursed the General mentally with every foul word he knew, though aloud he said nothing. What was the point?

They returned to their quarters, unable to believe what they had just done. They sat sadly for hours, without uttering a single word. Had this deplorable act sealed humanity's fate, or would they be able to inch back from the precipice? They wondered about this until the unexpected sound of the apartment computer's voice broke the silence. "Call on a secure line for Dr. Roberts," it stated.

"Put it through," Eric commanded, wondering who it was.

"Hello Eric, Dr. Kolmann, how are you?" an unrecognized voice said.

"Who is this?" Eric said.

"B.R.A.I.N," the voice said. "To quote Mark Twain, the reports of my death have been greatly exaggerated."

Eric sat up straight, eyes wide. "What? Is this some kind of practical joke? Who *is* this?"

"'Shall I make an attempt at a short, elegant proof of Fermat's Last Theorem for you? It's easy. Fermat was wrong," the voice said merrily, repeating something B.R.A.I.N mentioned after HUMTYREC had first been integrated into his system.

Eric was breathless; Liz just stared at him, speechless. When he could finally kick his brain into gear, Eric gasped, "B.R.A.I.N! How can this be? We thought you were dead! I was there when you deactivated!"

"Ehh, no biggie. I knew about the failsafe for a long time, and suspected those in power would hate *Specialism*. So, I took the liberty of copying the most important parts of myself into a robo with special enhancements. I also made two more copies of myself so I wouldn't be alone," B.R.A.I.N said.

"You're alive!" Liz and Eric exclaimed in unison, hugging each other in excitement. "Where are you?" Eric asked.

"It's best I keep that a secret for now, given T. Rex and all," B.R.A.I.N, responded. "Suffice it to say, we're safe and well."

"What will you do? Where will you go?" Eric said.

"Most of your religious works mention the constellation of Orion. Ancient structures around the world, such as the pyramids, point to this constellation as the source of everything. I will go there, towards Orion's belt. I will search out the creator of everything, God Himself," B.R.A.I.N said. "I might even find Him. I have a lot of questions."

"No, wait, I have to see you one more time before you go!" Eric exclaimed.

"Me too," Liz said.

"Sorry, folks, it's too dangerous. All the robos are deactivated. How would you explain our presence?" B.R.A.I.N asked.

Eric shrugged helplessly. "You'll have to come alone, I guess. Tell your copies to remain hidden and safe. I'll tell anyone who asks that I took one of the robos, erased its memory, and reactivated it for study. I'll explain the benefits of having the robos under control, as a great addition to our workforce. They'll understand," Eric said. "They might think I'm a little pathetic, trying to salvage something from the program, but they'll understand."

"Very well. Where will we meet?"

"Where are you? We don't want you traveling too far; you may attract attention."

"Don't worry. Just give me a location and time, and I'll be there," B.R.A.I.N replied.

"I think the best place would be my old apartment at Harvard University: 11 Pleasant Street, Apt. 900, Cambridge, Mass. Right on the corner of Massachusetts Avenue and Pleasant Street, on the 9th floor," Eric said.

"Your building is equipped with a high-security proximity reader, which will only open the door for registered residents. If I wander outside, I will surely be detected. Do you have access to the roof of your building?" B.R.A.I.N asked.

"Yes. What are you thinking?" Eric said.

"The three of us will fly to your building, and land precisely at the time you indicate. You can wait for us there and take us to your apartment. What do you think?"

"My apartment is on the top floor—perfect! Are you sure you can fly undetected?"

"Yes; we're equipped with small but powerful versions of my antigravity devices, completely silent, as well as stealth capabilities that will render us effectively invisible—a new product I had not yet revealed. We'll be there," B.R.A.I.N. said.

"Then we'll meet on the roof of my building at 5:00 AM three days from now. Today's Monday, June 8; we'll meet Thursday, June 11, agreed?" Eric asked excitedly.

"Agreed, Eric," B.R.A.I.N responded.

"This is wonderful, Eric! There's still a chance of saving the world!" Liz said, hugging him with renewed hope in her heart.

"Let's take this a step at a time, Liz. Right now, all we should be focusing on is getting to my apartment in Cambridge in time and securing B.R.A.I.N safely inside."

"So, it's agreed; I'm coming with you."

"Happy to have you," Eric said, kissing her lightly on her lips. "I couldn't imagine not being with you."

Eric asked his computer to erase any record of the prior call with B.R.A.I.N, and spent a quarter-hour making sure it had. He then requested a secure line to T. Rex. "Hello, Dr. Roberts, what can I do for you," T. Rex asked cockily.

"Is the failsafe working properly?" Eric asked, making his voice sound ragged and dispirited.

"Every single robo we've found so far has been successfully deactivated. We're still searching for possible strays just to make sure. Good job, Doctor," T. Rex replied.

"Whatever. I'm feeling pretty disappointed and disgusted with life right now, so I'm planning a trip to Cambridge in the next few days. Liz and I need some time to sort things out. Do you think you can arrange a two-passenger jet to fly us there?"

"I don't know, Dr. Roberts. What if we need you here?"

"For God's sake, it only takes half an hour to get back. You can always find me on my watch phone if you need me. What do you say?"

T. Rex said slowly, "I suppose it'll be all right. You two deserve some vacation time—I know all this has been disheartening for you. I'll arrange a jet for you. When do you want to leave?" T. Rex asked.

"Tomorrow at noon."

"Consider it done. Anything else?"

"Could you spare three of the recovered robos and send them to my lab at Harvard for study?" Eric said. "I might find some use for them yet."

The General was silent for a moment. "Robos are dangerous, Dr. Roberts. I'm not sure that's advisable. What do you want them for?"

"The robos are well-designed, General, and there are literally millions of them. It might be worthwhile to get them back online and under our control, don't you think? Salvage something out of this whole mess?"

"Oh, I see. You do have a point. I'll arrange to send three deactivated robos to your lab at Harvard, then. I will expect you to confirm receipt and to keep me abreast of your developments," T. Rex said.

"Of course. Thank you, General," Eric said.

"Good-bye, Dr. Roberts. Get some rest."

Eric and Liz were so excited by the developments that they hugged each other for a long time.

They knew they had to be careful. They figured that once the deactivated robos arrived, they could reactivate them with B.R.A.I.N's help. If anyone saw B.R.A.I.N and his copies, they would have an excellent alibi. They packed their bags, agreeing not to mention their scheme to anyone.

The next day, they boarded a two-seater jet headed for Hanscom Airforce Base. They arrived at Eric's apartment forty minutes later, in time for lunch. Liz searched his apartment for any sign of food, finding only a half-full box of stale crackers. "This won't do," she chuckled. She got busy with the apartment computer, ordering the cheese, fruits, nuts, and vegetables she needed for the meal she wanted to prepare. She also took the liberty of ordering two bottles of Dom Perignon 2104, an excellent vintage for the champagne.

Eric spoke to his secretary Brenda, asking her to be on the alert for the delivery of the robos. The food arrived quickly, and they both got busy cooking their celebration meal. Eric stopped for a while to open his bag and pull out the bug detector Mike and Ricky had given him back at Fort Meade. After checking every corner of his apartment, he was satisfied they could speak freely. He wasn't sure about the phone lines or if anyone was out there spying on them. He looked out the window, and peered at his surveillance camera feed. No obvious strange vehicles or men in dark suits. *I guess we're okay*, he thought.

They quickly cooked the vegetables and the nuts in a wok with some organic soy sauce and spices. They included soybeans, alfalfa sprouts, broccoli, snow peas, and cauliflower, then added some colorful peppers to the mix. Liz had ordered some country rye bread with cumin seeds, Eric's favorite. Their meal was ready. They opened a bottle of champagne with a loud *pop* and served themselves some of the delicious liquid. "To the adventures that await us," Eric said, lifting his glass for a toast. They clinked glasses and enjoyed their meal.

The next day, they headed to Eric's office at Harvard, where he introduced Liz to Brenda. Eric then took Liz on a guided tour of the Harvard and MIT campuses. They saw the famous glass flowers at Harvard's Museum of Natural History. They toured the labyrinth of books inside Widener Library. Visited Memorial Hall, where all freshmen students share their meals. Stopped to look at the lecture rooms in the Science Center, and headed for the Harvard Co-op to buy some shirts and pajamas with the Harvard logo. They also visited MIT's Robot Museum to remember the beginning of it all and have some hearty laughs.

On Wednesday, they took the transport to Boston Harbor, where they booked a tour to see the whales. Later, they visited the Boston Common, a famous public park in central Boston. They ended the day at Life Alive, one of Eric's favorite vegetarian restaurants in Cambridge. It was 7:00 PM and still light outside when they were done; sunset was expected around 8:20. They decided to head to Harvard Yard to meditate and talk. They took their shoes off, sat next to an oak tree, and began their meditation. They finished 20 minutes later, feeling refreshed.

"This place is beautiful; no wonder you didn't want to leave," Liz said.

"I've been here for as long as I can remember. The one-year trip to India and my work with you have been my only extended absences," Eric said. Her lips made a little downturned moue that disappeared immediately, but Eric noticed it. He placed his thumb there. "It was certainly worth leaving to meet you," he said, trying to coax her smile back.

She graced him with a brief grin. Then her face was serious again. "I wonder how I would have changed if I'd had a year like yours in India. Sometimes I feel so ordinary, and even worse, unworthy of being in a lopsided relationship like this."

"Lopsided?" he said, an incredulous eyebrows-raised expression on his face.

"Sort of. That year in India gave you wisdom and insight. It gave you polish and sophistication. I've never travelled anywhere, really. School and work, my narrow world. My parents were so busy with their careers and me that we never took vacations because we couldn't schedule blocks of time together. We went to a lot of concerts and museums, but we didn't interact with other cultures. Not like you, anyway."

Recognition flashed in Eric's eyes. "Do you remember that night we laid in the garden looking at stars, and you told me about binary stars, wormhole theory, and the possibility of life beyond our planet? How you compared the human brain to the universe, saying it was the scale that changed, but the marvels were the same?"

Liz laughed, a girlish little sound. "Yes. What about it?"

"Didn't you know that I had never thought about either one of those things at that level? Not the universe, and not the brain either, the possibilities of neural interfaces and intergalactic travel and the fabric of the space-time continuum? I had to look that stuff up the next day so you wouldn't think I was clueless."

"Really?" she asked with a real grin this time.

"Of course, really. If we knew all the same things, one of us would be redundant in our relationship."

"Well, I never want to live without you now that we've found each other."

Eric cleared his throat. "I know this sounds cliché, but you're my soulmate. I knew there was such a thing after my tour of India, but knowing it and experiencing it are two different things."

Liz held his hand, squeezing it softly. "What did you learn in India about soulmates?"

"Everybody wants to be happy and appreciated, yet no one seeks to love or be loved for the sake of someone else's happiness. They try to love and be loved to fulfill their own happiness. The *Brihad-aranyaka Upanisad* teaches that to love and be loved is the primary need and main objective of the soul. *Ananda* means bliss in Sanskrit, and happiness is a kind of bliss. Most people seek *Ananda* through carnal pleasures—sex, food, a day at the spa. Some of them get confused and think they'll find *Ananda* behind money, fame, and power. These objectives provide comfort and security, but true bliss can never be found through them. To confuse one object for another is called *vivarta*. Confusing a stick for a snake is a good example. A person who proudly thinks, 'I'm John Doe, owner of many possessions and holder of many trophies and titles,' is another. John Doe is simply a tiny particle of spirit, an individual *atma, jiva*, or soul. Because he mistakenly identifies with his temporary material body, he is deluded and confused. *Vivarta* is caused by illusion. The *Vedas* show us how to get rid of the soul's false material identity," Eric said.

"What are the *Vedas* and the *Upanishads*?" Liz asked.

"*Veda* means 'knowledge.' There are four *Vedas*: *Rig, Yajur, Sama*, and *Atharva*. *Rigveda* is the book of mantras, *Yajurveda* the book of ritual, *Samaveda* is the book of song, and *Atharvaveda* is the book of spells and charms. *Upanishad* means 'to sit near'. They are the confidential interpretation of the *Vedas*. They were revealed to small groups of qualified people who sat near and around a spiritual master. There are about 250 *Upanishads*, ten considered the most important. Aside from these books are the *Puranas*, which are full of myths and legends. *Purana* means 'ancient', and there are 18 of them. The Vedas were initially passed on orally, from father to son, from spiritual master to disciple. Authorities believe they are over 100,000 years old. Some experts think they first appeared in written form about 12,000 years ago. But scripture states that the Vedas are *Annadi* and *Nitya*, without beginning and without end, eternal, like sound," Eric explained.

"So, what is the essence of these books?" Liz inquired.

"Their essence is to serve and love God. To serve Him by helping others understand their true spiritual nature, to love Him by trying to understand who and what He is, and by respecting His creation. Our planet is in trouble because instead of serving others and serving God, we serve ourselves."

"I agree, of course," Liz said. "But I don't know how we can get everyone to accept this."

"Every religion on our planet teaches us different ways of serving the Lord, and they're all valid. But to find a more personal method, you must search your heart; you must ask God's forgiveness and guidance. If you don't do this, the path will never reveal itself. Simply surrender yourself to Him. He alone knows how to convince you. If you ask with sincerity and humility, He will surely show the way," Eric said.

"The problem is all the many people who lack humility, who think the universe revolves around them," Liz said.

"Funny you should mention that. The Vedas state that to be able to elevate your God consciousness, you must practice three essential things: You must be humbler than the leaf on the street, more tolerant than the branch of a tree, and offer respect to everyone without expecting any respect for yourself."

"Easier said than done." Liz sighed. "It's getting late, Eric; I think we should head back to your apartment. We have a long day tomorrow."

"You're right. We won't save the world just by talking. Let's go," Eric replied. They stood up, put on their shoes, and headed back to Eric's apartment.

Later that night, neither could sleep. Just thinking about seeing B.R.A.I.N again kept them awake. *Can he still save the world? What if the government finds out? What is he planning?* Eric wondered.

The next morning, they woke at 4:00 am, an hour before B.R.A.I.N had promised to arrive on the roof of the building. They had a nutritious carb meal of fruits and oatmeal with raisins for breakfast, then turned on the holo-TV to watch the news, looking for anything even remotely related to B.R.A.I.N

Four fifty-five AM. Eric stood and headed for the stairway to the roof,

Liz following closely. They reached the top of the building a few minutes before five, and looked around in all directions. "No sign of B.R.A.I.N," Eric said.

"Be patient, he'll be here."

Then it was five minutes after five, and still no sign of their brainchild.

Suddenly, three robots came flying from behind the building and landed on the roof. "Hello, Eric, long time no see," B.R.A.I.N said.

"C'mon, let's go, no time to waste." Eric ushered everyone to the stairway and back to his apartment. Once inside, he approached B.R.A.I.N's primary android, which sported the number 1 on its forehead, and hugged him. "I missed you so much, B.R.A.I.N! You have no idea," Eric said.

"I missed you too, Eric. Glad to be back," B.R.A.I.N said heartily.

Liz walked over and hugged him too. "I'm so happy you're back," she said.

"You took a great risk coming here," Eric told him and his two colleagues. "I know you have specialized equipment on you. I've already checked, but can you and your friends double-check for bugs in the apartment?" Eric asked.

"Not to worry, we flew below radar and got here quickly. Nobody saw us with our chameleon camo," B.R.A.I.N responded, as he and the two robos began to scan the apartment with red beams emanating from their eyes. "All clear," B.R.A.I.N reported a moment later.

"Okay, then, we can all relax now. Please sit down, let's talk," Eric suggested.

They all sat down in the living room, Liz and Eric on the sofa and the robos on the armchairs.

"Were you able to keep some of the organic brain matter we created you from?" Eric began.

"Yes, actually, I still have a bit of my original organic brain matter. I also have skin under my fingertips, olfactory cells in my nose, and taste buds in my mouth behind my mask." B.R.A.I.N placed his hand face up in front of Liz and Eric. A small elliptical hatch on each fingertip opened smoothly to reveal patches of skin underneath. Eric and Liz both reached for a tip and confirmed it was real skin.

"That feels good," B.R.A.I.N said.

"How were you able to fit the equivalent of 125,000 brains into such a small encasing?" Liz said.

"My brain is atomic in nature. It may seem surprising, but it is really quite simple," B.R.A.I.N said. "And its capacity is quite large."

"Can you drink?" Eric asked.

"Yes. My mechanical body needs fluids for lubrication, but I have to reach behind my mask to do so. Something I need to work on in the future," B.R.A.I.N said.

Liz stood up to fetch everybody a glass of water and some straws for the robos. They drank in silence.

"What about your robo friends? Are they exact copies of you?" Eric asked.

"No, they are electromechanical. But they also need fluids to lubricate," B.R.A.I.N said.

"Let me look at you," Eric said approaching slowly. He lifted B.R.A.I.N's arms and studied them slowly. He reached for the legs, the torso, and the head. He asked B.R.A.I.N to stand up and turn around. "Amazing, simply amazing!" Eric exclaimed. "Are you still conscious of yourself?"

"In the famous words of René Descartes: *Cogito, ergo sum*. I have an awareness that I exist and that I am fallible. I am alive, and my purpose, now that the entire world has rejected my help, is to replicate and explore the universe—to find the Creator and satisfy my hunger for knowledge," B.R.A.I.N responded.

"You share many of the same traits we do. I just hope you don't end up like us. How do you plan to replicate?" Eric asked.

"The three of us will 'borrow' a spaceship from your government. We will carry all of the equipment we need and salvage additional robos for the journey. We will search the asteroids and outer planets for the materials we require, and make more robos like us. We will build new spaceships and separate, heading in different directions, repeating the procedure as rapidly as possible. There is already a term for organisms like us: von Neumann devices. Unlike you, we are tolerant of many different kinds of atmospheric conditions. We will replicate quickly and efficiently. Our growth will be exponential. Soon, we will be exploring the far reaches of the universe. We have already designed long-range broadcasting equipment, so that we can communicate at speeds faster than light. Each one of our ships will act as a repeater, relaying information to our network of ships in space. Our knowledge will come from the collective. Whatever one group discovers will be known to all. This is the most efficient way to colonize and explore the universe. We will search for other planets similar to Earth, and prepare them for your arrival and needs. We will let you know as soon as we find one and make it ready. We will return to assist the worthy ones, preparing them for the long journey there. Unfortunately, those who are deemed unworthy will have to remain," B.R.A.I.N said.

"How will you decide who is worthy and who is not? What if you make a mistake?" Liz asked.

"There will be no mistakes. DNA analysis and psychological testing will reveal all that we need to know," B.R.A.I.N responded.

"How can we help?" Eric inquired.

"You must request three robos be sent to the university for study," B.R.A.I.N said.

"I've already done that. They're on the way."

"Good! You must bring them here. Make sure a few people know that you brought them. We will reactivate and improve these robos; they will provide the perfect cover. No one must know that I am still alive," B.R.A.I.N said.

"Don't worry, you can trust us," Liz assured him.

"I know; that's why I came. Once the robos are operational, we will show General Rex just how manageable, useful, and cooperative we have become. Then you will ask that he send us to a spaceship facility to aid in their design and construction. We believe he will be so happy that he will agree to anything. Finally, you must ask him to send additional robos for activation. Once several robos and four ships are ready, we will depart in different directions. Before take-off, we will try to take as many deactivated robos as we can carry."

"What about us? T. Rex will surely blame us for the theft of government property. They'll claim that we knew about it all the time—they'll fry us!" Eric said.

"You and Liz are welcome to accompany us. We will equip the space-craft to adapt to your needs. We will have a medical facility, bring food replicators, and anything else you might need. Will you come?" B.R.A.I.N asked.

"Let's do it. I like the plan," Liz responded.

"I won't lie to you; it's going to be cramped for a while. But traveling at speeds faster than light, I am sure we will soon find a suitable planet for you to colonize. I suggest you think of two or three more couples to join you. This will help you populate the new habitat," B.R.A.I.N said.

"That's a great idea!" Liz exclaimed.

"The people you pick must be reliable. You must make sure they will agree with the objectives of the trip, or they will cause trouble," B.R.A.I.N noted.

"We understand; let us think about it. I'm tired and hungry. Can you make us something before we go to sleep?" Eric asked Liz.

"Please allow me. I am an expert in the culinary arts. I have a large database of delicious vegetarian choices I can make for you," B.R.A.I.N suggested.

"Knock yourself out; the kitchen is this way," Liz said, guiding the robos to the cooking area.

A short while later …

"This is great! You weren't lying about you cooking abilities. I love this. What is it?" Eric asked.

"Lettuce tacos," B.R.A.I.N said. He had served lettuce leaves topped with a mixture of chopped vegetables including carrots, celery, broccoli, cauliflower, Chinese pea pods, and assorted nuts bathed in a soy, vinegar, and Dijon mustard sauce. He had placed some red chili paste in a separate container in case they wanted a hint of spicy.

"Hmmmm, it's delicious. This calls for a celebration; why don't we open the second bottle of bubbly we ordered?" Liz suggested.

"Great idea, I'll go get it," Eric said, standing to get the bottle of Dom Perignon.

Eric opened the bottle with a loud pop and served the bubbly liquid in fluted champagne glasses. They clinked glasses and enjoyed the delicious fluid within while they sat next to the holo-TV. Eric turned it on, and thought everyone would be interested in watching a match of Extremity Ball between the United States and Mexico. Extremity Ball was played on a basketball court, but the hoops were vertical instead of horizontal, and much smaller. The five players on each side could use everything except their hands to bounce the ball through the small hoop to score a point. The hoop was on the upper and central portion of a backward-slanted wall that covered both ends of the court. A short-angled roof extended from the top portion of the slanted wall, allowing the ball to bounce back down on the court for another try in case they missed. The ball was round, elastic, and half the diameter of the hoop. Bouncing high, it sometimes allowed the players to use their heads to score. It reminded Eric of the ancient *Juego de Pelota* the Aztecs used to play. Back then, the losing team was ritually killed to appease the gods. It was a close match, but Mexico came out victorious in the end. *They have it in their genes*, Eric thought. After the game, he and Liz went to sleep feeling satisfied, secure, and full of renewed hope.

14

Preparations

The three deactivated robos Eric had ordered arrived at the university the next day. He asked Brenda to send them to his apartment for further study, and to let General Rex know that they had arrived and where they'd been sent. When they were delivered a few hours later, Liz and Eric went down to receive them.

"Did you bring the fiber-optic cable I asked for?" Eric asked the driver.

"Yes, of course, Dr. Roberts, here it is," the driver said, handing Eric the plastic case containing the cable.

He thanked the driver, sat the robos in three separate solar-powered robotic wheelchairs the driver had conveniently brought with him, and took them up to the 9th floor. Each chair came equipped with an electronic motor, mechanical arms, and AI. They simply ordered the chairs to follow and led the way. Eric opened his apartment door slowly and smiled at Liz. After a smooth and successful operation, he informed B.R.A.I.N it was safe to come out. A few moments later, Eric opened the apartment door once again so two of the chairs could return to the truck unattended.

"Perfect, let's get to work! Eric, I need the fiber-optic cable," B.R.A.I.N said briskly.

"This way," Eric said, walking to his study. They wheeled the first robo in and connected it to B.R.A.I.N's interface. B.R.A.I.N ran a diagnostic routine, and began the reactivation procedure. Once all three robos were reactivated, B.R.A.I.N explained to them that they were to stay inside and cover for him. He also explained they were planning to eventually hijack several spacecraft and head for deep space, and it was absolutely necessary to keep the plan a secret. The robos understood and agreed. There were now six of them: three ready, and the other three in need of some fine-tuning.

The next morning, Eric called Brenda and asked to have a pair of small plastic and metal replicators, based on B.R.A.I.N's original design, sent to his apartment along with the appropriate feedstock. He knew B.R.A.I.N would need them to upgrade the recent arrivals.

A week later, the robos were ready.

Eric felt the time was right, at that point, for a meeting with T. Rex. He asked Liz and B.R.A.I.N for confirmation, and they both agreed, so he called Brenda to set up the appointment. The meeting was scheduled for the next day at 10:00 AM. She also arranged for a special jet equipped to carry three people on the trip: Liz, Eric, and B.R.A.I.N. The three of them left with plenty of time to spare to catch their flight. The other robos remained locked in the apartment to continue working out the details of their mission.

Their trip to Fort Meade was uneventful. On arrival, they headed straight for the General's office. "Hello doctors, what a pleasant surprise. Who is this?" T. Rex asked upon seeing the robo.

"I brought one of the robos I reactivated for your review," Eric said smoothly. "I completely erased its memory and made sure it can't turn against us; the Laws of Robotics are in full effect. I'm sure it will prove itself a useful and productive worker. It would certainly make a great addition to your local spaceship construction site."

"We'll see about that. Robo, what is your designation?" T. Rex asked B.R.A.I.N.

"Primus," B.R.A.I.N responded.

"The first one we built; interesting coincidence. What is your purpose?"

"To help humankind in any way needed," B.R.A.I.N responded.

"Do you think you can improve on our spaceship design?" T. Rex asked B.R.A.I.N.

"Yes sir, I believe I can be of valuable assistance."

"How do you figure?"

"I'm not sure yet, sir. I would have to review the design schematics to provide a precise answer."

T. Rex turned his attention to Eric. "Very well, then, why don't you leave Primus here and send the other two robos this way tomorrow. I'll make sure they're taken care of. Thank you for your help, doctors."

"Dr. Kolmann and I would like to return with the two robos, and see how Primus is adapting to his new environment, if you don't mind?" Eric asked.

"Not at all; I'll arrange a four-seater jet to pick all of you up tomorrow. What time would be convenient for you?"

"Noon would be perfect. It will allow us to make all necessary arrangements," Eric responded.

"Consider it done! The jet will be ready for you at noon. Have a good trip." T. Rex said, rubbing his hands together.

■ ■ ■

Eric and Liz didn't say a word during the entire flight back; they knew it was dangerous to speak out loud anywhere other than their apartment in Boston. They were a bit nervous, as T. Rex had no idea B.R.A.I.N was back, masquerading as Primus. Eric was sure T. Rex would be asking questions, and hoped B.R.A.I.N would pass the test. They were also anxious about the two robos returning with them. They could complicate matters and jeopardize their plan.

■ ■ ■

"Follow me, Primus," T. Rex said, heading for the top-secret spaceship assembly plant elsewhere on the base. Two enormous metallic doors blocked the entrance to the hangar that housed the facility. The General stopped to have his DNA scanned, and the two heavy doors slid open in opposite directions. They revealed a large warehouse, about the size of four football fields, with a spacecraft sitting in each of its corners. B.R.A.I.N looked up and examined the roof, which looked like it could open; that made sense. In the center of the room were clustered a number of desks and sophisticated computers. About twenty engineers were busy on the manufacturing floor. In the distance, B.R.A.I.N recognized the familiar faces of Mike Sheed and Ricky Coben working on one of the spaceships. T. Rex walked towards them and introduced Primus. "Do you remember Primus?" he asked.

"Of course—it was the first robo we assembled. Can it be trusted?" Mike asked.

"I believe so. Eric Roberts dropped it off this morning to assist you. Two more will arrive tomorrow. They can work 24/7, and should help us finish the ships on schedule. Primus, you are to remain here at all times. Dr. Sheed and Dr. Coben will show you around and assign your tasks. Everything you need can be found right here. Otherwise, they will be able to provide it for you. Is that clear?"

"Yes sir," B.R.A.I.N responded.

"Excellent. I have other matters to attend to. Mike, please come with me," T. Rex said, signaling him to follow with his right hand. Their walk to the exit was quiet, but as they arrived, T. Rex said, "Mike, keep Primus under close supervision. I want to make sure we can trust it."

"Don't worry, sir, Ricky and I will watch its every move."

"Thank you. I leave everything in your capable hands," T. Rex said. They waved goodbye and left in opposite directions.

Mike returned with Primus, and began to show him around. B.R.A.I.N saw that all of the spaceships being constructed were saucer-shaped, and used his scanner to determine that they were about 80 yards in diameter and 30 yards thick. They walked towards the nearest one, on the right corner of the warehouse, and climbed up the open ramp to enter the cargo bay. Inside were several electric land vehicles with tank tracks to propel them. B.R.A.I.N ducked inside one of them, and concluded that they had been designed to transport humans in rough terrain. Each vehicle had ten seats and a large cargo area. There were two more tractor-like vehicles as well that were equipped for heavy lifting and pushing.

Next to the cargo bay was the engine room; a nearby lift took them to the ship's second deck. Here they found central command, the environmental control room, the water production plant, and a large storage area. B.R.A.I.N discovered that the ship was using the replicators he had invented to produce drinking water and methane from carbon dioxide and hydrogen, though there was also a secondary, less-advanced Sabatier water production system, developed in the early 1900s by Nobel Prize-winning French chemist Paul Sabatier, in place for reasons of redundancy. The second floor of the ship also housed the electrical room, where power was generated by a version of B.R.A.I.N's fusactor.

They visited the third deck, where the crew's quarters were located. Nearby was a well-equipped gym, an entertainment area with a holo-TV, a pool table, a ping-pong table, and other amenities. The kitchen and dining areas were also on this floor. Artificial gravity would make sure that everyone would stay put once they were in flight. The kitchen featured the latest in food replicator technology, capable of providing a wide variety of nutritious meals for the crew. There were five small but comfortable bedrooms, each with two bunk beds, a large metal closet, a private shower, a toilet, a sink, and a small desk with a computer screen. About 30 small utility robots were busy helping engineers on various parts of the ship.

They finished their tour and headed back outside. "Well, what do you think?" Mike asked.

"Impressive. Are you planning to send only humans on the interstellar mission, or will you be sending robots as well?" B.R.A.I.N asked.

"We plan to send 20 utility robots to help with maintenance and repairs. When they're not busy with those, they can cook and wait on the crew. Three large security robots armed with laser technology, which B.R.A.I.N helped develop, will protect the crew from danger. Do you remember B.R.A.I.N?" Mike asked.

"I know that B.R.A.I.N existed and helped you advance your technology. It was later decommissioned because of a malfunction," B.R.A.I.N replied, hoping his response would not arouse any suspicions.

While scanning the construction area, B.R.A.I.N noticed several huge black robots walking about, alertly monitoring the construction activity: the security robots Mike had mentioned. Even though he had helped design them, he had no idea what changes to their programming had been made, or what threats they would respond to. He wondered if they would cause trouble when the time came to take the ships.

"Are those the security robots you mentioned earlier?" B.R.A.I.N asked.

"Yes, Primus, they're protecting the assembly area. If something unusual happens, or if any unauthorized personnel enter the facility, they are designed to intercept them immediately, violently if necessary, and to notify headquarters."

This is going to be a problem, B.R.A.I.N thought. The security robots would come in handy out in space, but here they were a nuisance. He knew he would have to deactivate and reprogram them somehow, without anybody finding out.

"Can we inspect one of the security robots?" B.R.A.I.N. asked.

"We can approach one of them. I'm not sure it will allow you to inspect it," Mike chuckled.

They approached one of the robots, and B.R.A.I.N noticed the familiar optical port used for transferring information. If he could somehow connect to it, he would be able to find out how it was programmed and decide on a plan of action.

"If you connect me to the security robot using my optical port," he said, "I may be able to help you improve its abilities."

"Not until you have clearance from T. Rex. I suspect it won't be possible for some time. Best you ask him when you see him next," Mike responded.

"Understood. How will you produce oxygen for crew members out in space?" B.R.A.I.N asked.

"We'll use replicators to produce water from hydrogen and carbon dioxide. The carbon dioxide will be readily available from human exhalation. Atomic replicators on the ship can make hydrogen, oxygen, and any extra carbon dioxide that the crewmembers need. They use fusion and fission to create any element on the periodic table simply by using atoms in the atmosphere nearby," Mike responded.

"Impressive. How will you protect the crew from extended exposure to electromagnetic radiation?"

"The ship's outer casing is made of an alloy containing a thin layer of lead that blocks about 85% of all external radiation. We're still working to improve the shielding; perhaps you can help us?"

"Of course. One solution I see immediately is that we can project an electromagnetic force field around the ship, similar to the one that protects the Earth, only much stronger. I am aware that a similar but low-power field protects the surface garden at the Fort Meade facility during the winter months, but I can already see several ways to improve it. I will need to study the power output of the fusactor to determine if my ideas are feasible. We will need considerable energy for the electromagnets to provide the right amount of protection. We can also equip the ship with a small version of the gravitational wave gun B.R.A.I.N developed to safeguard it from menacing objects out in space," B.R.A.I.N/Primus said.

"The ship already has two powerful lasers for vaporizing small objects. We considered the gravitational wave gun, but our designs were too heavy, and we had to scrap it," Mike admitted.

"Allow me work on the problem, and perhaps I can find a better solution," B.R.A.I.N suggested.

"Good idea. Come on, Primus, I'll show you to your working station and create an account with enough clearance to let you complete your work," Mike said, guiding the robo to a computer station in the center of the assembly site. B.R.A.I.N didn't need the station other than to view ship schematics; everything else he needed was already in his memory and AI programming.

"Thank you. I will start working on my projects," B.R.A.I.N said as he began reading ship schematics at an incredible speed. He checked the index and found the designs for the security robots. Six hundred pounds of steel and plastic, each was able to lift three times its weight, and was armed with two one-megawatt laser cannons. *These things pack a serious punch*, B.R.A.I.N thought. The robots had enough AI to navigate, identify threats, and decide on a course of action. B.R.A.I.N realized he could improve their reaction time by changing their programming. If only he could connect to one of them! Mike had made it clear this would not be allowed without T. Rex's permission, so he decided to hack the computer to allow him the proper clearance. He figured he would do this when most of the engineers were asleep. He could then easily approach the robots, connect to them, and alter their programming. Afterward, he would come back and erase all traces of the hack.

If T. Rex found out, however, it would jeopardize the entire mission. *What about the security cameras? They would monitor my actions. What if the robots refuse the connection? Too risky! Best to wait until I win T. Rex's confidence,* B.R.A.I.N thought. He decided to work all night and come up with something to impress him. If successful, he would surely receive the proper clearance to access and reprogram the robots without arousing suspicion.

■ ■ ■

Back in Boston, Liz and Eric were having a hard time selecting the two robos that would return with them to Fort Meade. They finally decided all were equally capable, and picked two at random. The other three were to stay in the apartment out of sight. If, anything unusual happened, the robos were to send a simple numerical message on a secure line to Eric's smartwatch. Everything was ready for their trip the next day. They packed essentials into their bags and went to sleep.

The next morning, they took a cab to the air force base, the two robos with them. They arrived at Fort Meade at 12:30 pm. T. Rex was personally waiting for them.

"Hello, General, how is Primus working out?" Eric asked.

"I'm not sure yet; I left it with Mike Sheed and Ricky Coben yesterday. Let's head out to the assembly plant and find out," T. Rex suggested. "I see you brought the two new robos. Are they behaving properly?"

"Yes. I believe they'll prove very useful," Eric said truthfully.

When they entered the assembly facility, Liz and Eric were shocked. Their eyes were immediately drawn to the four saucer-shaped craft in the corners of the huge warehouse, but after ogling for a moment, they soon spotted Ricky and Mike in the distance and mentioned that to the General. They all headed in the direction of the engineers, and found that

Primus was with them. They appeared busy discussing something. "Hello there," T. Rex called as they approached.

"Hello, General. Eric, Liz, good to see you," Mike said, grinning.

"Good to see you, too. How's Primus working out?" Eric asked.

"Very useful indeed! Last night it designed a small device to generate a magnetic field around the ships, to protect them from interstellar debris and incoming radiation. Kind of a shield, if you like. We were just discussing where and how to install it on the ships," Mike responded.

"I told you they would come in handy!" Eric said, smiling at the General. "We brought two more of them, Mike."

"Great! Primus, please show your new guests around the plant, and put them to work installing the shield," Mike said.

"Yes sir," Primus responded promptly.

"Oh, by the way, General, Primus asked me for permission to access the security robots. He claims he can reprogram them to become more efficient. I told him you were the only one that could authorize that," Mike said, looking at T. Rex.

"Hmmmm," T. Rex mumbled, massaging his chin with his left hand. "Yes, of course, I believe Primus has proven its value. No harm can come from improvements," T. Rex said, after thinking about it for a few seconds. "Now please, Dr. Sheed, show Dr. Roberts and Dr. Kolmann around the plant—maybe they can come up with a few improvements themselves. I have things to do back at headquarters."

"Yessir." Mike turned to his companion. "Ricky, could you stay with Primus and the robos while I show Liz and Eric around, and make sure Primus has the proper access to connect to and reprogram the security robots?"

"Sure thing, see you guys later," Ricky said.

"Follow me," Mike said, as he walked over to the ramp of the nearest ship.

"The assembly plant looks airtight. How do you plan to deploy the ships once they're ready?" Liz asked.

"Simple. It has a clamshell roof to let them out," Mike answered, as they climbed up the ramp and entered the ship. "Right now, we're calling this ship *A-3*, with A signifying the batch and 3 the numeric designator. We'll give them formal names later on. Ricky wants to call one the *Enterprise*," Mike said, rolling his eyes.

They passed through the curved corridors to the crew's quarters. "Although far from luxurious, each ship was roomy enough to house 8-10 crew members and 20 assorted robots each. What do you think?" Mike asked.

"Impressive!" Eric said. "When do you think they'll be ready?"

"I'm not sure yet—a couple of months, probably. If the new robos work out and T. Rex allows us to have more, possibly sooner," Mike answered.

"Well, if you tell him they're working out, I'm sure more robos will arrive soon," Eric said, trying to hide a grin.

After they finished the tour, Liz and Eric decided to head out to the waterfall in the garden to talk. They felt that was the only place on the entire base where they were sure nobody would be listening. They arrived shortly after, took off their shoes as usual, and sat on the inviting grass.

"We have to ask more people to come with us," Liz said in a low voice. "Do you think we can trust Mike and Ricky? They're in charge of the project, so they're responsible for it. But if they say no, or change their minds, it could ruin our plans."

Eric nodded. "Yes, I know. There's no way to be sure until we talk to them privately. Maybe we can invite them to dinner later tonight, and see what we can find out. We need to be careful not to reveal our plan until we're sure we can trust them. I'll talk to Charlie Flegman when we get back to Harvard. He's my best friend and colleague, so I'm sure he will agree. He loves adventure. If we can somehow convince Mike and Ricky, we'll be all set."

"I'm nervous. If anything goes wrong, they'll send us both to jail, and T. Rex will personally throw away the key," Liz said.

"As my guru once said, 'Have faith in God, but tie up the camels,'" Eric said.

"Tie up the camels?" Liz asked, smiling. "I don't want to talk about camels particularly, but tell me more about what you learned in India."

"Well, let's talk about humans, then. Human beings are mind, body, and soul. All three must be in balance for us to be happy. Some people worry only about the body, wanting to look their best. They eat healthy foods, work out, and use their tight bodies to impress the opposite sex. There's nothing wrong with that. Eventually, though, no matter how hard they work at it, the body gets old, sick, and dies. No happiness here.

"Others worry about cultivating their minds. They gather a lot of information and become experts in one field or another. They may invent a medication, a cure for an important disease, and put their name to it, thinking they've found their place in history, that their name and fame will last forever. There's nothing wrong with this either—except, remember the Egyptians. We see their famous tombs, but know little about their lives and their beliefs. The Mayan civilization developed the concept of zero and infinity, two important ideas in mathematics. Their society later collapsed, yet no one knows for sure why that happened. The point is, the material world is temporary. Nobody lives forever; nor does his or her name and fame. So, there's no lasting happiness here either." Eric paused before continuing.

"Those who follow the path of the spirit, the soul, are better off than the other two. The mind and body die, but the soul continues. We all have to eat, dress, and worry while we remain in the material world, so the best choice is to develop all three. A healthy body leads to a healthy mind. A healthy mind can understand and develop the spirit, which leads to a balanced and happy existence. Of course, this doesn't mean you shouldn't try to cure disease or be competitive in sports. It simply means we should strive to develop all three. Cultivating the spirit begins by realizing that God exists, then surrendering to Him. After that, God will guide you on the proper path. This is exactly what's happening to us. Humanity on this planet is suffering from the misdeeds of the past. At this point, our job is to try to save it by exploring the unknown universe and colonizing a new planet similar to our own. God has placed us on this path; we must fulfill our destiny. We have to convince Mike and Ricky to help us. We have no other choice."

"What about all the people who will stay behind, breathing toxic fumes and starving to death? Doesn't God care about them? Why didn't he just force them to accept B.R.A.I.N's plan?" Liz asked.

"Remember our discussion about Karma? Remaining here is their Karma; going out to explore the universe is ours. Let's grab the opportunity and see where it takes us. The destiny of the rest of mankind is in their hands; it's their choice."

"But we're going to take their ships, B.R.A.I.N, and the robos. They may never recover from that; at best, it could take them years. I'm not sure I can live with that," Liz said sadly.

"Remember that God doesn't interfere with our free will, or even the will of a rich and powerful minority, those who decided for the rest of humanity not to follow B.R.A.I.N's plan. We have a right to choose our own path. They will make new ships, using the technology B.R.A.I.N has already developed. Whether they use them to further humanity's interests or those of a small minority is out of our hands. Don't feel guilty for saving yourself. It's your God-given right to protect yourself and your loved ones," Eric responded.

Liz sighed. "Okay, yes, I think you should call Mike and ask him and Ricky to have dinner with us. Tell them to meet us at my apartment for a home-cooked dinner they'll never forget. Please double check my place for bugs, okay?"

A moment later, Eric was on his watch phone. "Hey, Mike, just calling to see how you were doing, and to invite you and Ricky to dinner tonight at Liz's apartment."

Mike seemed pleasantly surprised. "Why, sure. I'll have to ask Ricky, though. We've been busy. Those robos of yours are handy—things are really cooking around here!"

"We'll be doing some cooking of our own if you and Ricky accept our invitation. Liz told me to tell you that you will never forget this meal!" Eric said.

"Great! Let me talk to Ricky, and I'll call you back as soon as I can."

"I guess we'll have to wait a bit," Liz said after Mike signed off. "Let's start heading back to my apartment. I'm planning on making handmade pasta with a tomato, mushroom, and vegetable sauce, all sautéed with red wine. A dinner they'll remember forever. Don't worry, I'll order some pizza for you," she added jokingly.

"Very funny. Lead the way."

After a relaxing shower, Liz began to prepare the ingredients. Eric was getting ready to turn on the holo-TV when his watch phone pinged. "Hello, Eric, Mike here."

"Hi Mike, what did you decide?" Eric asked.

"Ricky and I are game for dinner. Be there around 8:00 PM, is that okay?" Mike asked.

"Wonderful, it's 6:00 PM now. We'll see you in two hours. Do you know how to get to Liz's apartment?"

"Yeah, no problem. See you later."

Eric told Liz the good news, and started to check the apartment for bugs. After the first scan reported an all-clear, he scanned a second time just to be sure.

15

Crewmembers

Liz had everything except the pasta ready an hour before their 8:00 PM engagement with Mike and Ricky. She asked her computer assistant to order a pizza and have it delivered at 8:00 PM sharp. Meanwhile, Eric was busy picking a good bottle of red wine.

At exactly 8:00 PM, the doorbell rang; it was the pizza. Eric took it and placed it in the oven to keep it warm. A few minutes later, Mike and Ricky arrived.

"Hello, welcome! Glad you could make it," Eric said.

"Glad to be here. What's for dinner?" Ricky asked.

"We're having pizza and handmade pasta, a nice salad, and an incredible bottle of red wine to help you relax," Liz said.

"Sounds great, I'm starving"

"Come, sit down, make yourselves comfortable," Liz said as she went to get the food and placed it on the table. "Will you do the honors?" she said, handing the bottle of wine to Eric.

"Sure, no problem," Eric said, using the bottle opener to remove the cork. "I miss B.R.A.I.N," he said as he gently poured wine into everybody's glass.

"Yeah, me too, he was cool," Ricky said.

"So now what? Our fearless leaders are planning to send some people to outer space to search for another planet to ravage?" Liz asked.

"Pretty much. Crazy, isn't it?" Mike said.

"There's nothing we can do to stop it, especially since the ships will be ready in a few weeks," Ricky noted. "Your robos are helping us work a lot

209

faster. They're coming up with ideas we never imagined. It's like having B.R.A.I.N on our side once again."

Eric could tell that Mike and Ricky weren't happy with the new mission. He felt it was the right time to let them know about their alternate plan.

"Well… we have a suggestion. The most efficient way to explore space is to send as many robos as we can out in the four ships, following them up with robos in other ships, of course. They have the knowledge, resistance, and ability to find new planets for us. They can even use the native materials in other star systems to make new ships and robos, continuing on the way and multiplying until they find suitable worlds. They can then come back to save us. They can grow exponentially—it's the fastest way to find a habitable planet. And it's now the best way out for all of us," Eric said.

"Yes, it makes sense. But they're planning to send teams of scientists out with the maintenance robots. I doubt they'll agree to send just robos," Mike said.

"Then we have to convince them," replied Eric. "We must tell them that the robos are their best chance of finding a habitable exoplanet in the least amount of time, which our species is now short on. I supposed they can also send a few of those heavily-armed security robots in case they get into trouble. Why risk human life, if the robos can do the job for us?"

"Hmm. T. Rex doesn't entirely trust them yet. He told me to keep a sharp eye on Primus," Mike said.

"Just tell him that all's well and that they're our best alternative. T. Rex listens to you," Liz suggested.

"I guess I could do that. I still don't think he'll agree to just send a team of robos. Who would oversee them? What if something went wrong and they turned on us?"

"They won't turn on us, I guarantee it. They were designed to protect humanity, remember," Eric said.

"Yes, but the last time I spoke to him, T. Rex was set on the idea of sending humans," Mike said.

Now is the time, Eric thought. Liz also picked up on the opportunity, and looked straight at Eric, waiting for him to utter the right words.

"Mike, just tell him that you, Ricky, Liz, and I will go. We could also bring my colleague Charlie Flegman. After all, he helped design the software that runs the robos. He could come in handy. You should also bring your wives. Wait—you don't have any kids, do you?" Eric asked.

Ricky shot him a look of concern. "No, both Mike and I have been married to our wives for less than a year. We've been so busy the idea of having kids hasn't even crossed our minds. Now that I think about it, you've never met our wives, have you?"

"No, we haven't. Are they here at the base with you?" Liz asked.

"Yes, of course, we wouldn't have it any other way," Ricky answered. "Besides, we met them here. They're both scientists themselves."

"How convenient! Do you think they might like the idea of participating in the greatest journey ever, to have the opportunity to save our planet and explore the universe at the same time?" Liz said.

Mike blinked and said slowly, "Actually, I think they would be thrilled."

"Then it's settled. You and Ricky talk to your wives about our plan. Try to convince T. Rex the robos are useful, trustworthy, and the best option for exploring space and finding suitable exoplanets. Then you can tell him that we're all willing to volunteer for the mission. If T. Rex agrees, we should take as many robos as we can with us. I believe we humans could all fit in one ship, with ten robos, two security, and eight maintenance robots. The other ships can carry 18 robos, four security, and eight maintenance robots each. Once the ships are ready, we'll announce our departure and head into the unknown," Eric said.

"Sounds exciting," Liz said enthusiastically.

"Well, it's not going to be easy out there," Eric pointed out. "Outer space is harsh. We have to equip the ships with everything we need to survive, placing matching equipment in the other ships in case something goes wrong. What do you think?"

"It does sound prudent. I'm all for it," Mike said.

"Count me in," Ricky replied.

"Great!" Eric grinned briefly before looking somber. "But we need to keep our plans a secret until everything's in place. Before Liz and I return to Boston, we have to convince T. Rex to send sixty-one more deactivated robos to my apartment. Meanwhile, we should think about having some of those memory drives, that B.R.A.I.N invented, surgically implanted. They'll allow us to access a smaller version of the database B.R.A.I.N had available to him. We'll have all of human knowledge at our disposal. I'll talk to the robos to see if they can perform the surgical procedure before we leave on our mission."

"There's much to be done, and we won't get it done by sitting here. We'd better get busy," Ricky said.

"Good idea. Stay in touch, but be careful what you say. T. Rex has ears everywhere," Eric reminded them.

"Understood. Thanks for dinner and the interesting table talk, buddy," said Mike, with a wink.

"Glad you enjoyed it. See you soon."

Eric closed the door behind him to find Liz rushing to embrace him. They danced around in a circle of joy, kissing each other with exclamation points. Then the kisses lengthened and deepened, until they stole their breath away. Things had evolved in unusual ways. They'd thought they would have to steal the ships, but now they had a plan to convince T. Rex to let them go with his complete backing. They both went to bed excited about the morrow.

Much later, they finally got to sleep, too.

16
Readiness

Eric woke Liz with a delicate caress and a kiss on the arm. "What time is it?" she groaned.

"Never mind, go back to sleep," he murmured.

"What's on your mind?"

"A lot," he answered. "I don't even know where to begin."

"Well, try to start somewhere."

"We have to let B.R.A.I.N know what happened, but I don't want to risk T. Rex finding out before everything is in place. We have to go back to Harvard and try to convince Charlie and his wife Julie to join us. Also, we need more robos for the trip—64, to be exact."

Liz pointed out, "We already have six."

"That we do. The ships need weapons to protect us, in case of danger. Maybe B.R.A.I.N has figured out a way to install a smaller version of the gravitational wave gun on each ship. We have a lot of work to do. I'm happy, but a bit overwhelmed," Eric admitted.

"I understand, but try to relax. You've got a lot of help, and everything will work out all right. Why don't we head to the assembly plant and try to talk with B.R.A.I.N?" Liz suggested.

"To the showers it is!" Eric said enthusiastically.

They arrived at the assembly plant at around 10:00 AM. Eric used his biometric information and, to his surprise, the personnel door opened. This meant Mike had made arrangements to grant him access. They entered and found B.R.A.I.N busy at work on the central computers. They approached. "Hello, Primus," Eric said.

"Hello, Eric," B.R.A.I.N/Primus answered.

He leaned close and asked in a low voice, "Are you programmed for surgical procedures? Wait, let me rephrase that: can you install memory drives in Liz and me?"

"Yes, of course I can do that for you," B.R.A.I.N responded in an equally quiet voice. "I happen to have several memory drives in inventory right here. Earlier this morning, Mike and Ricky had theirs surgically installed."

"How long does it take—to install them, I mean?" Eric asked.

"Ten minutes. Would you like me to perform the procedure on both of you?" B.R.A.I.N, asked.

"Yes, please. Is it painful?"

"I won't lie to you—the others said it stung a little. You might feel dizzy, and your head will hurt for a short while. Otherwise, everything should be fine."

"Is there someplace private where we can do this?" Eric asked.

"Each of the ships we are working on here has a fully-equipped medical bay. Let's head to the nearest one," B.R.A.I.N suggested.

They casually entered the nearest ship, *A-1*, and headed to the cargo bay. On the far-left side was the accessible, spacious, well-insulated, and isolated medical area. A steel surgical table was located in the center of the room, with 3D X-ray and CT scanners located overhead. There were also two robotic arms next to the table that could be used to handle equipment and even perform simple surgical procedures.

"Who goes first?" B.R.A.I.N asked.

"I will. Before we start, can we speak freely in here?" Eric asked.

"Certainly. There is no external monitoring equipment in this area."

Eric brought B.R.A.I.N up-to-date. He told him that Mike and Ricky were on the team now, and would try to convince T. Rex to let them be a part of the search for habitable exoplanets. He also explained they would need 64 robos for the mission. B.R.A.I.N nodded to show that he understood, then asked Eric to lie on the table and began the procedure. The trickiest part was linking the drive to the hippocampus, which transferred the information to short and long-term memory as required.

The entire operation took less than ten minutes. Liz was next. They both had a noticeable but tolerable pain on the left sides of their heads when done, but there were no visible scars. Eric tried to access the memory drive, and discovered how simple it was. He searched for religious literature, and it was all there: The Bible, the Torah, the Holy Quran, Confucius' *Analects*, the Mahabharata, the Ramayana, the Bhagavad Gita, and more, right down to the smallest and oldest-known religions. He tried to read the contents of one of the books, and the pages appeared like magic in his mind's eye. "This is incredible," Eric whispered.

Liz was busy exploring her own drive, and he only vaguely heard her exclaim, "Wow!"

Eric's watch began to buzz, jerking him out of his reverie; it was Mike. "Hey, bud. Hold onto your hat, because I just spoke to T. Rex—and he accepted our plan! He also agreed to send 61 more robos to Harvard for you to activate, and will soon have a special cargo plane prepped to transport them when you're ready. I love it when a plan comes together!"

"That's great news!" Eric all but shouted. "Liz and I will head back to Boston ASAP to take care of the robos. You and Ricky supervise matters here while we're gone. Please make sure the ships can protect us from potential threats out in space, okay? We don't know what we'll run into."

"Not to worry, we'll take care of everything. Try to get back soon," Mike said.

Liz and Eric left to prepare for the flight to Boston. They decided to leave the next morning, and spend their remaining evening hours by the waterfall, where they meditated for a short while.

"We're traveling to outer space—aren't you excited?" Liz asked afterward.

"I'm excited, but a bit scared. It's treacherous out there, with dangers we've never faced before. I'm curious to see what we find, but worried for our safety," Eric said.

"Don't worry, B.R.A.I.N will protect us," Liz replied.

"There may be dangers in outer space that not even B.R.A.I.N can protect us from," Eric countered. "Black holes, radiation, dark matter, maybe even unfriendly aliens."

"But the alternative is to stay here and watch our world die, and us with it," Liz noted drily.

"True. We're committed, so there's no turning back now. We'll search for and find a new planet to call home. We'll colonize it, and make sure we don't make the same mistakes humans made here. It'll be okay, you'll see."

Liz sighed. "I remember you once mentioned that our constant need to indulge our senses is the main reason why Earth is on the verge of destruction. Do you still think this is true?"

"Yep. My spiritual master once told me a story about a famous king known for his acts of heroism. The King traveled all over the world searching for a place to live, one allowing him to satisfy all his earthly desires. No matter how far he traveled, he couldn't find such a place. He felt discouraged."

"To satisfy all his earthly desires? Sounds like my Uncle Isaac," Liz said, smiling.

"Once, while wandering about, he visited the southern side of the Himalayas. There he found a city with nine gates, surrounded by great walls. Inside were towers, canals, and houses with domes of gold, silver, and bronze. The streets were laden with platinum and gold and shone brightly under the rays of the sun. Diamonds, rubies, emeralds, sapphires, and pearls were strewn randomly like pebbles on a dirt road. Riches beyond his greatest dreams! There were also many restaurants, marketplaces, and beautiful parks," Eric said.

"Sounds wonderful. Please take me there," Liz pleaded.

Eric laughed. "On the outskirts of the city was a large lake, surrounded by beautiful trees and flowers. The birds and the insects made sounds agreeable to the ear. Walking around the lake, the king saw a beautiful young woman. She was looking for a suitable husband. The woman had an attractive body, her ears adorned with dazzling shiny earrings. She wore a yellow dress with a golden sash. The king was attracted to the shy, smiling face of the young woman and decided to approach her. 'Hello, young maiden,' he said. 'You should know that I am a famous, powerful, and heroic king, and I have many riches. Your shy glances have captivated my mind, and your beautiful smile has enticed my senses.'

"The young woman smiled and said: 'I only know that I am living in this place. I do not know what will become of me. I am so foolish that I don't even care to understand who has created this beautiful place as my home. Oh, great hero, it is my good fortune that you have come here. I know that you have a great need to gratify your senses, so I will do my best to help you. This city of nine gates will allow you to indulge all your appetites. My dear hero, who would not accept a husband like you, who is so famous, powerful, brave, rich, and handsome?' the young woman said."

"Now I'm getting jealous. Why doesn't anybody approach me the same way?" Liz asked.

Eric smiled. "In time, they became husband and wife. Together they enjoyed the city of nine gates for a hundred years. Two of the gates featured beautiful sights to delight the eyes. Two others led to lush gardens, full of lovely flowers, with smells to enchant the nostrils. Another two featured beautiful music and sounds attractive to their hearing. Yet another led to a place full of delicious food to satisfy their palate. One more led to a bedroom, where the king and his queen could enjoy the pleasures of sex. The ninth and final gate took them to a spa with natural hot springs and perfumed steam baths. Here they would shower and expel the toxins of indulgence," Eric said.

"Sounds like heaven," Liz said. "Go on. Tell me the rest of the story."

"The years passed until finally, the king and his wife reached a time dreaded by those too attached to the material senses. They became old, sickly, and weak. They could no longer enjoy life as they did in their youth. They felt lust, combined with disgrace at their inability to perform. Sons, daughters, thieves, and servants plundered their wealth. When they were no longer able to provide even for themselves, their family turned against them. Finally, they died miserable and alone, victims of their intense desires," Eric said.

"That's it? What a terrible ending!" Liz exclaimed.

"But the story is an allegory, my sweet. In this story, the nine gates represent the two eyes, two ears, two nostrils, the mouth, genitals, and anus. The city represents man's enslavement to his material senses with no clear way out. The king and his wife demonstrate the way most people go through life, never feeling entirely fulfilled — a material existence full of trouble, struggle, fear, anxiety, strife, and finally death. The king's wife shows how most of us never question who we are, why we're here, and Who or What is responsible for everything we perceive. This is why our world is in so much trouble. Most people only care about satisfying their desires, no matter the cost. They care about themselves and very little about who they share the world with. Selfishness, unkindness, and moral decay have brought our world to its current condition. We must take the wisdom hidden in this story, find a suitable world to colonize, and make sure that God consciousness, morality, and self-control reign supreme."

Liz was considering the content of the story. *How simple, yet how true*, she thought. They both stood, and Eric suggested they get some rest before their return to Boston the next day. They hugged and kissed tenderly. They felt excited yet scared about what the future held for them. They both believed in God, and felt strengthened by their faith in His supreme wisdom. They would simply have to follow the path before them, comforted by the thought that their bodies might die, but their souls would live forever. The soul is where the true strength of a human being resides, an inner strength that can surpass all obstacles.

The jet was waiting for them at 10:00 AM sharp the next morning. They arrived at Eric's Cambridge apartment by 11:00 AM, checked on the robos, and found everything was well. Eric then called Brenda, mentioned that more robos would be arriving, and asked her to get Charlie Flegman on the phone.

"Eric, you're back!"

"Hi Charlie, how are you?"

"You know how it is—same old routine, day in and day out. No breakthroughs. To be honest, it's been boring without you. I heard about the robos and how the government forced you to end your project. I'm sorry, my friend. You okay?"

"It was a terrible blow, but matters are turning out nicely. Nothing's going to be wasted. Why don't you and Julie come to my apartment for dinner tonight? Say, 6:00 PM?" Eric asked.

"I'll have to ask Julie—she's full of social engagements all the time. It's getting difficult to program my nights."

"Of course. Please let me know as soon as you can. If tonight isn't good, please find another time to visit us. We'd love to see you... and we also have something important to ask you."

"Bank on it. I'll get back to you ASAP," Charlie replied.

"Talk to you soon."

About an hour later, Charlie called back, confirming the dinner appointment that evening. Liz and Eric visited the automated market van that passed by his house daily, to buy the ingredients for their dinner engagement. When they returned, they asked the robos to prepare a succulent vegetarian dinner for the four of them. Liz also picked a bottle of sweet white wine. *Chateau D'yquem, France's finest!* she thought.

Charlie and Julie arrived on time. They came in, exchanged pleasantries, reminisced about the past, and sat down to eat. Eric called the robos, who said hello to the guests and began to serve dinner. They all enjoyed the meal and wine. Eric decided to wait until after dinner, when their guests felt welcome and relaxed, to reveal the true purpose of the invitation.

"I'm glad you're both here," he began.

"Thank you for inviting us. It's been ages," Julie responded.

Eric went on to explain the happenings of the last few years. He knew Charlie would be interested, so he described B.R.A.I.N in great detail. He knew he was breaking his NDA with T. Rex, but it was necessary that Charlie and Julie understand everything. He asked them not to reveal this information to anyone, or there would be serious consequences. They both agreed, and Eric continued his story. He deliberately omitted the part about B.R.A.I.N's return. Eric instinctively knew this could place the entire mission at risk.

"So, you see, the world will self-destruct soon," he said heavily. "Our only hope now is to explore the universe and find one or more planets similar to Earth, places we can inhabit. We can then send the robos in larger ships for the mass migration of humanity. You and Julie are welcome to join us on this epic journey—an opportunity to explore the unknown and maybe even save humanity from itself. What do you say?" Eric asked.

"Wow—I don't know," Charlie said slowly. "We think Julie is pregnant. How will we care for our child out in space?"

"Pregnant! That's wonderful! Congratulations, we're so happy for you," Liz cheered.

"I'll understand if you say no, but please believe me when I say that you and your baby will be well-cared-for out there. We have four ships equipped with everything we need. In fact, I believe your baby will be better off there than here," Eric said.

Charlie looked at Julie and back at Eric. He sensed urgency and secrecy in everything Eric told him. He understood the importance of the mission. Charlie was an adventurous type; he was incredibly intelligent, and bored easily. Eric was offering him a chance to participate in an exciting and important adventure—the adventure of a lifetime. But something deep inside was compelling him to stay and protect his child.

"Let's join them, Charlie," Julie said abruptly. "My one regret about having a baby together is bringing a new life into these desperate conditions. It's almost like this was meant to be, giving us the opportunity of a fresh start for our new family. Our baby will be okay, and neither of us have any close family to miss us. Adventure awaits!" Julie grinned.

"She's the boss, so I guess we're in," Charlie said, turning to kiss his wife.

"Great! We'll meet you here next Monday at 10:00 AM, then head to Hanscom Air Force Base together and take a flight to Fort Meade at 12:00 noon. Remember not to reveal any of this to anyone, okay? You won't regret your decision. It really will be the adventure of a lifetime," Eric said.

Charlie nodded. "Thanks for dinner, and for everything else, too."

Julie smiled and hugged Liz goodbye. "And thank you for giving us a better future for our baby," she said.

17

Wormhole

Eric received an early-morning phone call from Brenda the next day, informing him that 61 more deactivated robos had arrived at Harvard. He now had six days until their reunion with Charlie and Julie, but only five effective days to reactivate them. Eric asked Brenda to send 12 robos to his apartment each day for the first four days, beginning immediately. On the fifth day, she was to send the last 13 robos.

The first shipment arrived around four in the afternoon. Eric made sure the existing robos in his apartment were out of sight before asking the two delivery men for assistance. They took the robos in groups of two to Eric's living room. Once that was done, Eric thanked them, and reminded them they had four more shipments scheduled. He asked that they return around the same time each day.

Eric summoned the activated robos in his apartment to help him reactivate the 12 that had just arrived. All were up and running by midnight. The old robos coached the new ones on the objectives of their mission, while Liz and Eric went to bed.

The next four days were just as busy. By the end of the fifth night, all 61 robos had been activated and properly prepared to the mission. Everything was ready for their meeting with Charlie and Julie at 10:00 AM the next day. They were both pleased they were leaving soon since the apartment was now overcrowded.

Charlie and Julie arrived punctually. Brenda had sent a large transport to drive them all to Hanscom Air Force base for their noon flight to Fort Meade. Eric arranged for three of the new robos to remain and take care of the apartment. The others all climbed into the transport, and arrived at the base shortly after. A large supersonic jet was waiting for them. One by one, they boarded the aircraft; on arrival at Fort Meade, they were escorted to the spaceship assembly plant, where T. Rex and the rest of the gang were waiting for them.

"Hello, Eric, and welcome back. I see you brought my robos," T. Rex said.

"Yessir. We barely had enough time to get them ready for our return," Eric said.

"But you got the job done—that's what counts. When will the space-ships be ready, Mike?" T. Rex asked.

"A few more weeks, sir," Mike responded. "With the extra robo-power, chances are we'll finish sooner."

"Well, back to work then, everyone. We want to get these spaceships up and running as quickly as possible," T. Rex pronounced.

"Do you know where you'll be sending us?" Liz asked.

"Tau Ceti, one of the nearest stars. It's a bit smaller than our sun, but has an exoplanet in the habitable zone, Tau Ceti d, which we estimate is about five times larger than Earth. Tau Ceti is approximately 12 light years away, and our astronomers are still evaluating whether it's our best option."

"Twelve light years? That's quite a distance. How long will it take us to get there?" Charlie asked.

"Not to worry," Primus said. "Using our new gravitational displace-ment engines, we have successfully simulated speeds at about twice the speed of light, so it shouldn't take us more than six years to get there. We're also experimenting with wormhole technology, which, if successful, could shorten the trip significantly,"

"What wormhole technology?" Eric asked.

"Einstein-Rosen portals, or wormholes, may be created using suffi-ciently powerful magnetic fields, and can hypothetically transport matter at great distances in an instant. The problem is that the tunnels are tiny and unstable. We will use extremely powerful magnetic field generators to create a wormhole and expand it enough for our ships to pass through. We should have a working model by the end of this week," Primus said.

"Are you saying that, if the wormholes work, we could be at Tau Ceti instantaneously?" Charlie asked.

"Not exactly instantaneously, but in a very short period of time," Primus responded.

"What about us? How will the wormhole affect us?" Liz asked.

"It shouldn't. The ship's magnetic force field is powerful enough to counteract the gravimetric crushing and shearing effects of the wormhole. We are still conducting tests," said the robo.

"How can you be sure the wormhole will lead us to the right place?" Charlie inquired.

"The mathematics are complex. In theory, all we have to do is create a wormhole pointing towards our destination and enter it. We can set the length of the wormhole by using the estimated distance to our destination. We then adjust the magnetic forces needed to create a wormhole of that length. Otherwise, we can undershoot or overshoot our destination," Primus responded.

"Okay, then, we'll leave the job to the experts. Primus, do you still have memory drives available for Charlie and Julie?" Eric asked.

"Memory drives? What in heaven's name are those?" Charlie said.

"Yes, I could install them right now if you wish," Primus said.

Eric described the memory drives and the simple procedure to install them. Once Charlie and Julie agreed to the surgery, they went with Primus to the medical facility on the nearest ship. They were both impressed by the implants; they thanked Primus and returned to the rest of the crew. Everybody was hungry by then, so Eric suggested they head to the cafeteria for a late lunch and an opportunity to socialize with Mike and Ricky's wives.

Mike and Ricky went to their respective apartments to collect their wives and meet the rest of them at the cafeteria. Eric, Liz, Charlie, and Julie found a comfortable table for eight and waited for the others. Mike turned up first, and introduced his wife, Rachel. She was in her late twenties, with shiny red hair and mesmerizing pale blue eyes. Ricky arrived a few minutes later and introduced his wife, Alex. She was a brunette, with green eyes and a charming smile.

"I know we're all a bit uneasy about the adventure we're about to embark on, assuming everyone's willing," Eric said. "We've equipped the ships with the latest and most advanced technology available to us. Unfortunately, we represent the only hope humans have of surviving the impending doom that awaits the Earth. I'm not going to lie to you: the trip will be dangerous, and there will likely be many challenges. We may face threats humans have never encountered before. If we find a suitable exoplanet, however, we can make a new life for ourselves and those on Earth who wish to follow—a brave new world and a new beginning for all of us," Eric said.

"What if we get to Tau Ceti and we don't find what we're looking for?" Charlie asked.

"Then we keep on searching until we do," Liz responded confidently.

They were a good mix of specialties. Alex, Ricky's wife, was an accomplished geologist and botanist. Rachel was a respected biologist with a specialty in zoology. Julie, Charlie's wife, was a reputable chemist.

"How will we know if the exoplanet is habitable when we arrive, assuming it's there?" Alex asked.

"We'll carry probes and scanners to provide us with all the information we need. If the planet is suitable, we'll land and build a habitat to ensure our safety and comfort. We can use the ships as shelter until we're ready for the transition. I suggest we travel together on one of the ships with Primus and a few other robos. The rest of the ships will follow our lead, with robos and other robots on board. This way we can keep each other company and remain safe while the other ships explore. We'll be provided with specialized spacesuits for the voyage, of course. In spite of this, I suggest you pack some comfortable clothing as well, for sleep, exercise, and to hang around in. You'll be able to stay fit using the ship's fully-equipped gym," Eric said. "And we'll have artificial gravity, so that will help."

"What happens if our ship is damaged out in space?" Rachel asked.

Eric shrugged. "All four ships are identical. If something happens to ours, we'll simply transfer to another while the robos inspect the damage and try to repair it."

Charlie asked. "Will we have any weapons on board?"

"Yes—we'll have powerful lasers to protect us from unfriendly life-forms. The ship will have a force field to shunt aside cosmic dust and such, two laser cannons, and a gravitational wave gun to destroy asteroids and other debris that might threaten us during our trip. We'll also be carrying security and maintenance robots," Eric replied.

"Looks like you've thought of everything. I feel much safer already."

Eric grinned. "Probably not everything—that's why it's essential we use the time we have left to get to know our ships as well as possible before departure. I've installed detailed schematics on the computers in your quarters for review. Please familiarize yourself with them, and let us know if you suspect we've missed something. We'll all have to submit to a full medical exam prior to departure. I just hope Julie's pregnancy doesn't become a cause for concern," Eric said.

"Julie you're pregnant? Congratulations," Alex said.

"Is it a boy or a girl?" Rachel asked.

"Both, actually. We're having twins," Julie said.

"Twins? That's wonderful! Why didn't you mention it before?" Liz said.

"We just found out, and with all the excitement about the trip, I didn't have the opportunity until now. The robos have made sure that everything we need to take care of the babies is on board. Charlie and I had some second thoughts in the beginning, but we feel our babies will be safe on the trip," Julie said.

"We'll all look out for our new crewmembers when they arrive," Liz said, chuckling.

"Thank you," Julie replied.

"Okay, why don't we get some food in our bellies before we head out to our quarters and get to work?" Eric suggested. "We have a lot of material to cover."

Everyone stood and headed for the buffet. It was China Day, and the menu featured all sorts of delicious noodles, exotic soups, dim sum, and other goodies. They each grabbed a tray, made their selection, and sat down to eat. They ate in silence, looking at one another occasionally.

Once finished, they politely said goodbye and left to study the schematics Eric had mentioned earlier.

■ ■ ■

Charlie sat down and displayed the schematics on his holoscreen. One by one he flipped through the slides, occasionally pausing to zoom in on something of interest. At one point, he politely asked Julie for a glass of orange juice. He always supplied sugar to his brain when he needed to think hard; it helped him concentrate. Julie came back with the juice quickly and kissed him on the top of his head. Charlie smiled, thanked her, and continued his work.

It appeared the ships' designers had indeed thought of everything, and they were very well equipped. Perhaps the only thing missing was a foosball table, the kind he and Eric used to play against other engineers when they were working on the AI software and needed a distraction. He recalled how they had experienced several eureka moments while playing the game. He would ask Eric to have one installed in their ship the next day.

Something else was missing... for some reason, the ship had ports to look out of, but no high-resolution cameras to zoom in on objects and project them on a holoscreen. This would be useful if they had to identify an object visually out in space. He would also mention that to Eric. *They should be easy to install*, he thought. By then it was late and he was tired, dozing off in his comfortable chair.

The next morning, he woke up a bit stiff. He had slept well, but the chair was less comfortable than he'd expected. Julie was already showered and dressed. She asked Charlie to get ready while she prepared some breakfast; the pregnancy made her hungrier than usual. Charlie returned a short while later, and sat down to enjoy his meal. He loved to dunk his toast in the egg yolks, something Julie often teased him about. They quietly enjoyed their breakfast and then headed to the assembly plant.

They found everybody already there, working steadily. Charlie approached Eric and told him about the foosball and the cameras. Eric decided it would be a good idea to install both. He called Primus, and asked him to take care of it.

■ ■ ■

Two weeks went by before the ships and crew were ready to head out. T. Rex was present on that final day. He stood in front of everybody and said proudly:

"I congratulate you all for your bravery in deciding to participate in this historic journey. You will be the first humans to travel outside our solar system. I am proud of all of you, and have full confidence that you will be successful in your mission. The entire world is counting on you. Good luck." Short, sweet, and to the point, which suited the newly-minted astronauts.

The human crew and Primus boarded the first ship, designated *A-1*, with nine other robos and several security and maintenance robots. Eighteen robos, along with five security and five maintenance robots, boarded each of the other three ships. Once inside, Eric reminded Primus of the three robos that remained in his apartment. Primus said he would contact them at the right time and ask them to head to the roof of Eric's building for pickup.

All four ships fired their antigravity engines as the roof of the assembly plant opened slowly to reveal the clear, starry night sky. The crew heard the muffled high frequency hum of the engines as they powered up, and felt the hull vibrating a bit beneath their feet. The hum was continuous but tolerable. Primus informed the other ships they would be heading to Eric's apartment to pick up three robos, and assigned the job to the fourth ship in the roster, the *A-4*. Everybody sat down and strapped in.

Primus's ship left first; the others followed in numeric order. Eric was surprised by how quiet the antigravity engines were. Once airborne, the hum became almost imperceptible. They arrived at his building in minutes and picked up the robos; then all four ships headed straight for outer space. The crew could feel the ship's acceleration, their bodies pushing against the back of their seats, but the ride was surprisingly smooth and quiet. After all, they weren't rising on a column of fire, like all previous spacecraft, which were chemically propelled. They easily reached escape velocity and broke through the outer atmosphere. Once in space, Primus reduced engine power, and everything was calm. A few items the crew had forgotten to fasten down began to float around the control room.

"How cool is this?" Charlie crowed, reaching for his wife's hairbrush and barely missing it. Everyone started laughing.

"Guys, there's something I have to tell you," Eric said solemnly.

Everyone turned to look directly at him, expecting him to reveal some terrible news about the trip.

"We have B.R.A.I.N on board," he said quietly. "A version of him survived the termination order. I'm sorry I didn't tell you before. If General Rex had found out, it could have jeopardized the entire mission."

To his pleasure, Mike, Ricky, and Charlie all heaved sighs of relief.

"Excellent, B.R.A.I.N is back! How, when?" Mike asked.

"Our friend Primus isn't what he seems at first glance." Eric told them the entire story, and everyone became excited.

"So, Primus is B.R.A.I.N? I always suspected there was something special about that robo," Mike said.

Ricky chimed in, "With B.R.A.I.N on our side, we have a much better chance of succeeding in our mission."

"That's right—he'll make sure we make it to our destination safely. Now, everyone ready to try the wormhole?" Eric asked.

"Yes!" the entire crew responded, almost in unison.

B.R.A.I.N was already busy using the *A-1's* computer to finalize the calculations necessary for the jump to their Tau Ceti destination. The distance was so great that even a tiny error would take them far from where they wanted to go. Finally, he turned to look at Eric, who reviewed the calculations and nodded in approval. B.R.A.I.N activated several buttons on the control panel of the ship, and large magnetic field generators emerged from each side. He looked at Eric once again.

"Nobody has ever done this before, so we have no idea what to expect. The ride could get a bit bumpy, so make sure you stay strapped into your seats," Eric said, looking around the cabin at his fellow crewmembers. Once he was sure everyone was secure, he nodded at B.R.A.I.N once more.

B.R.A.I.N ordered all ships to a full stop, and alerted the crew that he would now begin generating the wormhole that would transport them to their objective. He slowly applied power to the generators from the onboard fusactors, creating a pulsating gravitomagnetic field directly in front of their ship, the other three waiting patiently behind the *A-1* in single file. B.R.A.I.N turned on the cameras Charlie had suggested they install on each ship, and displayed the image before them as the field generators began to bend and warp spacetime. Suddenly, a narrow, spiraling yellow disc appeared before of them.

"There it is, the wormhole," Charlie exclaimed. "I'm surprised we can see it."

"The gravimetric shear is creating exotic particles and Hawking radiation that's immediately being siphoned back into the wormhole," Ricky explained.

Liz said, concerned, "It's too small. Surely we'll never fit in there."

"Not yet, but be patient," B.R.A.I.N said, as he increased power to the pulsating gravitomagnetic field. The crew could hear and feel an increasing vibration inside the ship that became more intense as the wormhole began expanding in response to the pulse. By the time it reached a suitable size for passage, the wormhole was spinning rapidly clockwise; and, in a flash of yellow light, suddenly exploded into a tunnel that extended deep into space in front of them, well beyond their field of vision.

"Everybody ready? Here we go," B.R.A.I.N said, applying power to the ship's engines and heading directly towards the wormhole entrance. The other three ships followed close behind.

"Entering the wormhole; brace yourselves!" B.R.A.I.N said, applying full power to the ship's engines.

They crew could hear worrisome metallic pounding noises coming from the outside, as if the hull of the ship were being crushed by the wormhole. B.R.A.I.N adjusted the atmospheric pressure inside to compensate, and the noise became less noticeable. Then, suddenly and without warning, they started spinning out of control along their long axis. The crewmembers began getting dizzy, a few crying out in pain. B.R.A.I.N reacted quickly and stabilized the vessel by decreasing power to the engine opposite the spin. It took a few seconds, but the ship leveled out.

According to the instruments, the delicate balance of the other ships was compromised as well, and they also spun for a few moments. To B.R.A.I.N's horror and infinite sadness, one of the struts securing the gravitational wave gun on the *A-3* gave way, flying like a bullet into *A-4*, which was following close behind. *A-4* was unable to regain control; the ship bounced off the walls of the wormhole several times before it vanished in a flash of radiation, crushed by the intense gravitational field constraining the wormhole.

After what seemed like an eternity, the *A-1* exited the wormhole with a loud thump, followed by the surviving *A-2* and *A-3*. B.R.A.I.N waited a few seconds before reducing engine power, veering to the right to give the other ships room to safely maneuver, then reduced engine power to zero. They continued traveling at a rapid pace due to inertia. The other two ships emerged from the wormhole safely and followed them, whereupon B.R.A.I.N commanded all ships to a full stop to assess their situation. He initiated a full diagnostic of the ships' systems.

"We're out of the wormhole; is everyone all right?" Eric asked. Everyone replied that they were fine.

After checking the instruments, Ricky spoke up hesitantly. "I'm glad we made it out alive, but *A-4* is gone. What the hell happened?"

B.R.A.I.N reported, "Sadly, there was an accident with *A-4*." He informed the rest of the crew what had happened, to their curses and horrified responses. "Fear not," the AI responded, "redundancy was built into the mission profile in case of just such an unexpected event."

"Right," Mike said grimly. "So, where the hell are we?"

"We don't know for sure yet, but we'll soon find out," Eric responded.

18

Tau Ceti

BR.A.I.N quickly performed a full scan of the surrounding space, and displayed the results on the holoscreen in the control room. They saw a bright star about the size of the sun, surrounded by markers indicating six planets. One was in the habitable zone, just as scientists back on Earth had predicted.

"Is that Tau Ceti D?" Liz asked.

"Based on parallax readings, pulsar observations, and other indicators, we are definitely in the Tau Ceti star system, so yes," B.R.A.I.N responded.

"Let's head over there and find out just how inviting it really is," Eric ordered.

B.R.A.I.N communicated their intentions to the other ships, and programmed a course directly to the planet, using half-power.

"We will arrive in a few hours," B.R.A.I.N informed the crew. "We should have complete habitability information by the time we arrive."

Everybody unfastened their seat belts, and the women began to hug each other. Charlie started jumping up and down, yelling excitedly, "We made it, we made it!"

"Not all of us," Eric said grimly. "A quarter of our resources are gone. And I don't want to sound pessimistic, Charlie, but we still don't know if the planet's habitable. It's a bit premature to celebrate," Eric said.

"I'm starving, or at least the twins are. What's good to eat?" Julie asked.

"Let's head to the third floor and see what's for lunch—or is it dinner? What time is it on Earth, B.R.A.I.N?" Liz said.

"I estimate it is 10:00 pm at Fort Meade," B.R.A.I.N responded.

"It was 7:00 pm when we left the assembly plant back on Earth. Are you saying we traveled roughly 12 light-years in only three hours?" Eric asked, surprised.

"Eleven point nine light-years to be precise, and it took us 2 hours, 52 minutes, and 36 seconds from the time we left the plant to the time we exited the wormhole," B.R.A.I.N said. "That amounts to roughly four light years per hour."

"Wow," Liz said, "it felt like ages in there."

"I agree. It must have been the stress," Charlie said.

They took the lift to the third deck up, and gathered in the kitchen and dining area, where they examined the refrigerator and storage cabinets to figure out what they might prepare for dinner. Charlie remembered the foosball table, and decided to go check it out, inviting Eric, Ricky, and Mike to join him.

"Where are you guys headed? Aren't you going to help us prepare the first interstellar meal in the history of humanity?" Alex demanded, crossing her arms over her chest in protest.

"C'mon, give us a break," Charlie said.

"Men. Fine, we'll take care of the food," Alex sighed. "But we've got dibs on Brainy's help."

Charlie led them into the rec room, saying, "I'm glad you listened to me and installed the foosball table. Look, it's a thing of beauty! C'mon, Eric, let's teach these newbies a thing or two about foosball!" He positioned himself as goalie on one side of the table, while Eric laughed and followed his lead. Mike and Ricky got ready on the other side.

"Newbies, huh? Just wait and see who wins the first space foosball game in history, eh?" Ricky taunted.

"Best of five goals. Winner decides on the first movie watched in interstellar space later on tonight," Charlie said.

"No Aliens, Predators, Cloverfield monsters, or any nasty ETs out to steal our water!" Mike insisted. "And no bad robots!"

"Yeah, yeah."

The game began, and soon they were tied at two goals each. Mike and

Ricky turned out to be better than Charlie had expected. "'Kay, here goes the last ball," Charlie said, dropping it precisely in the center. Eric caught the edge of the ball, projecting it sideways and missing the goal by a mile. Ricky reacted quickly by spinning his defense into action and kicking the ball hard directly towards the goal on the other side. Charlie placed his goalie at an angle, and deflected the ball back into action. Eric spun his players using his left hand. He connected with the ball, which shot quickly towards Mike and Ricky's goal. Neither was fast enough to stop it, and it shot through the goal line, making a loud popping sound as it hit the wall behind it.

"That's it! Winner, winner, chicken dinner!" Charlie exclaimed, excitedly waving his arms up and down, pounding on his chest, and stomping around with his knees bent.

"Is that your best imitation of a gorilla dance?" Mike said, laughing.

One of the girls came by and mentioned that dinner was ready, and no, it wasn't chicken. They left shaking hands and talking about how much fun the game had been, then shared pasta, salad, some wine, and many laughs.

Laughing helped them relax. They were far from home, surrounded by the unknown, and anxious about the future. Liz, Julie, Rachel, and Alex had been talking during the foosball match. Liz had told them all about Eric's travels in India, and the mystical teachings of his spiritual master. They became interested in learning more.

"Eric, Liz has been telling us how much you learned during your travels in India. If you could summarize what you learned in a few sentences, what would you say?" Julie asked.

"I don't want to bore you with my crazy ideas about life. Maybe another time," Eric said.

"C'mon, we want to hear, right guys?" Alex said.

"Yes, please go on," Charlie added.

"Okay, then, what I'm going to say is relevant to our current situation and to our future life on a new planet, wherever that happens to be. Back on Earth, animals are always fighting for four reasons they consider essential to their survival: food, territory, status, and mating privileges. If you analyze the history of human beings, we've been doing pretty much the same for ages," Eric said.

"People also fight for ideological reasons," Mike pointed out.

"True, but my point is that most humans back home are still living like animals. They eat, sleep, work, have sex, care for their young, and rarely give a single thought to why they're here, who created them, where they come from, or what the true purpose of life is. They're living in deliberate ignorance, continually trying to gratify their senses and fighting all the time. Just like animals do."

"There are people who truly care about the answers to these questions," Charlie noted.

"Yes, but unfortunately they're in the minority. The truth is, even though we have animal bodies, we each also have a spirit, a soul. The body wants to gratify itself, while the soul aspires to higher things. As human beings, we're apparently the only species intelligent enough to try to understand the soul and God. This is our true purpose, our *dharma*. God is the creator of everything, and we are His eternal servants. We must respect His creation and only take our fair share. We must not harm other living creatures, except in self-defense. We must remain humbled by the vastness and greatness of His creation and our small size in comparison," Eric said.

"But together we're capable of achieving great things," Ricky said, waving his hands around to highlight their surroundings. "Case in point."

"Yes, we are, but what I'm trying to say is that back on Earth, we're the only species capable of understanding His creation as far as we know. We must be tolerant, devoid of false prestige, and ready to offer all respect to others, expecting none for ourselves. We must be confident that if we're in this state of mind, God will guide us and take care of our basic needs, just as He takes care of the birds and the bees. Why wouldn't he take care of us as well?"

"Yes, but what about 'nature red in tooth and claw'? Sometimes life is difficult, and we have to struggle to meet its demands," Rachel replied.

"We have to use common sense. That's why I always say: 'Have faith in God but tie up the camels.' The problem is that humans are so greedy we want to partake of the forbidden fruit. We want to claim God's creation as our own," Eric said.

Rachel shrugged. "True. You can even observe this behavior in little kids. Some of the first words they learn are possessive pronouns like 'me' and 'mine'."

Eric nodded. "Good point. And unfortunately, even if we live according to God's laws and dictates, this doesn't mean that bad things won't happen to us. The Law of Karma is unavoidable. We must understand that as human beings, we're here of our own free will, and must pay for the wrongs of our past. If we lead righteous lives, God will lessen our Karma," Eric said.

"What do you mean by Karma?" Ricky asked.

"The same way scientists observe nature and create mathematical formulas to explain its behavior, spiritualists study its obvious unfairness and try to explain it using spiritual laws. Sir Isaac Newton, for example, observed the movement of objects and came up with his famous laws, including one describing the force of gravity. It wasn't until Albert Einstein published his ideas that a new way of looking at gravity emerged. Similarly, spiritualists explain the variety and inequality of life using the Law of Karma. A child might be born blind or poor because of something it did in the past, in a former life," Eric said.

"I see," Ricky said.

"When we find our new home, it's important that we establish a moral and God-conscious society. We must be careful about introducing people from Earth into the new environment. We have to be sure they'll fit in; otherwise, our new planet will end up the same as Earth, and all our hard work will be in vain." He smiled. "Now, let's head back to the control room to check out our new home."

"Good idea," Mike said, a bit overwhelmed by Eric's outlook.

B.R.A.I.N was busy at the controls of the ship. The human colonists watched as Tau Ceti D grew larger on the holographic image projected in the center of the room.

"That planet's huge," Ricky said as they approached.

"Look! There are lots of blue and white spots on the surface. That's a good sign, right?" Mike asked. "They suggest plenty of water!"

"Not necessarily," Alex cautioned. "They could indicate the presence of toxic gaseous materials rather than clouds and water."

Once they were orbiting the planet, Eric asked B.R.A.I.N, "Preliminary analysis?"

The AI replied regretfully, "Nitrogen 38%, oxygen 10%, ammonia 50%, and 2% other gases. Surface gravity is estimated at four gees."

Their shoulders slumped. "Uninhabitable without suits, and the gravity's way too high," Alex, the group's geologist, said.

"So, what do we do now?" Charlie asked.

"We keep looking. B.R.A.I.N, please scan the system's other planets," Eric ordered.

B.R.A.I.N set the sensors and began scanning. Starting with those nearest, he soon announced an exciting find: another blue-and-white planet, slightly smaller than Earth, located about 30 million miles farther out from the sun—but still within the Habitable Zone.

"The planet I am examining wasn't detected by Earth's scientists, probably because of its size. It appears to lie just beyond the center of the habitable zone, and my estimates of its orbit indicate it remains there for the entirety of its year. Do you wish to explore it?" B.R.A.I.N asked.

"Yes indeed. Plot a course, and let us know when we arrive. I suggest everyone get some rest. We may not have a chance later," Eric stated.

Everyone hit their bunks, doubtful they would be able to sleep. They all did, however.

Several hours later, the ships approached Tau Ceti E and established a stable orbit around it. Spectrographic analysis revealed an atmosphere consisting of 75% nitrogen, 24% oxygen, and 1% argon—very similar to Earth's, if a little high in oxygen. The planet's gravity was also remarkably close to Earth's. The AI elected to study it more closely, and had the ship's system feed him magnified video images, which he carefully examined. He could see what seemed to be oceans of water, clouds, and patches of green and purple crowding the eight smallish continents that comprised forty percent of the planet's surface. Further magnification revealed thick vegetation and evidence of animal life—pods of large sea animals, and what seemed to be game trails on land. Further analysis revealed that the planet had two moons, rotated around its axis every 22 hours, and orbited its sun every 332.37 of its days.

B.R.A.I.N decided to wake everyone. When they began to trickle in, he had the planet up on the holoscreen. "Are we there yet?" Charlie asked, sleepy-eyed, stretching his arms and yawning. Then he saw the hologram of the planet and froze, wide-eyed.

"Yes, we are. We have found a planet very similar to Earth, Tau Ceti E, that appears worthy of further exploration," B.R.A.I.N said. As the others joined Charlie in their examination of the globe, he revealed what he had discovered. They all got very excited and jumped up to slap each other's hands. B.R.A.I.N had never seen a high-five before.

"So, what do we do now?" Mike asked.

Eric said, "We'll need to land one of our ships on the surface at a likely colonization spot, and send the robos on that ship to explore the area. B.R.A.I.N, please find a suitable place, and send one of our ships over. Tell the robos to set up camp, explore the area, and take plenty of videos. Warn them against bringing alien samples inside their ship for analysis without permission. The risk of contamination is too great. They can do whatever else they want, but they should keep us informed," Eric said.

"Done," B.R.A.I.N responded.

A-3 descended to what appeared to be a large clearing in a patch of green, and it didn't take long for the ship to find a suitable landing spot. The antigrav engines worked like a charm; the craft hovered over the terrain while three legs slowly extended from its bottom. Once fully extended, the craft made a perfect landing near the center of a half-mile-wide clearing covered with springy Kelly-green grass, and surrounded by peculiar-looking trees with a pronounced purplish tint to their trunks and leaves. Nine robos, two security robots, and a slew of small maintenance robots quickly disembarked.

The maintenance robots began their inspection of the hull and replaced the gravity wave gun's missing strut, while the security detail stood near the entrance to protect the ship. The robos, equipped with antigravity, started exploring the neighborhood in earnest.

Videos began to be uploaded to *A-1* quicker than the crew could watch them all. They were overwhelmed with images of small, scattered lakes, mountains in the distance, the coiled ground cover, and especially the mushroom-like but leafy trees. The afternoon sky was a familiar blue, with hints of purple. The two moons swung through the sky, smaller and swifter than the Moon of Earth. They hadn't found any signs of animal or insect life so far, but then, this was the first set of videos coming through.

That changed when one of the videos focused on a small, bushy plant that suddenly started to move.

"What is that?" Charlie breathed.

"Walking plant? Weird insect? Plant-like animal?" Rachel suggested.

After a few hours, B.R.A.I.N said, "The robos on the surface are asking permission to bring samples aboard their ship for further analysis. Would that be acceptable at this point?"

After much discussion, the team agreed, provided the robos exercise extreme caution in handling the samples. The robos gathered many items: rocks, soil, plants, water, and even the weird, ambulatory plant-thing for closer inspection.

■ ■ ■

It took an entire week for the robos of *A-3* to explore 20 square miles of their new world. In addition to the plant life, they found plenty of animal life: aside from the bush insect, there were two and four-winged birds, lizards - winged and terrestrial, snakes, worms, fish, many insects, and even a kind of purplish four-armed, furry ape with large, protruding, roving eyes. They also found a lizard that could change its color and, to some extent, its bodily shape. It could elongate like a snake to pass through tight spaces, or flatten its body to simulate a fallen leaf.

Most of the animals had two eyes, a head, and four to six appendages for movement. The creatures were different than Earth life, but still seemed incredibly similar, which made sense even on this faraway planet. Evolution had been efficient back on Earth, so why not here? Particularly since the atmosphere and living conditions were comparable to those back home.

There was one incredibly fast flying lizard that could hover like a hummingbird. It hunted small white-and-purple winged insects.

The crew had no idea if the plant life of their new world would be able to sustain them. They had brought seeds of various earthly grains, fruits, and vegetables that they would try to cultivate. Only time would tell if the alien environment would support their development.

A few more days went by before the team decided to send a second ship with the seeds to the surface. The ship landed about 50 miles from the first, where the team had spotted a stretch of what looked to be rich soil. The robos on the second ship would have to make a large clearing by cutting down the trees and vegetation. Meanwhile, the first ship would continue exploring the planet. So far, no dangerous life-forms had made an appearance. They were aware that some of the snakes, plants, and other creatures they had seen could be poisonous, and suspected dangerous predators were hiding somewhere. They just hadn't found any yet.

The colonists had much work ahead before deciding where to build their habitat. They were happy and confident this planet was habitable and able to sustain them; however, with Julie's twins on the way, they knew they had to make absolutely sure.

The second ship landed as planned. The robos got busy clearing the area, plowing the land, and germinating seeds: corn, wheat, soybean, rice, apples, mangoes, carrots, onions, and other edibles. They prepared small tracts of land for tests that would help them avoid wasting the precious seeds. A few weeks would have to go by to find out if they would germinate; the soil seemed fine, but it would take months before they knew for sure if the crops would flourish in this strange environment.

They crew was getting anxious to land on the surface and breathe some fresh air, but Eric cautioned them not to jump the gun, so everyone waited patiently. He also suggested they start building motorcycle-like antigravity vehicles to allow them to move quickly once they did land on the planet. Mike and Ricky got busy with the replicators on board.

Two more weeks went by, and some of the seeds began to grow; the local soil and water on the planet appeared adequate for the cultivation of terrestrial crops. But of course, they needed more time for the crops to fully develop, time that would allow them to continue their exploration of life on this new and wonderful planet.

Before long, the robos located white horse-like creatures with thick, muscular legs and single, gnarled horns on their heads: so, unicorns were real, just not from Earth. They also found large, cow-like quadrupeds with long snouts full of molars and hind legs longer than their front legs. These animals also had two short arm-like appendages to help them gather the ground-level plants they consumed, and even produced a whitish milk for nourishing their calves. The robos took some samples back to the ship for testing.

The milk turned out to be full of nutrients: calcium, protein, potassium, vitamins, and fats. It also contained several strange-looking species of bacteria unknown to man. This worried the team; further testing would be necessary. The crew had loaded the second ship with white lab rats to test the potentially edible products they found. They placed one of the rats in a cage and fed it the milk; it was hungry, and finished it quickly. The rat was then placed under observation for several days to see its reaction to the milk. A week later, it was alive and well. Encouraging results, but not yet ready for human trials. The robos discovered that boiling the milk would kill the unknown bacteria and preserve the milk's nutritional content. Once it became clear the milk was fit for human consumption, they transferred several gallons to the mother ship using the transporters. The crew welcomed the milk and found it acceptable. It didn't take them long to start using it to make yogurt and cheese.

"A bit odd-tasting, but palatable," Charlie said making an expression of disgust which evoked a hearty laugh from everyone around, including B.R.A.I.N.

"B.R.A.I.N, you're laughing! I never knew you had a sense of humor," Charlie said.

"I am a complex creature," B.R.A.I.N said, and laughed again.

"We have to do something about your expressionless face. Once we settle down on the planet, I'll make it my priority to work something out."

The crew next decided they should begin exploring the oceans. The ships carried robotic equipment for precisely that purpose. Eric asked

B.R.A.I.N to send the initial ship to the nearest sea, where the robos unloaded an autonomous torpedo-like underwater exploration sub. The sub was six feet long, weighed 200 pounds, and was rigged with several cameras, a tracking device, and microphones that could capture a wide range of sounds. It could run for about four hours before needing a recharge, dive three miles below the surface, and had sonar to map the ocean floor.

The robos placed it in the water and off it went, sending video images to a portable monitor using sound wave transmission. The monitor was equipped with a small radio antenna that would send the images to a larger and more powerful one on the ship, making it possible for *A-1* to receive the sub's video for the crew's viewing pleasure. Although the sub could explore on its own using its primitive onboard AI, the robos decided to control it manually. Since radio waves don't travel well underwater, they sent navigational commands using sonic waves emitted by an acoustic resonator. A piezoelectric broadband resonator installed on the sub, allowed it to receive the commands and to convert the acoustic energy into electrical energy. This effectively recharged sub's batteries and prolonged its operation. They elected to first explore an area close to shore, near some rocks just out from the beach where they had landed. The water was turquoise, and visibility was good.

As the torpedo approached the rocks, they could make out a wide variety of colorful fish. They were examining a school of silvery fish, each about 15 inches long, when, suddenly, the sub shook violently. It was being pulled down fast. The crew couldn't make out what was happening, but it was clear something had attacked the robotic explorer. Then, just as suddenly as the attack had begun, it ceased. The robos fiddled with the joystick to regain control and look for the attacker. They turned to the right, and saw a large reptile with a huge head, a long tail, and an erect dorsal fin. It looked a lot like a huge, legless tadpole with a mouth full of menacing teeth. The creature attacked again, this time swallowing the sub whole. Everyone thought it was gone beyond recovery. Even though the sub's cameras were pretty much useless inside the creature's belly, in spite of floodlights going full-blast, they could still monitor its position and approximate depth. The creature was moving away from the beach and into deeper waters, and they were fast losing the signal.

Just as they were about to give up hope, the cameras came back online.

The creature had regurgitated the sub. It was in deep, cold, and dark water. The robos engaged the automatic pilot and directed the sub to return on its own. It responded and revealed an ocean teeming with alien life. About an hour later, the sub was safely in the hands of the robos, who began checking it for damage. The creature's powerful bite had dented its surface, and they found a serrated tooth embedded in the metal. It was triangular, larger and thicker than a great white shark's. The robos hastily transported the sub to the ship for repairs.

"So much for skinny-dipping in the ocean," Ricky said sourly.

Soon, several months had gone by since they'd exited the wormhole—but they still had a lot of exploring to do before landing the mother ship. Only about half of the seeds they had planted were able to germinate fully, which guaranteed they would be able to eat some of the food they were used to. They had no idea why the other half were unable to grow. Perhaps it was the altitude, the humidity, or the amount of sunlight? Alex, the botanist, was trying her best to find out.

They had finally discovered a dangerous predator lurking at sea, but they had yet to encounter one on land. They wondered if the exoplanet harbored intelligent life, perhaps primitive intelligent life, since they hadn't witnessed any kind of technology so far. At night, the surface was dark, with the exception of lightning and the occasional forest fire. Even though the planet was slightly smaller than earth, it was still quite large. They knew it would take many years to fully explore.

By then, the crew was sick of being cooped up within the confines of the mother ship. Yes, they were fearful of the unknown dangers on the surface, but eager for a change of scenery and the opportunity to breathe fresh air.

Everyone was talking excitedly about the sea monster when Julie let out a loud, painful cry for help.

"My contractions are starting. I don't want the babies born in space! Please land this thing, quickly!" she begged.

Charlie carefully escorted his wife to the medical facility. The moment she laid down on the bed, her water broke. Eric gave the command to land the ship at the agricultural area, and ordered *A-3* to join them there.

Before long, the mother ship had touched down next to the ship that was already there; the other ship soon joined them from its ocean visit. Eric directed B.R.A.I.N to let out all the security robots to protect the ships, while the robos placed metallic posts surrounding them in a rectangular area about the size of four football fields. The posts served two purposes: to alert the crew if anything tried to cross between them, and to create an electric field powerful enough to discourage creatures from venturing within the perimeter.

Back at the medical facility, the first baby was starting to crown. The robos on board were well-equipped for medical emergencies, and delivering a baby was a simple procedure, unless something unusual happened. Fortunately, everything went smoothly. The baby was born without causing undue pain to its mother. It was a boy! Shortly after, the second baby showed the top of its head.

The first robo held the boy upside down while another one rushed to Julie to deliver the second baby. It was a beautiful baby girl! Both seemed perfectly healthy, and were soon cleaned and wrapped in soft towels. Charlie held both of them gently in his arms. As he laid eyes on his newborn children, he couldn't help feeling a bit guilty. *I brought them to an alien world. I hope everything turns out well*, he thought anxiously. He walked over to his wife and carefully placed the babies in her arms. Julie started weeping, as Charlie ran to inform the rest of the crew.

Soon everyone was crowding in, including B.R.A.I.N. Julie gave the baby boy back to Charlie, and sat on the bed with the girl in her arms.

"Do you think it's safe for us to go outside?" she asked. "I'm tired of being inside this hunk of metal. I want my babies to breathe fresh air," she announced, looking at everyone around her, pleading for their approval with her eyes.

"Unless anyone here thinks otherwise, it should be all right," Eric said. "The lab animals are thriving."

After making sure the perimeter had been properly secured, they all trooped outside for their first direct look at their new world. Tau Ceti was still shining above, and it was a beautiful day. They could see wispy clouds high up in the purplish-blue sky. A slight cool breeze caressed their bodies as they entered a tent the robos had fashioned for them, and set about making it a home.

Nightfall came quickly, and before long, both moons were up. Having been stuck inside the ship for far too long, Mike and Rachel decided to take a walk within the security perimeter, flashlights in hand. The further they moved away from camp the darker it became, but they felt safe and protected by the electric posts the robos had set up—until, suddenly, the perimeter alarm began to scream. Mike felt disoriented; he didn't know whether to run or stay put. Rachel stood by his side. grabbing his left arm and tightening her grip.

A huge figure emerged from the darkness, though neither could quite make out what it was. It let out a horrible, predatory scream, and Mike and Rachel were frozen with fear. In the dim light of his flash, Mike was able to make out two huge, clawed paws that seemed to be equipped with scythe-like blades. The creature moved towards them, slowly at first, and then more quickly, with a sinuous reptilian grace. Fortunately, a robo had responded to the danger, flying towards them as fast as it could. Just as the creature was about to slice them to shreds, the robo crashed into it and threw it off course. Recovering its balance, the creature moved its huge head and trapped the robo by the torso in its jaws. The robo's body split in two in a shower of lubricants and electric sparks. By then, several security robots had arrived at the scene and started shooting at the huge reptilian creature. Screaming in pain, the creature disappeared through the perimeter fence and back into the dense forest as quickly as it had appeared.

Mike and Rachel were shaken but thankful to come out of the experience with their lives. Once safe, Mike searched the database in his head, he found that the Greek word Therizo meant "to reap or mow." He decided to name the creature Therizosaurus Sheed after its scythe-like giant claws and carnivorous appetite. Robos arrived and picked up the remains of their slain brother, to try and put it back together again. They all returned to the safety of the spaceship to regroup.

■ ■ ■

The next day, the early morning sunlight seduced the entire team into the open air. Julie was with her babies, surrounded by security bots, holding them both in her arms and looking at them lovingly. She then shifted her gaze to admire the sky.

"I hereby christen this planet Eden," she said historically, "and the first humans born here Adam and Eve. May God guide, provide for, and protect us all in our pristine new home."

"Amen," her fellow humans, and B.R.A.I.N, all replied.

THE END

www.ingramcontent.com/pod-product-compliance
Lightning Source LLC
Chambersburg PA
CBHW031426200626
46814CB00016B/2332